CONSUMED

THE SAVIORS OF SOULS BOOK 2

SHIRLEY O'NEIL

World Castle Publishing, LLC
Pensacola, Florida
Copyright © Shirley O'Neil 2019
Paperback ISBN: 9781950890101

eBook ISBN: 9781950890118
First Edition World Castle Publishing, LLC, June 10, 2019
http://www.worldcastlepublishing.com
Licensing Notes
Cover: Karen Fuller
Editor: Maxine Bringenberg

CHAPTER 1

After hearing the shocking news, Hayley Johnson molded herself into the gray leather passenger seat of Lee Franklin's Aston Martin. While he drove, she watched the road snake through the woods along Lake View Drive, heading north out of Sutterville, North Carolina. Towering oaks, poplars, and pines lined the pavement, blocking the late afternoon sun. She pushed her sunglasses above her bangs, closed her eyes, trying to relax, and listened to the hum of the engine as the car hugged the curves.

"Are you all right?" Lee asked.

Hayley nodded and opened her eyes. "I'm still thinking about what we've just learned. Because of me, while in Heaven, me, you, and everyone we work with today made a pact to be reborn into this lifetime. How astonishing is that?"

"I've always believed in reincarnation," Lee said. "I guess I'm not having as much trouble accepting it as you."

"Are you forgetting that I can see the past, present, future, and the dead? No one knows better than I do that there's more to life than meets the eye."

"So why do you look stunned?" Lee asked.

"I'm just having difficulty absorbing it. This is not a little thing. Less than an hour ago, I learned that just about everyone I've met in the last few weeks has been a best friend of mine throughout past lifetimes. What irony. Friends? I'm sure I've told you that I spent most of my life plagued with visions and screaming at people no one else could see. Everyone thought I was a schizophrenic. Until lately, I had no friends."

"You have control of your gifts now, and you have lots of friends."

"But all of us meeting as if it were a coincidence—who knew?" Hayley said.

"So it's bothering you because you never foresaw it?" Lee kept his eye on the road as it curved along the mountainside and followed Lake Tales. When the road straightened, he glanced at her out of the corner of his eye. "Am I getting close?"

"Yes," she confessed. "And that it's difficult to think of myself as a rescuer of souls when I've seen myself as a freak all my life."

"I've never thought that way about you."

"Of course not," Hayley said. "You're forced to care about me. It's in your DNA. We were lovers in other lifetimes."

"I don't believe that."

"What? That we were lovers?"

He shook his head. "No. That it's in my DNA. I believe we're born with free will."

She thought about how, in the last two weeks, their last investigation had taken them halfway around the world, allowing Lee and her to spend a vast amount of time together.

"I might've been destined to work with you," Lee said, "but I don't think I'm forced to love you."

His words sent shivers up her spine. He was right. As far as she knew, they were only brought together in this lifetime to investigate their last case. Mission accomplished. Because of that, she knew the relationship she and Lee had could end at any time. Plus, he'd made a pledge with Roger after their parents' tragic deaths never to marry, to avoid the possibility of losing another loved one. Since then neither Roger nor Lee had dated anyone for longer than a month.

I wish I were allowed to see my future. Can he ever love me, and for how long? Stop. Stop thinking about that. We're happy being together, aren't we? Why spoil it by thinking about losing him? She forced the thought out of her head and returned to their discussion.

"Another thing," she said. "Were we reincarnated to be saviors of souls in only our last case, or are we more than just ghost hunters now?"

"The reincarnated, saviors of souls. Sounds heavy."

"It does. But are we through? Is the last case the only one we were purposely born to solve?"

"Good question," Lee said. "Let's not think about ghosts and lost souls for right now. After the last couple of weeks we've had, we deserve some fun."

They'd known each other for less than a month. She wanted to know him better. Hayley brushed her hand across the posh car seat, noticing the extensive amount of leather throughout the interior, and wondered about Lee's life. She studied his appearance. He wore jeans and a white short-sleeved sports shirt. She saw nothing unusual about him other than how well his clothes fit his obviously hard body, and how his wavy brown hair appeared to have been styled. But that didn't mean anything except that he cared about his looks. What did she know of him?

He's part owner of a ghost-hunting business. His office is a former used-car dealership. Nothing screams, I can afford an Aston Martin. Plus, the money he makes from writing ghost stories for a magazine couldn't give him enough income to afford a car like this. It has to be borrowed or leased. Of that I'm sure. Not that it makes a difference.

"I'm taking you to a mansion off Lake View," he said. "I thought you might like to walk through the gardens."

He turned the car up a narrow road lined with maple trees.

After a short distance, Lee stopped at ornate wrought-iron security gates. They swung open, and then closed once he drove through.

Lee glanced at Hayley. She knew she appeared confused.

"We're expected," he said.

A curtain of woods on both sides of the drive gave way to reveal a sea of grass. They followed the drive lined with Norway spruce.

"This is beautiful," Hayley said. "How did you find this place? It's so secluded." As the drive curved, a mansion came into view. She gasped. "Wow! It's a castle."

She marveled at the architecture. The three-story, red-brick mansion had two wings extending forward, lengthened by three-story round towers protruding from each wing.

"I've known about this place since I was born," Lee said. "It's a smaller version of an English estate."

"Smaller? The one in England must be a palace."

Double-hung twelve-pane windows, regimented in size, looked as if they extended the height of each room. She leaned forward and peered out the windshield to search for a shade being drawn or a curtain being pulled back by someone curious to see if guests had arrived. Hayley felt uneasy, as if she and Lee had trespassed with the owner's back turned. But Lee wouldn't have brought her here without permission, she had no doubt.

She reached out with her senses. Her inability to sense a presence baffled her. In the past, she had never been able to foresee her own future. A divine rule forbade it, forcing her to live her life without a clue, like everyone else. And she'd failed to sense Lee's future, and perceived only bits and pieces of the other reincarnated due to conditions stated in the pact she'd been told about recently. *But why now?*

"It's weird, Lee. This place seems to be deserted. There

6

should be someone home—a maid, a butler, kitchen staff. But I'm not sensing anyone."

"That's interesting."

Lee drove to the side yard, parked, and got out, then walked around to open her door. Still looking up at the mansion windows, Hayley climbed out of the car. She shrugged off her bewilderment and followed Lee.

To the right of the house, high hedges surrounded the garden. An arched, weathered wooden gate with black iron hinges swung open easily as Lee pulled the handle. He stood aside to let her enter.

She followed a brick pathway between rose trees as round as lollypops. Perfume filled the air. Beyond the rose garden, in the backyard, she and Lee stepped up to a veranda bordered by a travertine stone wall dressed in urns filled with azaleas. Centered to the home's entrance, steps fanned downward, leading to a manicured lawn.

She looked across carpets of grass pathways crisscrossing between geometric designs formed by boxwood hedges and English holly framing colorful flowers. Topiary, some rounded, some coned, and others cubed, dotted the garden to the lake's edge.

"What do you think?" Lee asked.

Hayley took a moment, capturing beauty she'd seen only in magazines. "Stunning." Before she could say another word, wailing and a sense of anguish flooded her thoughts. She walked to the edge of the veranda and looked down, studying the grounds at the end of the rose garden. "Too bad it's haunted."

"Haunted?"

"Not a ghost I can see, but there's moaning and crying...a heavy feeling of sadness."

Lee followed her gaze. "Damn!"

She closed her eyes, intending to block the intense emotions, but instead, her curiosity tried to decipher what seemed to be words. "Next time you see the owner, ask him if he knows someone named Emma."

"Emma? So it's a woman?"

"No. It's a man's voice. He's wailing her name as if his heart were torn in two."

"Are you sensing something localized, or does it cover the entire garden?"

"Let's walk to the other side of the grounds, then work our way back this way. I'll try to find out where it's centered."

They crossed the veranda and stood at the top of the stairway. Hayley chose to ignore her imposed sense of melancholy. In the last couple of weeks, she'd had enough of mysteries and ghosts. All she wanted now was to have time to get to know Lee.

Before stopping at the mansion she had been on her way to Lee's home, and was looking forward to having dinner with Roger Hudson, the designated boss among the three partners—himself, Lee, and Jim Newton, who had created Paranormal Search and Analysis—and Dr. Laura Song, a renowned neurosurgeon from Hawaii.

This is supposed to be a relaxing evening with friends. Her defiance to the dead grew. *This is my day. I'm not going to let some moaning ghost ruin everything.*

At the bottom of the stairs, Hayley hesitated, reached down, and took off her sandals before her feet touched the grass.

"Will that help you pinpoint the haunting?" Lee asked.

She set her shoes on the steps and rolled up her pant legs. "No. I just want to feel the grass between my toes."

Lee laughed. "Need help taking anything else off?"

Her lips parted into a sensuous smile. "Maybe."

He reached for her waist, but she slipped away. She threw

the thought of the haunting, moaning ghost aside, giggling, and turned to run. Down the grassy pathways and around topiary she sprinted, looking for a place to hide. Behind a dwarf myrtle she threw herself to the ground. While catching her breath, she kept low.

Cautiously she raised her head, peeking over the low hedge, and spied Lee struggling to remove his shoes and socks, jumping on one foot. Barefooted, he looked her way, seemed to have spotted her, and ran toward her.

Hayley darted behind white ox-eyed daisies. Then, peeking over parrot lilies, she watched him sneak around the black-eyed Susans. But she had already moved.

As silently as the butterfly resting on the lily above her head, she crept forward. Her stomach rubbed against the grass as she peered around the corner of the boxwood while trying to find another hiding place. She looked again at the black-eyed Susans and found Lee was gone. Not knowing whether to run or to stay put, she waited. A growing sense of being watched filled her. Hayley glanced over her shoulder. Two long legs straddled her. She gazed up to see the grin on Lee's face.

Not willing to surrender, she rolled onto her back, reached up, and grabbed his hand, pulling him down on top of her. The weight of his body, and the memories of the previous night when he'd made love to her for the first time, sent her heart racing.

"Do you think the owner's watching?" she whispered in his ear.

"I guarantee it," he said, chuckling. His lips found her neck's soft skin.

The heat of his breath in her ear tempted her to give in to his desire, and hers. Her body surrendered to his touch as lust set flame to her common sense. She knew this was the wrong time and place. Seeds of paranoia grew until thoughts of prying eyes dampened her emotions. She tried to get up, but he had her pinned.

"Lee, we're going to get caught."

Lee rolled off her, his breath heavy, his eyes filled with disappointment. He sat crossed-legged and cleared his throat. "There's something I haven't told you."

She sat up, nervously glancing at the house. "What?"

He ran his hand though his hair. "I own this garden."

She glanced at him shrewdly. "Hah! Good try."

"No. Really!" Lee pulled up a blade of grass, rolling it between his fingers as he met her stare. "I'm serious. I know it's a lot to take in, but I wanted to break it to you slowly."

"It's not going to work. What if the owner sprints across the lawn, hoping to save his garden from being defiled? Wouldn't that ruin the moment?"

"I can defile my garden anytime I want." He sighed, stood, and reached for Hayley's hand, pulling her to her feet. "You're right. It did sound contrived. I wouldn't have bought it either. Come…let me show you the rest of the grounds."

Together they strolled hand in hand along the pond on the north side of the estate.

"This is beautiful," she said. "The colors along the banks look like a Monet painting. And that bridge going across — where does it lead?"

"To a garage housing a number of cars, a building full of garden equipment, and the tools to keep this estate running."

"You know a lot about this place. Do you know the owner?"

"It's all mine. I'm telling you the truth. And I don't know anyone by the name of Emma. Are you sensing anything?"

"No. Actually, it's really quite peaceful over here. Let's go back to the other side of the garden." She gave him a playful glance as they walked. "So, in this little fantasy of yours, am I

Marie Antoinette's naughty niece, the downstairs maid, or the king's mistress?"

He flashed a crooked smile. "I know where I could find a maid's uniform."

She stopped strolling, put her arms around his neck, kissed him seductively, then gazed up at the mansion's windows. "We should talk about this later."

They followed the path through the tapestry of evergreens and fragrant azalea blossoms to the south side of the yard, where she had earlier sensed paranormal activity. As they approached the area, Lee let her take the lead.

Hayley stayed on the soft grass path connecting to the rose garden and felt the negative energy rising from the soil.

"Nothing grows here but grass," Lee said.

She used her senses as a divining rod to find the origin of the negativity. "The soil's becoming progressively acidic. It's strongest here." Hayley wiggled her toes to get grounded, calmly took a deep breath, and closed her eyes to concentrate. The sadness of the weeping overwhelmed her. She stood silently for a moment, attempting to make sense of the distraught energy below.

Her breath caught in her throat and she gasped. Her eyes widened with panic while she tried to step back, wanting to run. Screaming, she stared down at a masculine hand, darker than the garden's richest loam, reaching out of the tainted soil and grasping her ankle, barring her escape.

CHAPTER 2

As abruptly as it appeared, the ghostly hand released Hayley and vanished.

Lee scooped her into his arms. He stared at the ground, and Hayley followed his gaze. Not a blade of grass looked out of place. Lee's upper lip curled up in revulsion. "What the hell was that?"

"Someone's buried here," Hayley said, her voice shaky.

"Can't be. I had this entire area dug up two years ago. I thought the soil had some kind of fungal disease, so I replaced it. There isn't a body there. I'm sure of it."

With what seemed like no effort to Hayley, Lee carried her to the veranda to a round hemlock wicker table, where, with a bare foot, he pulled out one of six chairs and set her down. Kneeling before her, he rolled her pant leg higher and ran his hands across the skin of her ankle. "Welts and handprints. They're red now, but I'm sure you'll have bruises." He raised his hand in summons.

What's he doing?

A thin man—who appeared to Hayley to be in his late fifties—wearing a black suit stepped out of the mansion's doorway. "Yes, Mr. Franklin?"

"Lewis, would you bring me a cold compress for Miss Johnson's injured leg?"

"Right away, sir." He turned and went back inside.

He was telling the truth! The blood drained from Hayley's face.

"Can you move your toes?" Lee asked.

She wiggled her toes and rotated her foot. "I'm fine. It's just bruised."

Lee stood, fumbled through his pockets, then pulled out a cell phone and texted a message. In minutes, gardeners were trimming hedges, and a woman wearing an apron arrived to hand Lee a towel and a small bag of ice.

"Thank you, Velma."

Beyond stunned by her comprehension, Hayley could do nothing more than stare at Lee while he bent down, wrapped the icepack in a towel, and draped it gently across her ankle.

"Will that be all, sir?"

Lee stood and stepped back, placed his hand on his chin, and studied Hayley's face. "Velma, Miss Johnson looks a little pale, don't you think?"

Hayley felt tongue-tied, her mind going in all directions, searching for the clues she somehow had missed in conversations with Lee. She watched the round-faced woman, her black hair streaked with gray, wipe her hands on her apron, lean closer, and, with squinting eyes, scrutinize Hayley's expression.

"I'd say she's in shock, sir. Maybe a glass of water?"

"How about a couple of the bottles of the wine I brought home yesterday, and five glasses? I'm expecting friends."

"Right away, sir." Velma hurried into the house.

Within minutes, the butler returned with two bottles of ZD cabernet reserve '06 and glasses. He set his tray on the table, scored the seal at the top of the bottle, then reached for the battery-operated electric corkscrew.

"Would you like an appetizer, sir?" he asked while removing the cork.

"No, Lewis. That'll be all. Mr. Hudson and Dr. Song will be arriving soon. When they do, will you show them out here? Oh, and if you see Jim, tell him we're waiting for him."

"Yes, sir." The butler stepped away and reentered the house.

Lee laughed when he returned his attention to Hayley. "I've never seen you speechless."

"You weren't joking."

He poured her a glass of wine. "I've been trying to tell you that."

She glanced at the workers in the garden, then at the doorway Velma had stepped through. "You made everyone hide?"

"Well, yes. When I showed you the garden, I wanted it to be a special moment just between you and me." He passed her a glass, then bent down, lifted the compress off her ankle, and touched her skin.

Hayley winced, nearly spilling her wine.

"Sorry." He replaced the icepack, then stood. "This house is two hundred years old. I've never heard of anything like this happening before. Do you have an idea what that thing was?"

She shook her head. "I'm not really sure."

Lewis stepped out of the doorway and cleared his throat.

Lee glanced toward him. "Yes, Lewis?"

"Mr. Hudson and Dr. Song, sir."

Laura, her thick black hair pulled into a ponytail under a white baseball hat, walked outside ahead of Roger. She paused, appearing to sum up the situation, then hurried to assist and removed her dark sunglasses before she bent down in front of Hayley. "Is it bad?" She lifted the icepack, studied the welts, and examined Hayley's ankle. "Well, it's just bruised, not sprained. How on earth did this happen?"

"Take a seat, you two," Lee said, "and have some wine. You're not going to believe this one."

14

~*~

Roger, Lee's best friend and business partner, set his wine glass down after hearing the story and walked to the area of the attack. "I don't see anything unusual."

"Maybe you should remove your shoes," Lee said. "Hayley was barefoot."

Lee winked at Hayley as Roger stripped off his shoes and socks.

"Now roll up your pant legs," Lee said.

Roger rolled his khaki pants to his knees, then ran his hand through his sandy blond hair. "Now what?"

"It happened exactly here." Lee pointed to the grass a few inches in front of Roger. "Put one foot forward and keep the other one back."

He followed Lee's instructions. "Nothing," Roger said.

"Try it with the other foot."

Roger put his other foot forward.

With confusion on her face, Hayley, sitting next to Dr. Song, sipped her wine. *What is Lee doing?*

"Now, try your right foot again and then your left, but faster. Oh, and hold this arm up over your head."

The moment Roger complied, Lee's and Roger's other business partner, Jim, walked through the rose garden. "How much have ya had to drink, Roger? Hell, ya forgot your damn tutu." He turned toward Hayley and Laura. "Ladies. I'll have what he's havin'."

Roger glared at Lee. "Thanks. You had me dancing on some guy's grave."

Lee grinned. Then, with a serious expression, he stared at the ground and told of how the area had been dug up two years earlier. "There were no bones, no grave. And the only thing that grows here is grass. Anything with longer roots dies."

15

~*~

They filled Jim in on the attack.

He looked up at the veranda, shaking his head at Hayley. "Well, darlin', I've never known anyone who could piss-off ghosts the way you can."

"How many years has the ground been sickened?" Roger asked, lacing his shoes.

"That's a good question," Lee said. "I have garden journals going all the way back to the time the estate was built. Maybe we should go into the library and do some research." He went to the veranda steps, picked up his and Hayley's shoes, returned to Hayley, and helped her slip on her sandals. "How's that? Are you okay?"

"A little sore, but fine."

He rushed to put on his own shoes and socks, stood, and looked thoughtfully at her ankle. "Can you walk? It will be a ways to the library."

Carefully, Hayley rose and took a step to test her ankle. "Feels okay."

Lewis returned and gathered the empty wine bottle and glasses.

Lee stayed close as Hayley stepped through the mansion's doorway. Her eyes widened when they entered an immense hallway with a large black and white marble-tiled floor and honeycomb pattern plaster bas-reliefs on the ceiling. At the hallway intersection, she walked with Lee and his guests down another corridor branching off the main hall.

Her eye caught a glimpse of a tapestry hanging against the gold Venetian-plastered walls and she drifted toward it, leaving Lee's side while he chatted with Roger. It depicted a garden similar to the garden in Lee's backyard.

Laura joined her. "Beautiful home, isn't it?" she whispered.

"Unbelievable," Hayley said, glancing over her shoulder at the French-style console supporting a two-foot-high vase filled with flowers she remembered seeing in the garden. Above them hung a painting of a young woman—by Rembrandt, she was sure—and in the center of the hall, a crystal chandelier dangled.

She and Laura followed the men while peeking into rooms that had eight-foot-tall windows and ceilings as elaborate as the hallway's. The rooms appeared to be designed for living spaces and entertaining with their formal, traditional, and French-influenced furnishings. When they turned another corner, open doors allowed Hayley and Laura to gaze into two bedroom suites.

"Roger's house is just as elegant," Laura told Hayley. "I have a wing to myself."

"I had no idea," Hayley said.

"Yes. I remember your clairvoyance doesn't allow you to see your own future," Laura said. "But wouldn't you want to be surprised? It's far more exciting."

"You're right. I would," Hayley said. *That's good to hear.* She'd written a prediction only a couple of weeks ago, foreseeing Laura and Roger's wedding, and had placed it in an envelope to be opened after the ceremony next year in June. Since then, she and Laura had become close friends, and Hayley worried how she would feel about the secret being kept from her. *I'm glad you like surprises.*

At the end of the hallway connecting to the tower at the south side of the estate, Hayley and the others walked toward a dark wood-paneled wall contrasting dramatically with the honey-colored walls on either side. Its aged rosewood paneling with filigree surrounded what she assumed to be the library's entrance. An inset arch with a cherub's face among carved roses crowned the sculptured door.

Lee held the door open for them.

Hayley felt small in the massive room. Its curved outer wall encased four twelve-pane bow windows stretching from floor to ceiling. With the full-length pale green drapes drawn back, sunlight helped to brighten the rosewood-paneled room. A floral print carpet lay beneath leather sofas and chairs in front of the huge fireplace. Near the doorway where they had entered, a spiral staircase connected to a second-level balcony where bookshelves reached to the embossed tin ceiling. The number of books amazed her.

A large, gold-framed mirror crowned the fireplace on the wall closest to the rose garden. Hayley, following her intuition, gravitated toward the carved mantel. She felt a hint of the negativity she'd experienced in the garden, and became aware of a pungent odor emanating from the wall on the left side of the fireplace. *What is that?* She played with the ends of her hair while she watched the others' reactions through the mirror. *Am I the only one who smells it?* No one but her seemed to notice. She kept silent. *What can I say? "Lee, your library stinks." It's bad enough that the garden's haunted. I won't tell him about this yet. Maybe I can figure it out.*

Lee climbed the spiral stairs to the second level and removed a thick journal from the bookcase. "There're ten volumes. Each contains twenty years of garden records." One at a time, he handed them down to Roger.

Hayley and Laura joined Roger to form a human chain. Laura passed the volumes to Hayley, and she handed them off to Jim, who set them on the long table in front of the windows.

"We can each take a journal and see if we can find anything about plants dying near the rose garden," Lee said, descending the stairs.

Standing in front of brown leather-bound books approximately ten inches by sixteen inches and at least four inches thick, Hayley moved her hands across each volume and chose one.

Lee winked at her as he pulled out her chair and then sat next to her. He flipped open a volume, leaned toward her, and whispered, "I promise we'll find out what that thing was, and before you know it, you and I will be playing hide and seek again."

The room fell quiet as the five of them dug through the garden's history. The butler brought a tray of glasses and another bottle of wine, then served.

"Thank you, Lewis," Lee said. "Just leave the bottle."

"Yes, sir."

Searching for a clue, Hayley brushed her finger along the handwritten lines. Her eyes stopped on the word *devil*. "I found it!" she shouted. Hayley read the passage out loud. "The devil himself has reached up from the bowels of Hell and taken hold of my garden on the southeast corner of the manor. There could be no other explanation. Within the count of three ungodly days, every healthy plant expired, wilted to rot until the earth itself became befouled."

"What year was that?" Lee asked.

Hayley turned back a page and searched for the date. "1855."

"Wow, that long ago," Lee said. "I'll read further back in the history. It should tell us if a body had been buried or if they dug up a grave." He glanced at Laura, who took the last sip of her wine. "Would you like some more?" He reached for the bottle in the middle of the table, but Roger beat him to it.

"Yes, thank you," Laura said.

Roger poured.

With her wine glass in hand, Laura stood, strolled to one of the leather chairs at the end of the two couches by the fireplace, and sat. Roger followed and rested on the arm of her chair. Jim also rose and crossed the room.

Looking past them at the carved mantle, Hayley studied the wood paneling while trying to ignore the sickening smell. "Lee, do you have the blueprints of this house? Maybe the problem's in this mansion."

He looked up from the journal. "No. We haven't been able to find the construction plans since my grandfather built the wine cellar when I was six. I sure would like to know where they are. You don't know how hard it's been renovating without them."

Holding his glass steady, trying not to spill a drop, Jim eased himself into the leather chair next to Laura's, took a sip, looked over at Lee and Hayley, and nodded. "It was harder than hell tryin' to figure out the electrical wirin'. One minute I'd find it strung through the walls, and the next...." Jim shrugged. "I didn't know if I should scratch my watch or wind my butt."

"Why did you put yourself through the frustration?" Hayley asked. "Lee could've hired someone to do the work."

"Renovation is a passion of mine. There's no way I'd let someone else have all the fun."

Lee turned back to Hayley and shook his head. "Inside? I don't think the ghost in the mansion has anything to do with what happened in the garden."

"Are you saying you have a ghost in your home?"

"Yes. I thought that's what you meant."

"Hell, he's a Casper," Jim said. "When I started doin' repairs 'round here, I expected him to get riled up just like other ghosts do durin' renovations. So, I started talkin' to him as I was workin', explainin' what I was doin' and all. I think he liked that. I could tell when he was 'round 'cause it was always colder than a witch's—"

Lee cleared his throat. "We have ladies present."

"Don't look at me that way. I was gonna say colder than a witch's heart. I swear."

Lewis came to the door. "Dinner is being served, sir."

"Thank you, Lewis." Lee set the volume aside and stood. "I'll go through this later." He led his guests from the library.

Before stepping out the door, Hayley, still thinking about the odor, glanced back at the fireplace. She closed her eyes and probed the wall with her senses, but perceived nothing. *I've got to figure this out. The stench is awful.* She searched for a light switch to turn off, but there wasn't one. She noticed Lee watching her.

"The lights and a number of other tasks are connected to the main computer system," Lee explained, reaching to close the door. Following the others, he walked with her through the hallway to the elevator, and added, "I hired Roger's nephews, John and Clint, last year to create an invisible computerized butler, you might say, to perform simple functions in the home's interior by using voice command. I call it Max. It controls motion detectors throughout the mansion, enabling us to enter or leave a room without turning on or off the lights."

"I knew John and Clint were smart, but that's impressive," Hayley said. *This place is huge. It must've taken them forever.*

"Max is amazing. It has the ability to know each of the household by photo analysis in order to track our location, which really comes in handy when I'm trying to find Jim."

"Does he live here?"

"Yes. He was a good friend of my parents. After they died, Jim moved in to help me run the estate and be my mentor. He handled the entire estate for a few years until he hired Lewis."

"That's a surprise. How did he know so much about running an estate?"

"Don't let Jim's colorful personality fool you. He was raised in a home nearly the size of mine."

They met up with Jim and the others at the elevator, and Hayley and Lee's conversation ended, leaving Hayley full of curiosity about Jim's past.

CHAPTER 3

The horror in the garden spun a nightmare, waking Hayley in a room dense with darkness. She blinked. *Am I still asleep?* Movement beside her startled her. Lying still, she pulled the cobwebs from her sleepy mind. She remembered coming to Lee's bedroom on the third floor.

Mahogany paneling gave the room a cozy feel, much like that of the library. Embossed bronzed tin tiles covered the high ceiling. Pale blue drapes dressed the twelve-pane windows. The vastness of the room dwarfed his huge bed, covered with a blue, brown, and bronze-colored chenille bedspread, pulled back to reveal brown Egyptian cotton sheets.

Last night, while she lay under soft lighting, her heartbeat hastening, desire quickening, feeling Lee's breath on the soft skin of her belly, he'd whispered, "Max, lights out." The room had gone dark. Her pleasures had soared—she warmed as she remembered.

After their lovemaking, she'd listened to the rhythm of Lee's breathing while he slept, not planning to fall asleep so soon herself. Before long, however, she'd slept, and the gruesome nightmare began. The hand reaching up from the garden soil had startled her awake.

Okay, okay, keep your mind on what you're doing. Trying not to wake him, she slid from beneath the covers and sat at the edge of the bed, raking her bare feet across the plush dark blue carpet. She knew Lee had placed a flashlight on the nightstand in case of emergencies. Old homes such as these often lost power, he'd told her. Blinded by the room's darkness, she had to figure out its whereabouts.

Without jostling the bed, Hayley stretched one leg out to the side until her foot struck a table leg. Carefully, she reached toward the nightstand. Groping to the right of the lamp, her hand bumped the flashlight. She pulled it to her and flipped the switch. Pointing its beam across the room, she glanced at the clock on the nearby fireplace mantel—two o'clock.

Hayley stood, putting weight on her foot and noticed her ankle injury had completely recovered. She gazed over her shoulder. In the dim reflected light, Lee looked peaceful, unaware of her plans.

The anticipation of investigating on her own stirred her adrenaline. *Good thing no one else can smell that odor. Lee's library would be unlivable. Who knows, maybe it doesn't have anything to do with the attack. But if it does…. Proof, I need proof, something they can see, too, not just me.*

She held the light in front of her and headed to the bathroom, where she'd left a few items of her clothes hanging in Lee's closet. Hayley softly closed the bathroom door, flashed the light around the room, then crossed the marble floor to the vanity, where she laid the flashlight down and dressed in the dim light.

Tiptoeing, she sneaked out of Lee's chamber. When stepping into the carpeted hallway, closing the door behind her, she triggered motion detectors in the hall. *Guess I won't need this.* Hayley tucked the flashlight inside the waistband of her jeans, rushed down the corridor until she came to a wider hallway, and followed it. Finally, she found the servants' stairs wrapped like a serpent around the elevator shaft. *The stairs are quieter.*

Hayley crept down two flights of stairs. Motion detectors lit her way, while the hall behind her returned to darkness. When she reached the final step, she noticed the gold Venetian-plastered walls and a vase filled with yellow roses on the Louis XV side table next to the servants' stairs. She realized her location. A little ways to her right she saw the black and white-tiled floor of the intersecting main hallway. *Good. Now I need to be on the other side of the house. Let's see. If I go straight to the south corridor, the library should be just around the corner.*

Glancing at several closed doors, Hayley hurried along the hall. *If I only had more time, I'd love to see what's inside.* Then she remembered. *Jim lives here, too, somewhere. I can just see myself walking into his room. Wouldn't that be great? He'd have a fun time telling everyone how I left Lee and snuck down to him. That would be worse than the nightmare I just had.*

She turned right at the next corridor and, at its end, saw the elaborately carved wooden door to the library. Hayley sighed with relief.

Gently turning the brass doorknob and opening the door, she crept into the room. The lights were on. "He said this entire mansion's installed with motion detectors," she said out loud.

"He's got more detectors than a dog's got fleas."

Hayley jumped. "Jim! What are you doing here?"

Jim peeked around the back of the leather recliner where he sat. "I was dreamin' 'bout one of those past lives we were supposed to have had. I'm sure it was Dodge City. At least I think it was. Anyway, I was in a room 'bove the saloon. I could hear music playin', kinda romantic-like. There was a voluptuous young lady with me, and I was just 'bout to.... Well, anyway, the next thing I knew, my...um...butt was on the floor." He swore under his breath.

"So, you're here because you fell out of bed?" Hayley asked.

"No, darlin'. I'm here 'cause Casper pushed me out of bed. Seems he wanted me to be here. Guess I'm supposed to help ya. Help ya do what? It better be damn good!"

"I'm not really sure."

"Well, that makes me happier than a judge in a fartin' contest."

She walked past him to the left side of the fireplace and ran her hand across the paneling. "Do you see anything unusual about this wall?"

He left his seat and walked toward her. "Like what?"

She glanced at him. Jim's tired expression made him appear older than his fifty-two. His short, graying brown hair stood on end, and he look crazier than usual. *He must've hurried to the library.* She almost felt guilty that he had been rousted from sleep.

"I sense negativity, and I smell something gross."

He came closer, squinting, felt the wall, then sniffed. "Feels all right, and I don't smell anythin' funny."

Hayley traced her fingers along the raised filigree trim laced with carved flowers. Her hand rested on a cluster of roses when she sensed a difference in the wood's texture. "There's something wrong with this. Take a look."

Jim leaned closer, his hand following the petals of the flowers. He pinched the carving and twisted it.

"What are you doing?" Hayley whispered.

"I'm checkin' to see if it's loose."

She heard a click. They jumped back. The paneled door creaked open, revealing a narrow passageway.

Jim's mouth gaped. "Well, I'll be a leapin' lizard!"

She took the flashlight from her waistband, focused the light into the darkness and, to calm her arachnophobia, checked for spiders. The odor seemed stronger. "You can't smell that?"

26

He sniffed. "No, darlin'. You must have an extrasensory nose, too."

She glanced inside. "Maybe we should see what's in there."

The hinges groaned as Jim opened the panel door wider. "Remind me to grease them things. Musta been decades since it's been opened." He walked to a table near the couch, opened a small drawer, and pulled out a flashlight.

They squeezed through the entrance and stepped into the narrow passage. In some places, wood lined the passage— elsewhere, brick. Higher up, bare beams revealed some of the mansion's structure.

"Mighty interestin'," Jim said, looking at the ceiling, his flashlight beam flickering. "Looks like my batteries are low." He gasped. "Somethin's got hold of my foot."

He shook his leg, lost his balance, and fell backward, dropping his light. The entry panel slammed shut.

Hayley aimed her flashlight beam at the floor next to Jim, trying not to blind him.

He looked up from the dusty floor. "Doesn't that just dill your pickle? Damn ghost. Remind me to thank Casper next time I see him."

"Are you sure it was him? I didn't see anyone."

"You didn't hear that snicker?"

"Yes, but I thought it was you."

"It wasn't," Jim said.

Hayley pushed at the door. "It's locked."

"What in the hell's wrong with that damn ghost?" Jim said. "He's never acted like this before."

The odor began to give Hayley a headache. She closed her eyes, shielded herself with white light, opened her eyes again, and breathed in the stale musty air. *Much better.*

The beam of light by Jim's side dimly lit his frowning face.

27

"Have you seen Casper materialize?" she asked.

Jim glanced at her. He wiped the dust from his hands. "A couple of times. Kinda looks like Ben Franklin."

"Do you think it was?"

"Don't know why it would be. His Franklin line is no kin to Lee's."

"Curious," said Hayley. "Why do you think he shut us in here?"

"Beats the hell outta me." When Jim tried to stand, placing his hand behind him for leverage, he bumped an object on the floor, sending it rolling.

"What's that?" She pointed the light toward a leather cylinder.

"Hell if I know." Jim scooted back, reached out, and pulled the cylinder to him. "Damn good leather. Must be somethin' important." Holding it in his lap, he unscrewed the cap and tipped the case. A scroll of paper slipped out. He lifted a corner. "A little more light on the subject, darlin'."

Hayley moved closer.

"Well, I'll be a cross-eyed jackass. It's the construction plans."

"Are you serious?"

Jim nodded, jumped to his feet, stuck the empty cylinder between his knees, and spread open the scroll. "Let's see. We don't need to see the whole castle." He leafed through the pages. "I only need to see this one for now." He pulled out the ground floor plans. "Why don't ya hold these while I take the flashlight and study 'em?" He handed her the drawing they needed and rolled up the others, stuck them back inside the case, screwed the cap on, and glanced around the floor. "Where's my damn flashlight?"

Turning in a circle, Hayley searched the dusty floor. "There. Against the wall under the cobweb where the bricks butt up against the paneling."

Jim picked it up and flipped the switch. "Seems okay now."

Hayley tucked her flashlight back into her waistband, then pulled the scroll taut.

"Uh-huh," he mumbled, twisting his mustache and studying the drawings. "Well, I'll be.... It shows the details of the passageway."

"So, can we get out of here?" she asked.

"There seem to be stairs leadin' down over that way." He motioned. "And there's stairs goin' up somewhere ahead."

"That stench is coming from the basement, and I'd rather not investigate what's causing it until after we find a way out. So let's go upstairs and see where we are."

"I'm with you, darlin'."

Hayley handed him the scroll, pulled out her flashlight, turned it on, and led the way. Without warning, she stopped.

Jim ran into her. "Ya might tell me when ya plan on brakin'," he grumbled.

Crossing her eyes, she watched a spider, its body the size of a walnut, crawl down her nose. Arachnophobia consumed her. Trying not to freak out, she held her breath, suppressing a scream, and swatted it. The spider fell to the floor. Aiming her flashlight down, she couldn't see where it had landed. She squirmed, panicking, imagining eight hairy legs crawling up her pants. Goosebumps spread across her skin. She swore under her breath. Inches in front of her feet, crawling toward her, she caught the creature in the light. Instinctively she turned to run, plowed into Jim, knocked him to the floor, and fell on top of him.

"I know I'm irresistible, but this ain't a place for dancin'."

She jumped up, flashing the light on herself. "Look, Jim, look! Are there any spiders on me?"

He stood, inspected her with his flashlight, and shook his head. "Calm down, darlin'. There's not a damn thing on ya."

29

"Sorry." Her heart pounded as she glanced around nervously.

"Come on. Let's get goin'." He squeezed by her, taking the lead. "The stairs should be real close. Keep your eyes open."

After a few steps, she froze. A squeak came from above her, and she glanced up into the darkness. A multitude of curses went through her mind again. Taking a deep breath, she flipped the beam upward and saw a rat the size of a small cat scurrying across a rafter. *Damn!*

Jim kept walking.

The rodent sprang in her direction. Hayley ducked. The flashlight slipped from her hands and rolled in front of her. Its light shone down a passageway branching off to their left. Hearing a squeak by her shoulder, she went to her knees and covered her head with her hands. *Damn, damn, damn, damn!*

"What's goin' on?" Jim backed up, glanced down the branching passageway, and toppled backward over her. "What did I do to deserve this?" he grumbled, sitting on the floor. "You okay?"

She reached for the flashlight. "I'm fine. Sorry."

"This here tumblin' act has got to stop. My butt's gonna have a lump on it the size of Dallas." He rubbed his rear end. "Gonna end up in the emergency havin' to tell 'em what caused my falls, and they ain't gonna believe it. Probably transfer me to some mental ward."

"I'm sorry, Jim. I really am." She stood and helped him up.

He brushed himself off and gathered what he'd dropped. "Damn Casper. I could be havin' sweet dreams right now." He led the way, mumbling.

A few steps into the left-hand passage, Hayley, with her flashlight aimed at the rafters, noticed raised stairs with a dangling rope. Jim reached up, grabbed it, and pulled. The stairs lowered. "I can't believe this rope's still in one piece and those hinges aren't rusted away by now." He looked over his shoulder and handed Hayley the construction plans. "Why don't ya let me go first so I can check to make sure it's safe? You stay there," he said firmly.

Jim climbed the stairs slowly. Cobwebs hung from the ceiling beams. He brushed them aside. At the top he pushed open a hatch, popped his head up, and shone his light around. "Another passageway." He reached out. "Hand me all those buildin' plans."

Gently putting her foot on each tread, she climbed seven steps and stopped. The old wood creaked as she shifted her weight. With a stretch, she handed him the cylinder and ground-floor plans. She watched him reach through the hatch, set the plans and case on the floor above, then finish climbing up. With one hand she gripped the ladder, and held the flashlight with her other. She lost sight of Jim. A sense of dread washed over her.

"Jim?" she whispered.

He didn't answer.

In the silence, the tight spaces seemed darker. Thinking about rats, Hayley gripped the ladder with both hands and her flashlight fell to the floor, so she eased herself down. Once on the ground floor and with the flashlight again in hand, she backed up to get a better angle to shine her light through the hatch. She saw Jim holding his flashlight and spreading the scroll on the floor. He stepped on its edges, squatted, and studied the drawings.

"It leads in two directions. Looks like there's stairs off to the left." He stood and lifted a foot, letting the paper roll up again, then picked up the scroll and motioned to Hayley. "Come on up, darlin'."

The steps groaned as she slowly climbed. She tensed. *Don't break now.*

He held out his hand and helped her step up.

"Let's go this way and head toward Lee's bedroom. The map shows it has a secret doorway, so we can get the hell outta here," he said, gesturing to the left.

After they reached the next intersection, a narrow stairway led them to the third floor.

"We should be somewhere 'round his room," Jim said. "Shine the light over here and let's see if we can find out where it is."

He ran his hand across a stud that looked to Hayley to be thinner than the others around it. She heard a click. Jim pushed on the stud and a door opened. They peeked inside. The darkness within didn't give a clue whether he'd guessed right.

He shone the flashlight around the room and grinned. "Well, darlin', looks like I brought ya home safely. Do ya mind if I exit through Lee's room? I'd be a fool goin' back through that maze. I bet that smell you're smellin' is someone who died after gettin' lost in there."

"That could be true. It's funny you didn't smell it."

Jim gave her the cylinder. "I'm heading back to Dodge. I think I've had enough for tonight." He rubbed his butt, then crept across Lee's bedroom and out the door.

Hayley hurried into the bathroom to undress.

~*~

After sneaking back to bed, she quietly slipped under the covers. As she nestled in, Lee whispered her name. She turned toward him. "Have I got a surprise for you," she said.

He rolled toward her. Reaching his hand up to her face, his fingers stroked her jaw tenderly. "And have I got a surprise for you," he whispered.

"Mine's bigger," she said.

"That's impossible." His hands read the shape of her body. She cleared her throat.

He sighed. "Okay, what's your surprise?"

Hayley lifted the leather case from beside the bed. "I found the construction plans."

She noticed his body quake as he chuckled. "You never cease to amaze me," he said.

She felt his warm breath on her neck, then melted as his kisses heated.

"Can we talk about that in the morning?" he whispered into her ear. "I seem to have a lot on my mind just now."

His kisses traveling across her skin ignited her desire. "I'm sure these can wait," she whispered.

The cylinder slipped from her hand.

CHAPTER 4

A forest of trees blurred into a sheet of green as Hayley gazed out the window of Lee's car. They were only a twenty-minute drive from downtown Sutterville and their office at Paranormal Search and Analysis. Not long enough for a nap, she imagined. Instead, she thought about yesterday.

If I have another day like that, I'll be able to sleep for a week.

As the car hugged the curves, she nestled into the leather seat and yawned.

"You must be exhausted," Lee said.

"Extremely."

"We won't have to stay at work the entire day. We'll be closing the office early. John, Kathy, Roger, and Jim are going out on a case tonight. They won't be needing us, so we can have a nice relaxing evening."

"I'll believe it when I see it," she said, her hand covering another yawn. "I've been curious. You mentioned that Jim grew up in a mansion similar to yours. Was his family wealthy?"

"No. His father was the chief butler. Jim was groomed at an early age to follow in his dad's footsteps, but his real interest was restoration. He hung out with the master builder who restored and repaired the mansion. That's where Jim picked up his colorful grammar."

34

"Interesting. Was his dad upset that Jim didn't choose his profession?"

"No. Jim could talk his way in and out of any situation. He even charmed the family who owned the mansion into enrolling him, along with their son, in a private school."

"He hasn't changed much. Pretty smart guy."

She closed her eyes. The next thing she knew, Lee was nudging her awake. He had parked in front of the office.

"Are you up for this?" he asked.

"The nap helped. I'll be fine."

After reaching behind his seat and grabbing the cylinder, Lee climbed out of the car and went around to open her door. Once she stepped out, Hayley glanced at the office's showcase windows facing the parking lot. The drapes were drawn. She sensed the other investigators were patiently seated at the conference table waiting to start the morning meeting.

Lee held the office door open and followed Hayley inside.

"It's about time you two showed up," Roger said, standing at the head of the table. "What's in the case?"

"The master construction plans of my estate." Lee pulled out a chair for Hayley and sat beside her, setting the cylinder on the floor next to him. Jim sat across from them.

"So, where'd you find them?" Roger asked.

"Didn't Jim tell you about what happened with Hayley and him last night?"

"No." Roger gave Jim a hard stare.

Jim shrugged and turned to Lee. "Did she tell ya how many times she knocked me on my butt?"

"That wasn't entirely my fault," Hayley said.

Roger raised his hand. "Wait. Would someone tell me what the hell's going on?"

"Hayley snuck down to the library while I was asleep last

35

night," Lee said. "I guess Jim was there when she arrived."

"That damned Casper," Jim grumbled. "I don't know if he heard me, but I had a few choice words for him on my way back to bed."

"Seems my resident ghost woke him last night so he could help Hayley," Lee said. "They ended up finding a hidden passageway in the library and getting trapped inside."

"Damn ghost tripped me and locked us in," Jim said.

"They found the construction plans in a cylinder lying on the floor inside. I guess the old guy fell down a few times while they were trying to find a way out."

Jim's eyes widened. "Old guy, hell."

"I never knew there was another way into my bedroom," Lee said. "Anyway, they found it. Hayley showed me this morning."

"Did she tell ya someone's dead in there and they're stinkin' up the place?"

"I said it *could* be a body," Hayley interjected.

Lee rose to his feet, reached for the leather case, and unscrewed its lid. He slid out the scroll and leafed through the pages. Once he found the ground floor plans, he spread the plans on the table and located the library. "Look, Roger. They discovered the secret door here in the panel left of the fireplace. It seems to lead to several rooms on all four levels."

Roger stepped to Lee's side and studied the drawings. "You said there could be a body in the walls? Think it belongs to the ghost that attacked you, Hayley? Where's the smell coming from?"

Kathy Lane, their historian and research investigator, left her seat and stood behind Jim.

Hayley said, "Even though everything that's happening seems to be on the south side of the mansion, both situations might not be related. It's a very old house." She glanced at the yellowed paper. "All I know is the odor's coming from the basement. There is a basement, isn't there, Lee?"

He nodded. "A very big one."

The construction drawings consisted of six pages. The first showed the house and surrounding grounds. The following five pages showed the details of the basement, ground floor, second floor, third floor, and attic.

Roger took a closer look and pointed. "May be stairs leading down. Lee, anything unusual in your basement we should be checking out?"

"Unusual?" Lee set the first-floor plans aside and spread out the basement's. "Nothing besides structural supports and storage areas. How about the wine cellar?"

"The wine cellar." Roger ran his finger along the basement drawings. "I always thought it was odd your grandfather built it so far from the kitchen." He glanced up at Lee. "It isn't here. Take a look."

"It wouldn't be. It was constructed over a century-and-a-half later than these plans," Lee said.

Roger flipped through the other pages. "Strange. I'm surprised all the plans weren't kept together."

Kathy took notes. "I can go to the hall of records and see if I can locate any information on the estate."

"We tried lookin' in the hall of records," Jim said. "Either the plans were never filed or someone misplaced 'em."

Roger slid the first-floor drawings in front of him on top of the basement's.

"Wait!" Kathy said. "Let's see the basement again. I thought I saw something."

Roger pulled out the basement plans. "Show me."

Kathy pointed to the basement's southeast corner. "Look closer. Something's been erased." She ran her finger from the basement's outer wall and into the yard.

"You're right," Roger said, examining it close up. "Maybe they planned to add on and changed their mind."

"As I recall," Lee said, "when I was little, I hid behind a large crate watching my grandfather close and lock a secret door. There were stairs leading down below the mansion's foundation. My father denied that such stairs existed. The next time I crept down there, the door was sealed behind a wall of shelves inside a wine cellar. I forgot all about it."

"Perhaps the plans were altered for a reason," Hayley said. "Maybe there's something down there they don't want anyone to know about."

Lee narrowed his brows. "Do you think there's a body under the foundation?"

"Could be," Hayley said. "It's below the rose garden where I was attacked."

"It's a far distance from the southeast corner of the mansion to the tower in the front of the house," Jim pointed out. "Best if we start by trackin' the stench in the passageway to see where it leads. Then we gotta decide which anomaly to investigate first. What does it smell like, darlin'?"

"Rotten eggs."

"Wait a minute," Lee said, looking at Hayley. "If Jim or I can't smell it, doesn't that make it paranormal? Can't you block it?"

"I have, but I can only block it for a short time. It's too strong."

"I second Jim's suggestion," Roger said. "If the two anomalies are unrelated, let's investigate the wine cellar first."

"I think we should investigate both," Hayley said.

"What kind of scenario are we looking at if the two cases are connected?" Lee asked.

"My best guess is that the smell is residual, a memory from the past," Hayley said. "Maybe it's the odor of rotting flesh and the memory is attached to the remains, not to the ghost. I should know more once I'm in the basement."

"If it's the ghost's remains and you can get a vision of him, will you know his identity?" Kathy asked.

"Hopefully. I don't always sense a name. But if I do and I can perceive what made him attack me, I hope to figure out how to avoid getting hurt again."

Roger tapped his chin with his index finger. "In that case, we'll need the geological assessment and the history of the area around the estate to learn more about what we're walking into. Do you have anything like that in your records, Lee?"

"I have no idea. I'll have to check."

"It might be faster if we let Kathy research it," Roger said. "Hopefully, we'll find out if there's something like an Indian burial ground or some ancient place of sacrifice." He looked at Kathy. "Today will be a short day because of our investigation in Stern tonight. Do you have time to check into this?"

She nodded. "I'll get right on it." Kathy stuck her pencil through the platinum blonde bun at the back of her head, walked to her seat, picked up her purse, and left.

Roger turned to Hayley. "What's your take on your being attacked in the garden? Do you think you'll be in danger while you're in the wine cellar?"

"I was born a magnet, attracting the dead. I'm sure whoever attacked me will feel my presence. In that case, I'll have to hurry to get the information and get out of there."

Lee rolled up the drawings and returned them to the cylinder. "If we have to hurry, do you think I'll have time to check out the entrance to that hidden room? I don't plan on opening it. I just want to take a look."

"You and your staff have never had problems going down there," she said. "Whatever that thing is, your presence doesn't upset it. Go before I join you. I'm pretty sure that as long as I'm not there, you'll have all the time you want."

"So, no arm reaching out of the wall to grab me?"

Hayley shook her head. "No, I don't think so, but I could be wrong."

"And if you are?"

"Run like hell!" Jim said.

CHAPTER 5

Hayley took the last bite of her grilled salmon and placed her knife and fork across the gold-rimmed dinner plate. Glancing out the second-floor window to the north, past a grove of oaks at the edge of Lee's estate, she watched the mid-afternoon sunlight glisten off Lake Tales. It was nearly three o'clock. Across the lake, along the banks dense with white pines, a goshawk flew from the woods and circled above the inlet. Upriver, almost out of sight in the July heat, the *Old Queen* paddle wheeler made its way toward town.

With a contented stomach, Hayley relished the peacefulness. She sat back in her chair and looked at the elaborate ceiling in Lee's dining room. Embossed designs of grape leaves and vines ornamented each cornice, and double-crown molding framed a coffered ceiling. Three chandeliers, each easily four feet in diameter, hung evenly spaced along the length of the room. The largest dangled in the center of a double-ringed medallion above the dining table.

She glanced around. "Seven, eight, nine—"

Lee wiped his mouth with his linen napkin and cleared his throat. "What are you doing?"

"Math. The ratio between your dining room and mine."

"So what's the quotient?"

41

"Maybe ten times the size of mine. The height of your ceiling is throwing my calculations off."

"Understandable," Lee said.

"Isn't it traditional to have the dining room on the same floor as the kitchen?" she asked.

"No. You're forgetting how old this mansion is. Back then, when this place was built, it was common for kitchens to be located in other areas of upper-class homes. The smell of smoke and cooking food permeating through social gatherings was unacceptable."

"One, two, three—"

Lee lifted his fork and moved a piece of roast beef into the gravy on his plate. "What are you determining now?"

"The number of chairs around this table."

"Thirty-two," Lee said.

While Lee finished eating, she continued to admire the second-floor room. Along the pale yellow walls, five twelve-foot-tall windows draped in green velvet permitted views to the garden pond. Under the dining table a multicolored Persian carpet ran the length of the room. Above the carved marble fireplace, seven feet high and ten feet wide, hung a gold-framed oil portrait of Ben Franklin, its size commanding a place of honor.

"I think you should take a couple of days to show me your home."

"You're exaggerating, Hayley." Lee smiled. "Maybe a day at the most." He pulled his napkin from his lap and placed it on the table. "But not this afternoon. We still have to investigate the wine cellar."

"How do you plan to move the shelving?"

"I'm recruiting Lewis, my butler." Lee pushed away his plate and leaned back. "He helps us on cases once in a while. Ghost hunting excites him. Seeing an apparition is a ten on his joy meter." Lee shook his head and chuckled. "If you ever notice his hands shaking, it's a giveaway he had an encounter with my resident ghost and he's trying to contain his excitement."

"Jim told me he saw your ghost," Hayley said. "Said he looks like Ben Franklin."

"I've seen him myself," Lee said, "and he does."

"Any reason why Ben Franklin's haunting your house? Jim told me your line of Franklins isn't related to his. Also, if that's the case, why's his portrait above your fireplace?"

"Jim didn't get it quite right," Lee said. "Ben had a grandson, Temple, who had a son. Unfortunately, the baby died and that ended Ben's male Franklin line and his surname. But he did have a daughter, Sarah. She married. Through her line, her genes were passed to my mother, who married my dad, William Franklin, of German descent, no relation to Ben's bloodline."

"Until now."

"Yes, by coincidence, and my mother named me Benjamin Franklin. Lee's my middle name."

"You're joking," she said. "You're Ben Franklin? So he's a distant grandfather?"

"Yes, in an ironic, roundabout way."

"That would be enough to pique Ben's curiosity. Could be why he's visiting you. You never told Jim?"

"No," Lee said. "Jim's jokes would be never-ending. And if Frank Thompson learned about the connection, he'd mention it in the Sutterville society page, the town historian would read about it, and my home would become a local attraction."

"It doesn't seem right," Hayley said, thinking back to how the publisher had tailed them on their last case. "Just because Frank owns the largest newspaper in town, he gets away with snooping and invading your privacy."

"A real licensed pain. Hopefully we'll be able to keep him

out of our business, away from this case, and off my property."

She glanced at the portrait above the fireplace. "Ben would know who attacked me in the garden and what's underground. I should talk to him."

"Well, good luck with that. I hardly know he's around."

"I'll keep my eyes open. He helped us find the construction plans."

"If anyone can find him, you can." Lee looked at his watch. "Let's get to the wine cellar."

He pulled his cell phone from his pocket, touched it, and waited. Lewis slid open the pocket doors to the north hallway.

Hayley smiled as she watched him approach. *He looks so butler-y. Is that a word?* His slender nose suited his long face, she thought, and his black suit and dress shirt fit perfectly on his thin frame, making him seem tall and stately.

"Yes, sir, you vibrated?"

"Lewis, we're down a few investigators at work. John's back in college, and Clint's in the hospital. I was wondering if you'd be interested in joining us on a case."

"Yes, sir, I would. Would you excuse me for one moment, sir?"

"Certainly, Lewis."

Hayley took a sip of water, swallowed, and nearly choked with laughter when she looked through the open dining room entry and saw Lewis dancing in the hallway.

"What's he doing?" Lee asked.

"He's jumping up and down, pumping his fist, saying, 'Yes, yes, yes.'"

"Now, what's he doing?"

"He's not there."

Lee nodded. "Give him a minute. He's running up and down the hall. He should be back soon."

44

Lewis, wearing a sober expression, walked stiffly into the room and stood at Lee's side. "When would you like me to start, sir?"

"Once you finish here. Join us and I'll fill you in on the details."

"Yes, Mr. Franklin." Lewis gathered their dishes. "Coffee or wine, sir?"

Lee glanced at Hayley. She shook her head. "No wine. I want to keep a clear head, and coffee will make me jittery."

The butler stood with his arms full of dishes, waiting for Lee's decision.

"No, nothing. Thank you, Lewis. Hurry back."

Faster than Hayley thought possible, Lewis stepped away then returned, pulled the doors closed, and hurried to the table. He sat next to her, across from Lee. Sitting motionless, he listened to the details of her attack, the secret passageway, and the meeting at the office this morning.

"I'm going to need your help periodically throughout this case," Lee said.

"I will notify the staff, sir," Lewis said.

"Please do. Hayley and I plan on going to the basement to see how much work it will take to get into the hidden room. I'll need your help to move a few things around, so you might want to change clothes."

"Yes, sir."

"Are you sure you want me to participate?" Hayley asked. "I'm the magnet. You're asking for trouble."

"My relatives were architecturally obsessed," Lee said. "The basement looks a lot like a Roman underworld. Most of the masonry work is below ground, limestone arches everywhere. You'll need a tour."

"Okay, I'll go with you, but when I say run, run."

Lewis's eyes widened. "Sounds like my kind of fun. I'll meet you in the kitchen in, let's say, ten minutes?"

"Perfect," Lee said.

~*~

Lee led the way down the staircase behind the kitchen pantry. Hayley glanced over her shoulder at Lewis, who had dressed down by removing his suit coat. He followed closely, wearing a long-sleeved white shirt, black pants, gray vest, and black tie. She watched his slender nose for reactions to the putrid smell. He didn't react.

The stone stairway hugged the limestone walls on its way to the basement. Once at the bottom of the stairs, Hayley looked out at a sea of arches creating an underground maze. *I'm glad I didn't come alone.*

Lee pointed to a metal door nearby. "That's the cold storage." Along the outer wall, an alcove lined with pegboard displayed tools of every shape and size. "Jim's workshop. He has every tool known to man, it seems."

In the heart of the basement, Hayley could dimly see the limestone arches and columns. Farther back, vast darkness. She searched the shadows for hidden danger. *This is creepy.*

After she hiked from the kitchen at the northeast side of the mansion toward the southeast corner, the area brightened and she saw the wine cellar door. The farther Hayley walked, the more she noticed the odor. Nausea rose in her throat. She put her hand to her mouth and gagged. "Stop. I can't get any closer without blocking this smell."

Lee and Lewis stood quietly while Hayley closed her eyes, gathered her energy, and surrounded herself with white light. After a moment she opened her eyes, took a deep breath, and gasped. A knowing washed over her, giving her unquestionable knowledge of what lay ahead. Her mouth gaped. She stared in astonishment and disgust at the wine cellar door.

"Are you all right?" Lee asked.

"I was wrong," Hayley said, glancing at Lee, then at the door. "The smell's not coming from human remains."

"Then what's its source?" Lee asked.

"It's attached to the ghost that attacked me."

"'It'?" Lewis asked.

"Yes, 'it'—an entity formed entirely of negative energy," Hayley said. "Why didn't I understand this before? The smell— negative energy doesn't dissipate. It grows."

"Like something that's alive?" Lewis asked.

"It is alive, and it feeds."

The butler's eyes widened. "Feeds on what?"

"It consumes its host's mind and attacks anyone in its path. It's rare to find someone living in a negative environment that hasn't been infected."

"Infected? You mean affected," Lee said.

"No, *infected*. It infects the mind, creating fear to feed on." She noticed Lee's frozen stare. "Don't worry. I can protect you with white light."

Lewis raised his hand. "May I ask what you mean by white light?"

"Of course," Hayley said. "I'll silently ask God for His protection, then envision His white light surrounding us."

"So it isn't an actual beam of light, like a spotlight, engulfing us?" Lewis asked.

"Only in the movies—special effects," Hayley replied. "It's not visible. It's a mental image. I picture pure light washing over us and becoming a shield. And as long as I shield you, the entity can't infect you."

"So it can't hurt us, even if Lewis and I can't see it?"

"Not mentally," Hayley said. "But the entity controls the

ghost and can manipulate him to kill. And once it separates from the ghost, it could materialize. Then we'd have trouble."

"So we're not safe," Lee said.

"I never knew that negativity exudes an odor," said Lewis. "Do you find most people unpleasant to be around?"

Lee shook his head and chuckled.

Lewis raised his chin. "Miss Johnson did say I could ask her anything."

"No, Lewis," Hayley said. "The negativity has to be massive before I can detect an odor. But I'm sure you know that dogs smell it. Over the years, extensive studies have proven their sensitivity."

"Oh, yes," Lewis said. "I hadn't thought of that."

"Since I blocked the odor," Hayley said, "I'm able to sense the spirit's location. We were right. It's below the foundation. We're safe for now."

CHAPTER 6

Through the glass door Hayley saw shelves with countless wine bottles lining the walls, from the wood floor to the vaulted ceiling. A ladder, similar to one she had seen in the public library, moved along a rail, allowing access to the topmost alcoves. A marble table surrounded by several cushioned stools stood in the center of the room. In the left-hand corner, Hayley noticed a door. *A bathroom.* In the right-hand corner, Hayley sensed another small room, its door blocked and hidden behind six-foot shelving.

"It's in the back right-hand corner," Lee said, pointing.

She nodded.

"Do you want to go in or stay out here?" Lee asked her.

She took a moment to study the surroundings. The size of Lee's collection shook her. *Either he's one hell of an alcoholic or he throws some pretty fierce parties.* She glanced at him, then gazed at the room. "It's so huge. Do you entertain often?"

"I've been known to have a few people over once in a while," Lee said.

What does he call a few? It looks like he entertains hundreds. She recalled the thirty-two chairs around his dining room table.

"What do you think?" he asked.

She glanced at her attire, trying to visualize what she'd wear to one of his parties. "I think I need to go shopping."

"That's not what I meant. Do you want to stay out here?"

She moved aside. "You two go ahead. I can see everything from here."

Once reaching the far corner, the men started to remove the bottles from the shelves and placing them on the island. After handing nearly forty bottles one by one to Lewis, Lee hesitated, looked intently into one of the empty cubbyholes, and reached inside. Nothing happened. He retracted his arm, stepped back, and shook his head.

While they worked, Hayley took a deep breath, released her shield, and opened herself up to the surrounding energy. Again the overwhelming smell enveloped her. Ignoring it, she concentrated on the negative entity's host, and a vision engulfed her.

She left her reality, as if stepping into a movie, and stood in a dimly lit limestone tunnel. Looking for the source of the light, she glanced to the left. A dark-skinned man, dressed in a blousy, dirt-stained, white cotton shirt, tramped by her. With each step he took, she heard loose rocks crunch beneath his feet. Following him, a thin, pockmarked man with matted blond hair and a mustache carried a flickering lantern. His shirt appeared filthy and his vest looked muddy brown.

Their words echoed off the walls, distorting their conversation. She followed them. Soon she sensed a small chamber at the end of the tunnel, and wondered if the men knew they were coming to a dead end.

They trudged on. Their muffled conversation became clear.

"Not much farther," the trailing man said.

Although trying to grasp the situation, Hayley couldn't sense what they looked for. She witnessed the trailing man nervously twisting his mustache with his dirty fingers. His eyes darted everywhere as the tunnel ended, widening into an area roughly ten feet by fifteen feet. With his focus on the man ahead of him, he reached beneath his vest, unsheathing a hunting knife. He raised the weapon and brought it down with brute force, stabbing the dark-skinned man in the back.

Hayley watched as blood soaked the victim's white shirt. He stumbled forward and went to his knees. The blade struck him again and again. While he lay moaning in a widening pool of blood, the perpetrator kicked him in the ribs, rolled his body over, and chuckled.

"Shut your mouth, boy. You're the property of your master, and he wishes you dead." Turning, he walked away, taking his lantern.

Standing in the darkness, Hayley heard the dying man call, "Emma, Emma." Then instantly, her vision ended.

She opened her eyes, and in the energy around her sensed his overwhelming anguish. Hurriedly, Hayley surrounded herself again with white light, protecting herself from the emotional debris. Taking a deep breath, she slowed her racing heartbeat, and with the back of her hand wiped away the remnants of a tear.

So the ghost was a slave and an entity is wrapped around him, manipulating and feeding on his emotions.

Through the glass door, Hayley studied Lee and Lewis's progress. They gazed at the shelves as if stumped. Panic made her antsy. She sensed they had little time. Every cell of her being perceived the impending danger.

Lee ran his fingers through his hair. Lewis walked forward, stood on tiptoe, reached up, and ran his hand along the top of the nearly empty shelves. He jumped back when the set of shelves shifted, moving outward like double doors, exposing a hand-hewn wooden door.

"They found it," Hayley whispered to herself. "The door to the foundation room."

Lee hurried to the door and tugged on its brass handle. It didn't open. He studied the large keyhole.

While Hayley anxiously watched their discovery, the energy around her became heavy. The odor shattered her shield. Dread washed over her. She pounded on the glass and reached for the doorknob.

Lee glanced over his shoulder.

"Run! Run!" she screamed.

Lewis stared transfixed at the bottles remaining on the shelf as they began to vibrate. His eyes grew wide. Lee grabbed the butler's shoulder, jerking him out of his stupor. They turned and bolted through the wine cellar and out the door. Without slowing, Lee took Hayley's outstretched hand, and the three sprinted across the basement and up a flight of stairs, stopping only when they reached the kitchen.

Bent over, breathing hard, Lewis looked at Lee. "That was exhilarating, sir. Can we do it again?"

Hayley fell into the first chair she saw, her legs spent, lungs burning from the run.

Lee stood next to her, leaning on the pantry door, appearing as exhausted as she. "Yes, Lewis," he said between labored breaths. "When I find the key, I intend to go back."

"Good plan, sir. I think we should meet it head-on."

"I know who the ghost is," Hayley said.

They turned toward her.

"He's a murdered slave consumed with anguish," she said. "If you're planning to go down there, you'd better take the team with you. Maybe a show of strength will keep him off balance and he won't attack."

"I'll talk to Roger in the morning," Lee said. He glanced at Lewis, who smiled broadly. "Yes, Lewis, you're going, too. You're part of the team now."

"Thank you, sir. I'm anxious to be of service."

Lee smiled. "I know you are, Lewis."

CHAPTER 7

Later in the afternoon, Lee gave Hayley a partial tour of his home. Before leaving the parlor, situated in the heart of the home, she hesitated, gazing again at the eclectic furnishings the Franklin family had collected through the decades.

Lee held the door for her, and she stepped into the south hall.

"You've seen just about all of the ground floor," he said, and pointed to the doors across the hall. "Those suites belong to Lewis. The entire wing, except the library in the tower and also the security room, where Kathy's new love interest Thomas works, is taken up by Lewis's chambers and sitting room."

"Almost the entire wing. Isn't that a lot of rooms for just a servant?"

"But Lewis isn't 'just a servant,'" Lee said.

"He's not?"

"No. Besides being the most considerate man in the world, he has a photographic memory, which allows him to take care of the entire estate. That's why Jim hired him. Plus, as I said, he handles my investments. In the late seventeen hundreds, a relative of mine found a gold mine on this property. Later on, with the profit from the mine, he invested in the railroad." Lee strolled with Hayley toward the library. "Since then, the mine has run dry, but not before leaving our family substantially wealthy, not to mention the early investment in the railroad that expanded with the growth of the country. Lewis helps me manage my stocks and bonds. He plays the stock market like a fiddle. He says a little voice tells him when to buy and sell. I'm thinking it's Ben."

Hayley nodded. "Could be."

He chuckled. "You'd think that Lewis and Jim would kill one another the way they carryon sometimes. But they're really good friends. In their spare time, they strategically play the stock market, trying to hide the fact they're getting inside information. By now, they're almost as rich as Gates."

"No doubt. Ben's a genius." She glanced at the carved library doors at the end of the hall and saw a transparent figure walk out of the adjacent wall and through the aged door. She blinked. "I saw Ben go into the library."

Lee grabbed her hand. "Come on."

They rushed toward the library door and Lee opened it. Hayley hurried in. She glanced around, catching motion out of the corner of her eye. Looking to her left, she saw Ben's misty figure step into the wall next to the fireplace.

"He went into the hidden passage," she said.

Once they crossed the room to the secret passage, Hayley touched the panel's decorative filigree and triggered the entrance mechanism she and Jim had discovered. The panel opened, and they peered into the darkness.

Lee pulled his phone from his pocket. "Let me call Lewis. We need a flashlight, and if that door closes with us inside, I want someone here to let us out."

Lewis hurried into the library, his face lit with excitement. He handed a flashlight to Lee and turned to Hayley. "I've never seen the ghost myself," Lewis said, "although he has made his presence known to me on many occasions." He walked up to the paneling and ran his hand across the open door. "Amazing. All these years and I've never noticed." He looked at Hayley. "Do you think he wants you to follow?"

"Yes." She glanced into the passageway. "If I hadn't sensed something different about this area of the wall, no one would've found it either. I need to show you how this panel opens in case we get trapped inside." She closed the panel door and ran her fingers across the filigree. "See these carved flowers? If you pinch the cluster and turn, it releases the lock." She twisted the flowers, and the secret door opened.

Lewis nodded. "Seems easy enough."

Lee slipped through the narrow entrance, Hayley following. He shone the light up and down the dusty passageway. "Whoever made this used leftover building material. The wood on the floor is from the upstairs hallway, and there's even some paneling from the library." He aimed the flashlight at the wall near a stairway leading down. "Those bricks in the wall came from the home's exterior."

A noise caught Hayley's attention as Lee turned the light away. "Wait! Did you hear that?"

"What?"

"Shine the light on the wall behind you."

He turned toward a grating sound and aimed the light upward. Very slowly, a brick inched its way out of the wall. Lee reached up and tugged it from its recess. As he examined it, something fell from it.

"The brick's center had been carved out," Hayley said.

Lee pointed his flashlight at the floor. "I heard something hit. Do you see it?"

She shook her head.

Lewis peeked through the hidden doorway and pointed. "It's a key, sir. It's there, enveloped in cobwebs on the floor. I'll get someone to clean this place thoroughly, sir."

"Might be nice, Lewis," Lee said, bending to lift the key from the dust.

"If you don't mind, sir, I would love to investigate and see if any repairs are necessary."

"Good idea, Lewis. Just make sure you let someone know you're going in here, and carry your cell phone in case you get trapped. I don't want you to get lost."

"Yes, sir. Thank you, sir."

"I need to see this key in better light."

Lee put it into his pocket and moved aside, allowing Hayley to reenter the library. He followed her across the room, placed the key on the table in front of the window, then pulled out a chair for Hayley before he sat next to her.

Lewis stood stiffly. "Would you care for tea, sir?"

"Take a seat, Lewis," Lee said. "You're part of the team, remember?" Lee held the three-inch rusty key in his palm. "It's heavy." He looked closer. "The design on the bow is simply an F in the center of a circle, and the bit is tumbler cut. This might be the key to the foundation room."

"So, why do you think Ben helped Hayley, Jim, and now you?" Lewis asked, pulling out the chair across the table from Lee. "He's never helped anyone else before, has he, sir?"

"Not that I'm aware of. Hayley said the murdered man was a slave. If that's the case, it could be the answer. Ben opposed slavery. Even though he owned slaves earlier in his life, as he got older, he agreed with the Quakers that slavery should be stopped. Just before he died in his eighties, he became president of the Pennsylvania Society, which promoted abolishment of slavery."

"I remember reading about that in school," Hayley said.

"Over the last couple of centuries, my relatives have collected Ben's writings. We even have a copy of the petition he introduced to Congress, and a notation describing his reaction when Congress tabled it. Congress claimed that the Constitution restrained them from prohibiting the importing, and also the freeing, of slaves."

"It sounds like they were being manipulated," Hayley said.

Lee's brows furrowed. "I lost you."

She shifted in her seat, getting ready for a long explanation. "I'll try to explain. Next to positive energy, negativity is the oldest viable entity that exists. It might help to visualize a yin-yang symbol—simply for its contrasting colors, not its spiritual meaning. Let's say the white is positive energy and the black is negative. It's the gray area between where the two energies coexist, and so do we."

"I must say, you're very knowledgeable about this subject," Lewis said. "May I ask how you learned about such a thing?"

"Growing up a medium was scary for me, Lewis," Hayley said. "To keep my sanity, I asked my guide, Elaina, lots of questions."

"Please forgive me, Miss Johnson," Lewis said. "I didn't mean to bring up such painful memories."

"It's okay, Lewis," she said, sensing his uneasiness. "I'm serious. You can ask me anything. I really don't mind."

Lee set the key on the table and sat back in his seat. "Okay, so Earth is where positive and negative energy coexist. What does that have to do with the decision they made about slavery?"

"Negative energy is never satisfied with balance," Hayley explained. "Its nature is to grow and control. In its collective state, it's balanced with positive energy and there's no threat. But negativity's desire to control causes bursts of it to break away from the collective, forming separate entities."

"And Congress?" Lee asked.

"Each entity has a concentrated desire to control, and an insatiable urge to feed and increase its mass. In order to do that, each consumes a host. An entity will sway its host's thoughts until controlling the host's mind. Negativity has had forever to learn to bend the truth, and it manipulates so well that its host doesn't even know he's being lied to. During the time of slavery, Congress actually believed it had made the right decision."

Lee raised a brow. "You're saying the entire United States Congress was possessed?"

"Everyone's possessed to a degree," she said. "If you quiet yourself and listen you'll be able to hear your own negative thoughts. And when you become more aware of the negative entity's lies, you'll be able to see how it distorts the truth."

"That's extremely scary. Why haven't we all been consumed?" Lewis asked.

"We were born with the ability to balance the two energies, although some people are better at it than others. Those who are unbalanced can become hosts. Once finding its victim, the negative entity creates hatred and makes a person believe he's justified in his feeling."

"Something on the lines of the KKK?" Lewis asked.

"Exactly. And while hatred grows, the entity feeds and increases its mass, over time taking complete control over the host's mind."

"A leech," Lee said.

"Yes," Hayley said. "Children are attacked frequently, their balance tested. Some are easily swayed, perfect targets. Once the seed of negativity starts to grow, it has years to feed on the child host. The worst cases grow up to be serial killers. Negativity loves to feed on fear."

"Since it's an entity, can you see it?" Lee asked.

Hayley nodded. "Yes. It's a black mass."

"Wow!" Lee said. "That hits home. We've investigated a number of places where children have lived and clients reported seeing a black mass."

Hayley exchanged glances with Lee and Lewis. "It's scary, isn't it? Even after a person dies, negative energy can still victimize a soul. I think that's what's happening to the slave's soul. The leech, as you call it, is distorting the slave's anger — brainwashing, so to speak — and manipulating his mind to change his anger into hatred."

"Pardon me," Lewis said. "But, if I may say, I believe being murdered would create hatred without an outside influence."

"You're right, Lewis," Hayley said. "In that case, Leech found the perfect victim, and all it has to do is turn the slave's hatred into an obsession. In the process, without knowing he's being swayed, the slave creates pure negativity while being consumed. The more Leech consumes, the more he controls the slave's thoughts, using him to provoke our fear so Leech can feed off us."

Lee's eyes widened. "Is there any way to stop the feeding? Am I going to end up with that thing in my home?"

"As much as I can figure out," Hayley said, "the slave hasn't been thoroughly consumed. If he were, he wouldn't be calling Emma's name. Whoever she was, he loved her. As long as he holds onto that love, he won't lose himself completely. That's good news. Leech won't leave him alone until the slave is totally consumed." She looked toward the secret passageway. "It's arrogant and reaching out, looking for its next victim. I can tell, because its odor is spreading into some areas of your home. In places it's so strong it gives me headaches."

Lee's face paled. "Where? How bad are your headaches? Why didn't you tell me?"

Hayley met his gaze. He was right; she'd purposely kept it from him, too painful a subject to discuss. If her headaches didn't stop, she'd never be able to set foot in his home again. *I can fix this. I'll find the answer. I have to.*

"As long as I'm shielded, I feel fine," Hayley explained.

"How long do you envision the light?" Lewis asked.

"Only for a moment. The key is clearing my mind and focusing, then holding onto the awareness of the shields surrounding me. Sometimes that's hard to do, especially when I have a headache."

"This is indeed interesting," Lewis said.

"Your headaches...." Lee pushed his chair out and stood. "We should get out of the library and stay away from the south wing."

Hayley nodded, yawned, and rose.

Lee offered her his arm. "It's been a long day. Why don't we go upstairs?"

~*~

While she slept, Hayley tossed and turned, wrapped in a vivid dream. In Ohio, on a dirt road lined with white pines, the slave she'd seen in her last vision stood with his wife and son, the forest behind them.

"We's free." The black man reached into his shirt pocket and took out a folded sheet of paper. "Says here."

Sensing danger, Hayley stirred and watched a rider dismount, step forward, and rip the document from the black man's hands. After a moment of reading, seemingly satisfied, he looked at the family and handed the document back. He turned, spoke to his two traveling companions, and remounted. "It's a blessed day for you, Abel Smith," he said, glancing back at the free man. His companions chuckled and moved their horses forward.

Hayley sensed that the men patrolled for escaped slaves, but something was not right. Abel realized it, too. He turned and shouted to his wife, "Emma, run."

Before Emma could respond, a fourth patrolman came out of the woods, approached Abel from behind, and knocked him unconscious with a small club. Emma pulled her son to her side and backed away.

The leader gazed around. "There's nowhere to run, girl."

Hayley jumped in front of Emma. The leader advanced and stepped through her as if she were a ghost. Startled, Hayley remembered this was a night vision, a dream. Frustration washed over her. She could do nothing.

The leader snatched the boy. "Noah!" Emma yelled.

"Keep your tongue tied and I'll refrain from killing the boy."

Emma nodded and stood silently with a pained look in her eyes.

Two more men drove a flatbed wagon out from behind the trees. Those mounted climbed down from their horses. One helped the attacker carry Abel's limp body to the wagon, while the other grabbed Emma.

Hayley screamed her protest. In a haze, she felt Lee gently rock her awake.

"You're yelling in your sleep," he said. "Are you okay?"

She sat up and quickly reached for the pad of paper and pen on the nightstand. "I've got to write this down before I forget. I think I just found out what angered the ghost who attacked me. It upset me, too."

After filling three pages, she put pen and pad away and covered her yawn with the back of her hand. She lay back, resting her head on the pillow. "I'll tell you about it in the morning."

"So, you're going to make me wait?" Lee asked.

Hayley yawned again. "Have to. Too tired." Her eyes closed and she drifted into sleep.

CHAPTER 8

The wind whipped Hayley's hair across her face as she stepped out of Lee's Porsche Cayenne. If all worked out as she and Lee planned, the team would spend the day investigating the hidden room in the wine cellar. She looked up at menacing clouds.

The only thing that might stop us would be if the coming storm knocks out the electricity. It doesn't look good.

Gray billowing clouds blew in from the southwest, the remnants of a hurricane in the Gulf of Mexico spreading into North Carolina. Listening to the news this morning, she'd heard that a thunderstorm would hit their area. *No. I can't let the weather stop us. This is too important. I have to get rid of the headaches.*

Lewis climbed out of the SUV's backseat, then rushed to open Lee's door.

An amused smile crossed Lee's face as he slid out. "You're not a butler today, Lewis. You're part of the team, so I don't want you to wait on me. Got that?"

"Yes, sir." When they approached the office, Lewis reached for the door, glanced at Lee, and jerked his hand back. "Sorry, sir. Old habits are hard to break."

Hayley stepped inside and watched Lee and Lewis decide who would enter next. Finally, Lee acceded to Lewis and stepped past him.

They were the last of the team to arrive. Roger sat at the head of the conference table, with Kathy at his left and Jim sitting across from her.

Roger lifted a voice recorder from the table. "Lee, I need your opinion."

Lee went to the head of the table and talked to Roger, while Lewis took a seat next to Kathy and Hayley sat with Jim.

"Good mornin', darlin'. Why's the butler here?" Jim asked.

"We're short-handed," Hayley said, "so Lee thought Lewis would like to help us."

"Help us do what?"

"Investigate what's beneath Lee's estate."

"That thing attacked ya. Can't ya just turn off your sensors and forget about that damn ghost?"

"So I can walk through the garden and be attacked again? Or even worse, be bombarded with headaches until I'm blind?"

"You're gettin' headaches?" Jim asked.

"Extreme."

"Does Lee know?" Jim asked in a low tone.

"Yes, but not how bad they are."

"Ya need to get outta that place before you're as crazy as the rest of us."

Hayley frowned. "Right now, I'd kill to be just like the rest of you. Being psychic is becoming a real pain. What am I going to do? If it is a negative entity and we don't get it away from Lee's estate, I won't be able to set foot in his home again. Especially when the thing keeps growing."

Jim's eyebrows shot up. "Entity? What are ya talkin' 'bout? I thought it was a ghost under the rose garden."

"It's both. I think a negative entity, kind of like a leech, has attached itself to the ghost. But I won't know for sure until we investigate."

"Well, that's enough to give a man gas. How are we gonna get rid of that damn thing?"

Hayley sighed. "I wish I knew."

She glanced up when Lee sat beside her. Lee looked at Roger and cleared his throat. "Can we get going? Hayley's got something to tell everyone about the apparition beneath my estate."

"There's nothing I have to say that can't wait," Roger said. "Okay, Hayley, the floor's yours."

She glanced around the table. Kathy wore her platinum blonde hair pulled back in a ponytail, revealing the phone device hooked to her ear, while her red-framed glasses rested above her forehead. A notebook, its cover folded back, lay on the table in front of her.

Across from Kathy, Jim swiped his fingers through his thinning, slightly graying brown hair. His tattoo of Neptune and his trident, a souvenir acquired in the navy back in the day, decorated his raised arm.

Beside Kathy, Lewis, wearing black dress pants, a white shirt, black tie, and gray vest, opened his eyes wide with excitement.

At the far end of the table, John pulled his cell phone out of his pocket, set it on the table, and stared at it as if expecting a call.

And, of course, Laura's not here. She's preparing for Clint's surgery. No one here has any idea what they're about to encounter under Lee's home.

Neither did Hayley. She'd only heard about the entities, but never encountered one. If her suspicions were correct, the consumed spirit could do more than give them bruises and welts. *It could be deadly.*

Hayley stayed seated. "Let me start with the vision I had in the basement yesterday. I witnessed the murder of a slave. A thin, weasely-looking man with a mustache and pockmarked face followed him into what I think was a cave. The slave walked ahead without glancing over his shoulder. When they came to the dead-end, the weasel reached under his vest, pulled out a knife, and stabbed the slave in the back. Said it was the slave's master's wish that he should die."

"How brutal!" Roger said. "Was it like that? Could a slave owner kill a slave or have one killed just because he wanted to?"

"Legally, yes. Slaves were considered property," Lee said.

Kathy raised her hand. "I have some information about the cave."

"Let's hear it," Roger said.

"I found out the bedrock around Lee's estate is limestone," Kathy said, "and numerous caves were discovered in that area. Seems most of North Carolina was part of the ocean floor at one time. Anyway, I researched the estate and unearthed, so to speak, something very interesting." She pulled her glasses down and glanced at her notes. "While they were getting ready to lay the foundation, the southeast corner collapsed into an underground cave. Instead of stopping construction, they erected brick walls inside the cave, creating the room you discovered, then laid the foundation over it. All those limestone-brick arches and columns in his basement were meant to help relieve the pressure from the weight of the house." She looked at Lee. "The cave is under your estate just where Hayley was attacked."

Lee sat back in his chair and crossed his arms. "Well, that answers a lot of questions—why they went to all that trouble to fortify the basement, where that locked door in the wine cellar leads, and where the apparition's body might be. Hayley and I found the key to the locked door last night, so we'll be able to see what's down there."

Kathy raised her hand to the phone piece at her ear. "Paranormal Search and Analysis."

66

"Anything important?" Roger asked.

"It's Clint," she said.

"What's up?" Roger asked.

"Hi, Clint." She listened. "He said it's on for tomorrow."

"What time?" Roger asked.

"Seven in the morning," Kathy said.

Roger looked at Lee, who nodded. "Tell him we'll be there before he goes into surgery," Roger told her.

"So will I," John said.

Kathy relayed their message, gave Clint her blessings, told him she would be there too, and hung up.

Roger continued with the meeting. "Anything more, Hayley?"

"Yes. I had a dream last night. I found out the slave's name is Abel Smith. He was married to Emma, and they had a son, Noah, around eight or nine years old. They were freed slaves living in Ohio, carrying their papers with them so they wouldn't be picked up as runaways. While they were walking down a dirt road on their way into town, three men, patrolmen on horseback, rode up alongside and asked their names."

"What kind of patrolmen?" John asked.

"Bounty hunters after runaway slaves. Abel showed them their papers, explaining that they were free. The lead man took the papers, studied them, and handed them back. It looked as if they were going to be left alone until a fourth bounty hunter came up behind Abel and knocked him unconscious. They grabbed Emma, Abel, and their son, bound them, and loaded them into the back of a wagon the patrollers had waiting across the road."

"Ohio was a free state, but that didn't matter," Kathy said. "*The Fugitive Slave Act of 1850* stated that if a slave ran from his owner, the owner was allowed to go into the free state to retrieve his property. Unfortunately, in most cases, they didn't need to show proof of ownership. Their word was good enough. Because of that, bounty hunters were able to kidnap freed slaves and sell them."

"That's what they did to Abel and his family," Hayley explained.

"So that's why the ghost is so irate," Roger said.

"Yes. But there's more," Hayley replied. "I believe Abel's being consumed by an entity—possessed, so to speak. If I'm right, the entity's like a leech, and it's inflaming Abel's anger so it can feed on his negativity."

"Is it dangerous?" Kathy asked.

"Yes. It could be deadly."

"Sounds scary," Kathy said.

"So what now?" Roger asked.

"We gotta go down into that foundation room for starters," Jim said. "Somehow, we gotta get Leech to leave. Our sensitive here is too damn sensitive, and what Leech is doin' to her sounds serious. She's havin' nasty headaches."

"Are they getting worse?" Lee asked her.

She nodded.

"Well, we haven't unloaded the vans from last night's case," Roger said, "so why don't we head over to Lee's and show that ghost what we're made of?"

Jim turned and looked out the window. The wind blew briskly through the trees. "Ya better pull out those flashlights and propane lamps, Lee. I'd hate to get caught in that dark, spooky basement of yours." He looked at Hayley. "I've always felt someone was watchin' me whenever I was down there."

"And now you know you were right," she said.

"Well, let's get going before the weather gets worse," Lee suggested.

"I'll gather up all the necessary equipment when we get

home, sir," Lewis said. "With some luck, the lights will go out. Sounds incredibly fun!"

CHAPTER 9

While getting out of Lee's car, Hayley heard the thunder and saw the trees bending in the wind. She and the team made it inside the mansion just as the rain began. As Hayley had feared, the storm knocked out the electricity. The six of them gathered in the kitchen in the light of flashlights and propane lamps.

Roger distributed voice recorders, cameras used to capture images in the dark, and flash cameras. "This is all we need for now until we find out what we're up against."

Lee brushed a wayward hair from Hayley's face. "Sure you want to do this?"

"What else can I do?"

"You can stay here where you'll be safe and let us investigate."

"What good will that do? We already know he's down there. And I'm the only one who can communicate with him. You need me."

He wrapped his arms around her, pulling her snug against him. "If it gets to be too much for you let me know. I'll do anything to keep you safe."

Hayley stepped out of his embrace, a sudden awareness coming to mind. "That might be a good idea. Abel tried to protect his wife and son. He would see your reaction as a sign of love. Your protectiveness may be the key to winning his trust." She looked around at the others. "Lewis, you need to take off that vest. The man who killed Abel wore one and carried a lantern. Jim, the murderer also had a mustache, so stay back. In Abel's condition, he won't just leave a scratch. He has the strength to kill."

Each held a flashlight. Kathy and Roger also carried lamps.

Lewis led the way to the basement and through its maze to the southeast corner. Once inside the wine cellar, Lee pulled out the found key and unlocked the hidden door.

Lee turned to Hayley. "Are you ready?"

Taking a deep breath, she said a prayer asking for protection, then mentally surrounded herself with white light. She nodded. "Ready."

A stone stairway led under the mansion's foundation. After descending several steps, they reached a stone balcony above a dark room that Hayley estimated was around seventeen feet below. The walls, made of huge limestone slabs, lacked windows and doors. To their right, a stone staircase awaited their descent. Aiming their flashlights at the stairs one by one, they descended into the empty room, then used their lights to explore the dark shadows and high ceiling.

Hayley, looking for Abel, stared into the shadows. "He's not here, but I feel his presence on the other side of that wall."

Scant furnishings lined the room—a small desk, a couple of wooden chairs, and a bookshelf against the wall Hayley pointed to.

"He's coming! Move back," she shouted.

They huddled into a corner and watched the bookshelf heave in and out. Jim and Roger aimed their cameras; Kathy held out her voice recorder. As the apparition forced its way into the room, the shelf exploded, shattering into numerous pieces, exposing a doorway leading into pitch blackness. Hayley saw the oscillating

71

leech feeding on Abel's body, covering him like a cape, leaving only Abel's mighty arms and fierce face exposed.

Aiming his light into the darkness, Lewis stepped forward. Flashlights and lamps instantly went out, sucked dry by the entity's insatiable appetite for energy, leaving everyone in the dark. Lee swore, and in moments Hayley saw him on bent knees, lighter in hand and his propane lamp relit. Jim and Roger did the same.

From across the room she heard a snarl. Before she could shout a warning, Abel lifted the butler off the ground. Lewis peddled his legs in midair, his screams echoing. He squealed as his body slammed against the wall and slid limply to the floor.

Kathy gasped, while holding the recorder firmly in her shaky hand.

"Stop it! Leave him alone," Hayley shouted. She saw Abel turn and posture for an attack. Glancing over her shoulder, she whispered, "Lee."

Lee jumped in front of her, spreading his arms to protect her, while searching for his invisible adversary. "Leave her alone! Don't hurt her!" He glanced over his shoulder, locking eyes with Hayley.

She felt the depth of his love. The warmth of his affection wrapped around her. She looked at Abel, hoping he'd release his anger and remember how he'd tried to protect his wife. Hayley wished he'd share an understanding with Lee, and maybe realize they weren't a threat.

"I love her," Lee said, his gaze embracing Hayley.

Hayley stared at Abel's changing expressions, noticing, too, the negative entity's curious reaction to Abel's memories of love. She whispered to Lee, "It's working. He's calling Emma's name and pulling back into the cave."

Lee turned to Lewis, who stood brushing himself off. "Are you okay?"

"Yes, sir. Do you think we can get him to do that again?"

"Ya need some serious therapy, ya crazy loon," Jim said. "He could've smashed your puny brain."

"Yes, but he didn't. I don't think he intends to hurt us," Hayley said. "We just caught him off guard." She looked at Lee's concerned expression as he stared toward the blackness leading to the cave. "You know we have to go in there," she said.

He nodded.

Silence filled the stone chamber. The apparition had retreated into the darkness through the gaping hole in the wall.

"Are we going in now?" Lewis asked.

Hayley could no longer hold her shield—the entity had drained her energy, and the white light protecting her dissipated. Pain pounded in her head. Trying to ease her throbbing headache, she raised her hands, hiding her eyes from the lamp's light. When the wretched smell returned, the pain intensified, overwhelming her. She gagged and winced, gasping for breath. On the verge of unconsciousness, she collapsed. In her haze, she felt Lee scoop her into his arms.

The others followed Lee, who carried Hayley toward the staircase. Dashing in front of him, Lewis cleared a path, kicking away the wooden bookshelf's debris, then, taking the lead, lit the way with a lamp.

Once again in the wine cellar, Lee adjusted Hayley's weight in his arms and studied her face. She met his gaze, her head pounding.

"Are you okay?" he asked.

"I can't breathe. The stench is gagging me. I need to get out of here."

He held her tight, headed to the wine cellar entrance, and stepped aside, letting Lewis open the door. After waiting for everyone to exit, Lewis then led them through the maze of basement arches, barely visible beyond the glow of their lamps. At the bottom of the stairs leading to the kitchen, he stopped, opened a breaker box, and reset the main switch. The basement lights went on. 73

"I can walk from here, Lee," Hayley said.

"Are you sure?"

"I'm sure."

He gently set her feet on the ground.

Lewis rushed up the stairs and held the door. When Lee and Hayley ascended and entered the kitchen, the others filed in.

Jim swiped his mouth with his shaky hand. "That thing was so scary I was fartin' like a pack mule."

"I say we meet it head-on," Lewis said.

Jim glared at the butler. "Then what? That makes as much sense as a squirrel up a bear's butt."

Roger picked up his camera. "We've got the leech on video. I think we should take a look at it before we proceed."

"I agree," Hayley said, sitting on a nearby chair. "I noticed something curious. I want to take a look."

Twisting the end of his mustache, Jim stared at Hayley's face. "Maybe we should wait on that. Ya look greener than gourd guts, darlin'."

"He's right," Lee said. He took Hayley's hand as she stood, and he led the way to the elevator in the central hallway.

Roger caught up with them. "Where are we going?"

When the elevator door opened, Lee followed Hayley inside. "My sitting room."

Roger nodded. "We'll meet you there." He turned and joined the others climbing the servants' stairs.

From the elevator, Lee and Hayley entered the third-floor hall. With her hand in his, she counted each door they passed, trying to take her mind off her lingering pain. Once they turned into the north wing hallway, she focused on the decor. The hall's dentil crown moldings were the colors of champagne and gold. Cranberries and vines bordered the ceiling. In its center, swirls of golden threads laced around a medallion where a chandelier hung in front of the door to Lee's sitting room. At the end of the hall, walls the shade of honey surrounded two long windows dressed in wine-red drapes.   74

Everything's reminding me of food. Her stomach rumbled. She hadn't eaten all day, worried about her reaction to the inevitable pain.

Lee opened the double doors to the tower's room. "Would you like some lunch?"

"You read my mind. And maybe some wine." She sat on the overstuffed pale blue suede couch.

Lee pulled out his cell phone.

Hayley glanced toward the sunlight streaming in through the long windows encased in the tower's curved wall overlooking the front lawn. *I love this room.* The walls were painted the green of the apples on her tree at home just before they blushed red. The carpet reminded her of a blue sky reflected in a crystal pond, and the drapes of espresso with cream. She assumed motion detectors triggered the lighting. She sighed.

More crown molding. Martha Stewart would love this place.

Feeling safe, Hayley imagined herself sitting in the glow of the white marble fireplace on a snowy day. *Not very likely if this headache keeps up.* Her hand brushed across her forehead, trying to sweep away the last traces of the pain. She put her head back, gazed at the light blue ceiling, and waited for the rest of the team to join them.

Lewis rushed into the room, went straight to the bar, and loaded a tray with drinks.

Lee took a glass of red wine from the tray and passed it to Hayley. "Still have a headache?"

"It's nearly gone."

"Can I do anything for you?"

"You can take me home after lunch. I need to get some rest and try to figure things out."

When Roger, Jim, and Kathy arrived, Lewis offered them drinks.

"Lewis, tell Velma there'll be five for lunch," Lee said.

"Right away, sir." Lewis quickly left the room.

"Because of Clint's surgery, I'm closing the office until noon tomorrow," Roger said.

"Call before you leave." Lee looked at Hayley. "Think you'll be up to going to the hospital tomorrow?"

"I'm not sure how much sleep I'll get tonight. Why don't you give Clint my love and call me when he's out of surgery?"

"Will do," Lee said. "I'll meet you at the hospital, Roger."

Roger sipped his wine and nodded.

"If Hayley's up to it, we can make plans to go back into the foundation room tomorrow night," Lee said.

"If I'm up to it or not, I have to go over that footage."

Jim rolled the stem of his glass between his fingers. "Gettin' Leech to leave is gonna be 'bout as easy as nailin' a snowflake to a tree."

"Might be harder than that," Hayley said.

CHAPTER 10

Hayley stepped out of Lee's car, gazing at her Victorian home with its coned turret and wraparound porch. Even though she'd recently found out she'd grown up in this house during a previous life, her fondness for the home in this lifetime couldn't be more genuine. To her, coming home always felt like stepping into a hug.

Lee picked up her suitcase and followed her, neither speaking. The gusting winds thrashed her rain-soaked flower garden. Leaves on the old apple tree rustled. Dark clouds threatened more rain, and thunder rumbled in the distance as she stood on the porch unlocking her front door.

Hayley hesitated inside. "Lee, you can leave my things here. You don't have to take them upstairs."

"It'll only take me a second."

He followed her up to her bedroom. She pointed to the rocking chair beside the fireplace across from her bed. "Right there's good. Thanks, Lee."

Lee set her belongings down, turned, and put his arms around her. "You okay?"

She snuggled against his warm chest. "Yes. I'm just tired."

He drew a deep breath, then released it with a groan. "Damn it! This whole thing turns my stomach! I can't stand the fact my home makes you feel like this." He ran his fingers through her hair and kissed her forehead.

"We'll figure this out somehow," she told him.

He led her to the edge of her bed, motioning for her to sit. "Tomorrow, when Clint's surgery is over, I'll call you. If everything goes well, we'll open the office at noon. Sleep in. Try to get some rest." He leaned in. His lips brushed across her cheek, then met her lips, lingering. He pulled away and sighed. "I hate leaving you alone like this."

"I'm okay, Lee. Tell Clint I'm thinking of him."

"I will. I'll pick you up for work around eleven thirty."

He turned to leave.

After hearing the front door close, she opened a dresser drawer and pulled out a nightgown. On the wall above her head, her grandmother's antique clock chimed softly. Hayley glanced up, surprised to find it was only two in the afternoon. The day weighed on her. Her body felt heavy, as if the last of her energy had evaporated. She needed a nap.

Hayley undressed, tossed her clothes onto the rocking chair, and slipped into her nightgown. She pulled back the bed covers and slid between them, eyes ready to close. With her head nesting on the feather pillow, she whispered, "Grams, I need you." She closed her eyes.

Hayley dreamed she walked along the beach by Hotel del Coronado, where she'd had her first date with Lee. In the wet sand, imprints formed beneath her bare feet, and the rhythm of the waves felt as relaxing as the breeze. Seagulls soared over the water, and from a cluster of large granite rocks behind her came the barking of seals.

She followed the shoreline toward a woman in a flowing white dress who stood on the wet sand, gazing at the ocean. The woman turned to face her.

Hayley marveled again at her grandmother's youthful appearance. She recalled the first time Grams had appeared to her in spirit. She'd said, "I no longer have to wear a rotting carcass, dear. My soul is ageless." Since then Grams had continued to help her make sense of her abilities, while telling Hayley about the hereafter.

"I love you, Grams. Thanks for coming. I need help."

"I know, dear. That's why I'm here." The gentle wind played with Grams's golden hair. "I've consulted with others about your dilemma, and there *is* something you can do. First, to avoid getting headaches, you need to meditate before confronting the entity. Give yourself at least ten to fifteen minutes."

"Why?"

"It will increase your stamina so you can protect yourself longer, and enable you to have more time to drive away the negativity."

"Drive away? Can't it be killed?"

"No, honey. Your universe has laws. Neither positive nor negative energy can be destroyed. But the good news is that positive energy always dominates negative. Always! It will take time, maybe a week. You'll have to get Abel to keep his mind on the pleasant aspects of his life so the entity won't be able to feed."

"So, I should get him to talk about his wife?" Hayley asked.

"Yes. But make sure it's about a happy time, before being kidnapped, or Abel's anger will be manipulated into hatred."

"A week? Are you saying the entity will pull away?"

"Yes, maybe less," Grams said. "Eventually, when Abel's will becomes stronger, the entity will surrender its host and go in search of another."

"What if I can't get it to leave? My relationship with Lee, would that change?"

"Do you think a drug addict planned to be born a drug addict? Honey, life doesn't always go as planned. Free will can change things, and the manipulation by negativity can destroy a person's life purpose."

"So, there's a chance my life with Lee will end?" Hayley looked down at the sand and, although in a dream, felt tears well up.

"You can't allow yourself to think about that alternative, dear. The entity will use it against you. It's not going to go willingly. You need to protect yourself at all costs. That's why you can't confront it for more than thirty minutes at a time, though as many times a day as you feel comfortable, until Abel builds up his strength against it. The important thing is to keep Abel's mind on the love he has for his wife and son. It's the only way."

"Thanks, Grams. I love you."

Hayley woke, reached for the notepad on her nightstand, and wrote everything down before she forgot. After finishing, she slipped under the covers and thought about her adversary. "I won't let you take my life with Lee! I'm coming for you. You'd better run!"

CHAPTER 11

At the office, Roger hooked up the thermal-imaging camera to the laptop computer and slid it in front of Hayley. She watched the video of Abel posturing to attack her. Focused intensely on the screen, she waited for the moment Lee had defended her, and the odd reaction of the negative entity consuming the slave.

Hayley pointed at the monitor. "There! Look! Leech is oscillating. Play it back. I want you to see this."

Spinning the laptop around, Roger reset the video and turned the monitor toward Hayley. Lee, sitting next to her, leaned closer. Lewis, on her other side, pressed his chair to hers, while Roger and Jim looked over her shoulder. Kathy remained at the hospital with Clint's mother, Roger's sister, John, Clint's cousin, and Laura, who'd performed Clint's surgery.

"Keep your eye on the density of the negativity right here," she showed them, "where it's feeding on Abel. There!"

Lee played the video again. "Its temperature is fluctuating. It's moving," he said.

Hayley nodded. "Yes. It's shifting, pulling away, and waiting."

"Waiting for what?"

She sat back in her seat. "Waiting for the instant it can turn Abel's thoughts away from his wife so it can manipulate him to focus on the circumstances of his murder and being separated from his family."

"What happens if Leech pushes Abel's memories of his family to the back of his mind and keeps his thoughts on hatred?" Roger asked.

"That's Leech's goal. If that happens, Abel will lose himself completely. When Abel appears as a ghost, it won't be him any longer, it will be Leech, and Leech will be looking for another victim."

Jim squinted at the monitor. "Ya got some kinda plan to get rid of that thing?"

"I asked Grams for help. She told me we need to keep Abel's mind on the happy times before those men kidnapped his wife and son. She said if he thinks about the love he feels for his family, his free will becomes stronger, and Leech weakens."

Lee rolled his chair back from the desk. "Hayley and I plan on communicating with Abel for brief periods around the clock. It's going to be tough, but we have to keep at it."

"How long do you think it will take?" Roger asked.

Hayley shrugged. "Maybe a week."

He stared, his mouth gaping. "Day and night?"

She nodded. "Yes. We'll start out strong and spend thirty minutes with Abel every two hours."

Lewis frowned. "Thirty minutes? Why not longer?"

"It could be dangerous," Hayley said. "We have to remember Leech's insatiable appetite. It'll try to attack us, plant seeds in our minds. I can shield myself and two others for only so long. With practice, I'll be able to increase the protection. I'll shield Abel as Leech recedes. By the time Leech turns to fight, he won't have anything left to feed on."

"While we're communicating," Lee said, "we should video the entity's reaction so we can see if our plan's working."

Hayley patted his leg. "Good idea. And we'll need an EVP so we can record Abel's answers. We might be able to piece together what happened to Emma. As we go along, we can find out what questions work best."

Lewis raised his hand. "I'll volunteer to video, since I'll be nearby twenty-four hours a day."

Jim glared at Lewis. "Ya don't think I'm gonna let your bony butt be the only one to have all the fun, do ya?"

"I beg your pardon! I am not skinny!"

Jim grunted. "Hell, ya can stand under a clothesline in the rain and not get wet." He reached over and disconnected the camera from the computer, then held it up to Lewis. "I'll show ya how to use this, and we can take turns. How's that sound?"

"Sounds good to me. There's more than one way to skin a fish."

"Cat."

"Excuse me?"

"Cat. There's more than one way to skin a *cat*."

Lewis crunched his nose in disgust. "Sir, *you* are a Neanderthal."

"Lewis, you're nuttier than a squirrel's turd."

"If you guys are through insulting each other," Lee said, "I suggest we end this meeting so we can go back home. Ready, Lewis? You, Hayley, and I have to confront our nemesis."

"More than ready, sir."

CHAPTER 12

On the balcony overlooking the windowless foundation room, Hayley, Lee, and Lewis stood shining their flashlights into the darkness of the stone chamber.

"Who's the genius who thought of putting plastic chairs down there?" Lee asked.

"It wasn't a genius, sir," Lewis told him, holding up a lamp. "It was Jim."

Shadows beyond the propane lamp's light kept the three of them alert and skittish. Lee took a step toward the stairway leading down.

"Keep the light away from the cave's entrance," Hayley said. "We don't want to scare Abel again." She took a deep breath to slow her hurried heartbeat. *Calm. Remember to keep calm.*

From the top of the stairs, Lee gazed into the still room below, turned, and studied her face. "Are you ready for this?"

"Yes." *I hope so.*

Earlier in the wine cellar, before they entered Abel's domain and the consuming entity's, Lee and Lewis had left her to meditate while they gathered flashlights and lamps. Now, before descending into the den, she stood above the putrid-smelling room and closed her eyes, saying a prayer to ask for protection, and mentally surrounded the three of them with white light.

Opening her eyes, she looked toward the dark, gaping hole leading to the cave and took a breath. The air smelled clean again.

She nodded. "Ready."

Clad in his butler apparel minus his black suit coat and vest, Lewis, holding a flashlight and lamp, led the way down the stairway. Lee carried two lamps. Once they reached the bottom, they gathered behind the chairs.

"These could be lethal weapons," Lee said, placing his hand on the chair in front of him.

"I will tell Jim to remove them, sir," Lewis replied.

"I'd wait on that," Hayley said. "When Jim went to the trouble of putting these down here, he was following an instinct."

"So, some kind of divine intervention told him to do this?" Lee asked.

"I don't have time to go into that right now, but yes. Things happen for a reason. So let's just go with it."

"Chairs it is then," Lee said.

Lewis set his lamp on the floor and exchanged his flashlight for Hayley's thermal-imaging camera. Keeping his eye on the cave's entrance, Lee set his lamps down and took a voice recorder from Hayley.

When they were organized, she cleared her throat. "Abel, we'd like to talk with you, please."

The room grew cold as the slave approached. Lee took Hayley's hand, and they stared into the mouth of the cave.

"He's here," she whispered. Her words flowed in a cold mist. She saw the slave's dark face distort with hatred. She glanced at Lee, then at Lewis. "I wish you could see him."

"What does he look like?" Lee asked in a low voice.

"If I were Jim, I'd say he looks like he's chewing on a hornet," Hayley said. "He's strong, and scarier than hell."

Abel stood in front of them with glaring eyes and teeth

grinding. "Where es my Emma? I'se free! Emma an' my boy, dey's free like I is."

"We don't know where Emma is," Hayley told him.

"Youse ly'n'!"

Lewis watched the negative entity on the camera's view screen. "Leech is growing denser and increasing its size."

"Would you let us help?" Hayley asked.

"Youse workin' fo Massa Wheeler," he said through clenched teeth, "jes like Sam. He gone 'n' stab me in de back. Evil man. Youse evil, ly'n'."

Hayley watched the black mass grow, engulfing more of Abel's body, covering his neck and shoulders. It reached its tentacles toward her, smelling her energy, and she prayed to God for more protection.

The entity drew back.

Lewis glanced up from his camera. "It seems to me that this line of conversation is not going as planned."

Hayley spoke. "We're not going to give up. You can't scare us away." She rubbed her arms and whispered to Lee, "Look around. The room's starting to fog. It's sucking the warmth from the air."

The chair she rested her hand on started to vibrate, startling her. *Is Leech willing the chair to move? Can it do that?* She jumped away.

The chair jerked, spun, then with great force flew above her head, crashing against the wall. With camera in hand, Lewis darted to a corner of the room and turned to Hayley for instructions.

"Near the wooden chair, a couple of feet in front of the desk," she said.

Lewis looked through the view screen and continued to record.

Lee grabbed Hayley's hand. Putting her against the stairwell wall, he stood in front of her with his back toward Abel, then studied Hayley's face. "Headache?"

She shook her head.

"What's he saying?" he asked.

"He thinks we're lying to him."

Lee moved aside, giving her another chance to speak.

Hayley stepped forward. "Is Emma your wife, Abel?"

The slave threw his arm up, covering his face as if Hayley's words harmed him. "Leaves me be!"

"Please, let us help."

"Youse ly'n'."

A second chair spun on one leg, then edged toward Hayley. Lee grabbed her by the waist, wheeled her around, and stepped in front of her. The chair sailed over them, hit the staircase, and bounced off a few steps, landing at Hayley's feet.

"Now I see," Lee said. "Better the chair than us."

Hayley nodded. "Exactly." She stared at the dark mass and noticed it moved as if restless. "Abel, do you remember what Emma looks like?"

She turned toward Lewis, who raised his head from the camera's view screen and gave her a thumbs up.

"Was she pretty?" Hayley continued. "Did you love her the first time you met her? Did she laugh a lot?"

"My Emma es a perdy woman. I'se a lucky man. She loves me. Emma told me dat every mornin'. I does shurly miss her." He lowered his head.

"We're going to help you find Emma," Hayley told him. "You'll see her again. I promise."

"Youse ly'n'."

"No, Abel, I'm not. Think about how great it will be to see her again."

The distrust on his face diminished slightly. He seemed confused, then smiled. The dark mass momentarily pulled away from Abel's body, then reclaimed its host.

"Repulsed by the taste of untainted love?" Hayley asked Leech. She whispered to Lee, "Leech didn't like our conversation. I think we should go now. Hopefully, the visions I've embedded in Abel's mind will make him think of his wife until we come back."

"Lewis," Lee said softly, "let's go."

Lee and Lewis handed their tech equipment to Hayley and picked up the lamps, keeping their eyes on the chairs in case of another attack. They ascended the staircase and nervously looked back from the balcony. Their lamps dimly lit the chamber, while Hayley stared down at the negative mass. The entity had slid below its host's chest, leaving Abel's body visible from head to waist. Leech pulsated. Hayley saw it reach out with a tentacle to taste and feed on the traces of the energy hers, Lee's, and Lewis's bodies had left behind.

It's waiting for its chance to regain its control over Abel.

The smile on Abel's face lingered and, by the leech's reaction, Hayley believed he was thinking of Emma. "Good for you, Abel. Keep thinking about your wife. We'll be back."

CHAPTER 13

Lee's sitting room on the third floor of the tower overlooked the spruce-lined drive that curved through the sea of grass in the front yard of his mansion. Hayley rested on the soft couch. With her bare feet in Lee's lap, she wondered, *If a lawn mower left the far corner of the front yard at ten A.M., and another with a loose rear wheel left the south side fifteen minutes later, how long would it take them to meet at the train station?*

"What are you thinking about?" Lee asked. "You have a strange look on your face. Headache?"

"No. I'm relaxing, taking my mind off dimensional realities. I think I'm getting better at blocking the negative energy. How about you?"

"I can't relax until that thing's gone. What do we know so far?"

Hayley touched her index finger to her lips. "Let's see. Abel Smith, his wife, Emma, and their son were kidnapped from Ohio. He mentioned a Master Wheeler, so I'm guessing they were sold to a plantation owner. Who knows how long after that, in the 1850s, a man named Sam murdered Abel in the cave under your estate. Sometime after Abel's death, the negative entity took him as its host and wrapped its dark mass around him to feed. Then, more than a century-and-a-half later, for some reason, Abel, dominated by the entity, reached up through the garden and grabbed me. That's about it."

"That's not much to go on. I'm wondering how Sam knew about the cave."

The answer came to Hayley as a whisper in her mind. "The Underground Railroad."

"We have a couple of hours," Lee said. "I think we should search the library to see if we can find proof that my family was involved in helping slaves."

"Your library is as big as my entire home. It'll take a while. Maybe we can ask Jim to help us."

"Good thinking."

Lee pulled out his cell phone and texted Jim and Lewis. The double doors swung open, and Lewis stepped into the sitting room, resuming his duties.

"Would you care for a drink or something to eat, sir?"

"Lewis, you don't have to jump from ghost investigator to butler. Choose one or the other. We're meeting Jim in the library to search for clues. Want to join us?"

Without hesitation, he removed his black suit coat and draped it across his arm. "Yes, sir!"

"I'm hoping to find evidence of the Underground Railroad. Hayley believes my family was involved. If so, there has to be some kind of record or correspondence somewhere."

"Yes, sir. Maybe I can search the secret passageway. I'll look for hidden compartments."

"That sounds great, Lewis. Maybe you and Jim should take a look."

~*~

Jim stuck his head out of the secret doorway leading into the passageway. "Lee, come here a minute. I want ya to see somethin'."

90

Hayley tucked a book back into its place on the shelf, turned, and followed Lee down the spiral staircase and across the room. Wanting to stay out of their way, she waited while Lee joined Jim. She leaned inside the passage to see what had caught Jim's attention.

Lee looked around. "Where's Lewis?"

"Ah, he's off investigatin' the stairs leadin' to the basement," Jim said. "The weirdo looked happier than a gopher in soft dirt." He aimed his flashlight at an area of the wall and brushed his hand across the bricks. "Take a look at this. See how the bricks are protrudin' in some kinda decorative detailin'? I think it's a façade."

Lee examined the bricks, each square pattern extending an inch beyond flush. He glanced at Jim. "What makes you think that?"

"Buildin' decorative masonry in this rat-infested hidden passage makes as much sense as hangin' a chandelier in an outhouse."

"Actually, I could see my family doing that," Lee said. "Have you seen how many chandeliers there are in my home?"

"I agree your family's a little on the prissy side, but I still think this is a sham." Jim knocked on the wall. "Should make a different sound if it's hollow behind one of these." Then he rapped on the center grouping of protruding bricks. "Hear that?"

"You're right. It sounds hollow."

Jim pressed firmly against the right edge of the extending bricks. "Hear that click?" He looked closer. "Well, looky here."

Lee leaned in.

Jim ran his finger across a newly formed gap running along the seam between the protruding bricks and the flush wall. "The entire bunch of bricks is top cut and set into a metal plate." He examined them closer. "Some kind of wire." Jim pinched it and yanked. "What've we got here?" He pulled fake mortar from between the bricks and shone his light into the crevice. "Hinges."

"They sure went to a hell of a lot of trouble trying to hide something," Lee said. "Hopefully it's what we're looking for."

Jim reached to the left side, slid his fingers into the gap, and pulled. The cluster of bricks swung open like a door to a safe. Reaching inside, he brought out yellowed papers, envelopes, and a brown leather-bound book and handed them to Lee.

Lee glanced at Hayley. "Think this is our evidence?"

She nodded. "I'm sure of it."

After the men stepped out, she released the panel and let it close. Across the room, the morning sunlight brightened the carved mahogany table in front of the library windows. Hayley, excited about their discovery, followed the men to the table and sat next to Lee, while Jim took the seat across from them.

Lee spread out their findings and took his glasses from his shirt pocket, then put them on and hesitated, glancing across the room. "Did you hear that?"

Hayley heard it too: a series of raps.

"Someone's knockin' on the door," Jim said, looking over his shoulder.

"Sir." The voice came from behind the wall.

"Oh damn! We forgot Lewis," Lee said. "Jim, let him out, please."

"Can't we just leave him in there so I can take his turn down in the dungeon?"

"I heard that!" the voice said.

Lee looked over the rim of his glasses. "Just let him out."

Lewis knocked again.

Taking his time, Jim walked to the secret panel. "All right, keep your damn shirt on. I have three speeds—on, off, and don't push your luck." He turned the carved filigree and the panel swung open. "Come out, you damn fool."

Lewis stepped out of the passageway with his chin high and followed Jim to the table. They sat across from Hayley.

"Find anythin' interestin', nutcase?" Jim asked the butler.

"I did find an excellent way to get to the wine cellar. We no longer have to cross the mansion to take the kitchen stairway."

Lee looked up from the documents. "Good to know, Lewis."

He returned his attention to the book. Yellowed pages slid out when he opened the cover. He carefully picked them up from the table and examined them.

"It's a journal. This is a list of people's names with numbers beside them. Maybe it's a code."

"Does it mention a state?" Hayley asked.

He examined it closer. "No. Could be they're all in North Carolina. I'd think something like this would be on a need-to-know basis so there's less chance of leaking information." Among the papers strewn on the table were posters of wanted slaves and a couple of hand-printed flyers advertising slave auctions. "There doesn't seem to be anything here stating outright that my family was involved with the Underground, but it looks quite likely."

Jim picked up a large envelope and opened it. He slid out folded sheets of paper, looked inside the envelope again, and pulled out a photo. As he twisted the end of his mustache, he read the letter. "Well I'll be a son of a jackass!"

"You already are," Lewis said, glancing up from a wanted poster.

"Take a look at this." Jim handed the letter and photo to Lee.

Lee carefully separated the letter's two pages, handing one to Hayley.

After reading, she looked at the photo. "According to this letter, that picture was taken by a man in Greensboro, North Carolina. The four men on horseback are patrolmen licensed to catch runaways. The black boy standing by the horse, holding the reins, is a slave belonging to that man with a mustache."

Lee read the page he held. "I think this letter proves our theory. It's a warning. The men in that picture are helping slaves run, then tracking them for a fee. In some cases, they're kidnapping free slaves, crossing borders, then selling them. My ancestors *were* involved in the Underground. Why else would they get a letter like this?"

Looking closer, Hayley focused on the man whose horse stood forward from the others. Her mouth gaped open. "This is the man I saw in my dream, Lee. He's the one who killed Abel. I'm sure of it." In her mind's eye, she could clearly see his pockmarks, shabby mustache, and dirty clothes.

"There's a list of names here," Lee said. "His name was Sam, right? There's a Samuel Digger on this list."

"So we know he's a patrolman, a kidnapper, and was hired by Master Wheeler to kill Abel," Hayley said.

"That makes sense," Jim said. "I bet Wheeler knew the guy was two-faced, and had some kind of deal to buy all Digger's illegals." He leafed through some of the paper, then scratched his cheek. "Why don't I take this stuff to the office and give it to Kathy? She can start lookin' for clues to the whereabouts of Wheeler's plantation."

Lee looked at Hayley. "What do you think?"

"It's a good idea. We can use all the information we can get to find out what happened to Emma."

Lewis glanced at his watch. "Sir, it's time for another confrontation, and I've mentioned I know of a quick way to get there."

All turned toward the secret passage.

"Jim, you'll sit this one out," Lee said.

He nodded. "Got things to do anyhow."

Lee pushed his chair back. "Before we go, let's give Hayley some private time. She has to meditate so she can form a shield. We'll need protection. That thing knows we're coming."

CHAPTER 14

Looking through the glass door, Hayley saw the wine cellar was still and peaceful. Once inside, she found the stench seemed less invasive, and the energy in the room seemed different somehow. Her psychic senses nudged her consciousness, telling her to go slowly. Something was wrong.

Lewis lifted propane lamps from the shelf, lit them, and handed a couple to Lee. The two men took the lanterns and flashlights, while Hayley carried the thermal-imaging camera and voice recorders. With everything in hand, they walked to the corner of the wine cellar and the entrance they had uncovered leading to the foundation room, Abel and the entity's domain.

When she neared the door, Hayley froze, staring down in disbelief.

Lee followed her gaze. His face paled. "What the hell is that?"

Dark red fluid seeped into the wine cellar from under the door. Visions of Abel's death flashed once more through Hayley's mind. She saw the knife plunge into his back over and over until he fell.

"Blood," she whispered. "Don't panic."

They rushed back across the room.

"Give me a minute." Hayley set the equipment on a chair, closed her eyes, and envisioned herself standing with Grams.

"I'm so glad you're here."

"Of course, dear. I'm as concerned about Abel as you are."

In her vision, she and Grams walked beyond the wine cellar's boundaries and down the steps to the balcony. They stood looking out at the entity's creation. Blood dripped from the foundation room's limestone walls, pooling on the floor, while a red mist filled the air.

Hayley blinked away the moisture gathering on her eyelashes, and felt the crimson mist beading on her hair and dripping down her face. She looked at her clothing. Her jeans and yellow short-sleeve blouse appeared to be soaked in blood. When she looked at her arms, small puddles on her skin gave her the impression she'd been stabbed many times. The gruesome sight turned her stomach.

"This entity has the ability to distort a person's thoughts," Grams said. "By using the humidity of a stream flowing through the cave and the warmth in the air, the leech formed a recipe for condensation, gathered the moisture, and froze it inside this room. What you're seeing is melting ice, not dripping blood. By manipulating your perception, the entity can make you or anyone believe a lie, trying to create fear so it can feed." She hesitated, watching Hayley look around, and added, "It won't give up its host until it has consumed him. It needs to feed off your fear to increase its energy mass so it can finish with Abel once and for all. Then it will look for a new host. You must explain this to your friends."

Hayley glanced around. As she comprehended her grandmother's words, the deception melted away, revealing the truth. The illusion was water.

"Thank you, Grams."

Her vision ended. Hayley returned to her own reality and saw Lewis and Lee's strained expressions.

"It's a trick," she told them. "The entity's distorting your reality. Come. Let me show you."

They returned to the entrance and stared at the liquid bleeding into the wine cellar. Hayley closed her eyes, said a prayer for protection, and mentally surrounded them with white light. The pool of blood turned to clear water.

Lee looked up with raised brows. "What just happened?"

"Now you're seeing the truth."

"It's only water," Lewis said, sounding disappointed.

She put her finger to her lips. "We have to stay quiet. We can't let it know we're aware of its tricks."

Lewis and Lee followed her across the wine cellar. They gathered by the chair where she'd set the equipment.

"We're going to have to change our plans a little." Hayley thought a moment. "Lewis, we're going to need raincoats."

He grinned. "Right away."

When the glass door closed behind him, Hayley watched Lewis run across the dimly lit basement. She turned, picked up the voice recorder and camera from the chair, and sat, taking a moment to strategize.

She glanced at Lee. "The entity will be waiting to feed on our fear. But Leech will need only a second to realize that's not going to happen. So I'll go in first. I need to film its density to compare it to our last video. If I'm right, this little stunt has drained quite a bit of its energy." Hayley checked the thermal-imaging camera, making sure its batteries were charged. She sensed Lee's trepidation. "I know how shocking things will appear, but whatever you do, don't react or Leech will feed and increase its mass."

Lee stared at the doorway. "Is it dangerous? Will it attack?"

"No. There won't be any point. If we're not afraid, it can't feed."

"What if it decides to kill us?"

Hayley shook her head. "I don't think it will. We're just an annoyance so far, not a threat."

"So far," Lee said.

Lewis returned with an armful of raincoats. He handed each a full-length slicker. "These were hanging by the basement door leading to the garden."

She checked the size and swapped hers with Lee's. "I'll go first," she said. "Then I'll let you know when to follow. If I'm right and that trick drained the entity's energy, it isn't going to be happy. Keep your eyes on me so you'll know where it is."

Lee held her coat while she slipped her arms into the sleeves. Hayley flipped up her hood, waited until they were ready, closed her eyes, and strengthened their shields by once more surrounding them with white light, then reopened her eyes. With lanterns and equipment in hand, they crossed the room.

Reaching around her, Lee opened the door and they followed her down the stairs. Before they reached the balcony, she gave them a sign to wait. She went first, tiptoeing down the remaining stairs and across the water-covered balcony. Through the camera's lens, Hayley stared into the mist at the entity clinging to Abel, and she began to film.

In a moment, Hayley realized Leech knew its plans were foiled. When she lowered the camera, Hayley saw Abel looking up at her, his face twisting with hatred. Then he turned, entered the cave, and disappeared into the darkness.

Cold, wet, and trying to hurry, Hayley hung the camera strap around her neck and tucked the camera under her raincoat. Glancing over her shoulder, she motioned to Lee and Lewis, then headed to the staircase.

Equipped with flashlights and lamps, she followed the others creeping down toward the foundation room, keeping her eyes on the mouth of the cave. Through her shields, she saw and felt water pelting her slicker. With her head down and hood pulled forward, she reached the bottom of the stairs.

"Leech convinced Abel to hide," Hayley told them. "Abel won't be back."

Lee patted his arms. "Why is it so cold?"

Aiming her flashlight upward, Hayley gazed through the rainstorm into the misty cloud hugging the ceiling. "Grams said the cave has an underground stream. The entity took the humidity created by the stream and the warmth in the air to use the principles of condensation. It pulled all the moisture into this room and froze it, creating a winter wonderland, and then waited for us. Now it's melting. If we weren't shielded, we'd see it as blood."

"What would happen if you lowered our shield?" Lewis asked, teeth chattering.

Lee and Hayley stared at him as if he had lost his mind.

"J...just wondering," he said, stuttering from the cold.

Hayley looked at Lee. "Want to see?"

"Will we be affected?"

"No. You'll only see the distortion for a few moments until your rational mind tells you it's a lie."

"That'll work for me." Lewis shone his flashlight around the room.

She had seen the entity's creation through a vision. Did she really want to witness the gory deception in reality, where her mind would process the same distorted truth that Lee and Lewis's would? Again, she would see the illusion as blood. Gathering her nerve, she closed her eyes, and in her mind released the protection surrounding them, then reopened her eyes.

Looking at the illusion, Hayley knew what Lewis and Lee were seeing. Thick drops of blood fell from the ceiling through a red mist. The walls around them wept crimson tears.

Lewis extended his hand, catching blood in his palm. Hayley watched him rub the liquid between his fingers, sniff it, and scrutinize its texture under the beam of his flashlight. "This is awesome!"

Lee looked up into the rain. As he glanced down, the beam of Hayley's flashlight lit his face. She held her breath.

Blood drenched his face. His moist eyes, welling with crimson liquid, glowed like rubies. Blood streamed down his cheeks, dripping from his mouth and chin.

It's not real. It's not real.

As Hayley's mind rejected the lie, she saw by Lewis and Lee's wide-open eyes that their minds had exposed the truth as well: the blood had become water to them.

Lewis's breath turned to cold mist as he rubbed his arms. Aiming his light upward, he stared at the defrosting ceiling. "Wow! What an illusion."

Lee looked behind him, then looked up. "I heard something fall." He squinted, as if trying to see through the dissipating mist. "Ooh, look! The ceiling's covered with icicles."

Ice fell, hitting one of the three plastic chairs near the stairwell. To their left, another icicle dropped, shattering, spraying them with shards of ice.

Lee grabbed Hayley's hand and they sprinted up the staircase, with Lewis at their heels. Momentarily, they stood on the balcony watching the fog dissipate. More and more ice plummeted from the ceiling. Remnants of the illusion melted away.

Grams was right, Hayley thought. The negative entity held tightly to Abel. But now its antics would lead to its downfall. Using so much of its energy to create the illusion, counting on an abundance of fear to feed upon, hadn't worked. Hayley smiled with satisfaction.

An icicle imploded on the balcony just a few feet away. Out of the corner of her eye, she saw Lee reach for her arm and Lewis turn to flee.

"Wait a minute. I can't leave and let the entity feed on Abel."

She cleared her throat and flashed her light toward the dark entrance of the cave. "Abel, I know you can hear me. We still want to help you. Do you remember when you courted Emma? Do you recall holding her for the first time?"

Instantly she felt the change of energy. She turned away from the balcony. "I hope that will give him something to think about until morning," she whispered to Lee.

"So, that's it for today?" Lee asked.

Hayley nodded. "I got a good look at Leech through the view screen on the thermal-imaging camera. It lost a lot of its mass from creating this illusion. Most of Abel's torso is exposed now. Since Abel's going to be thinking of his family, I'm pretty sure there's no chance the entity will feed tonight."

Before entering the wine cellar, Hayley turned and whispered, "I promise, Abel, we're not giving up. We'll be back. Whatever it takes, you'll see your wife again."

CHAPTER 15

Lee climbed out of bed and strolled to the ten-foot-tall window overlooking the pond on the north side of his estate. Hayley rolled over in bed and gazed across the room. While Lee stretched in the soft morning light, she studied his long muscular back and appreciated his tight sexy cheeks.

Turning, he met her gaze. She rubbed her hand on the warm vacated spot next to her and patted the bed. Lee walked back across the room and slipped in between the sheets.

He ran his finger across her lips and kissed her. "Do you want to sleep in?" he whispered. "Our plans for today won't start for a while." Before she could answer, he brushed his lips across the round of her breast, then feathered kisses along the curve of her shoulder.

His touch tempted her, but something in his words made her think. "What do you mean about 'our plans'? What are we doing besides helping Abel?"

He rolled away from her. "I've invited Roger, Laura, and Kathy for brunch. And of course, Jim will be joining us."

She looked over her shoulder at the clock on the nightstand, adjusted her pillow, and sat with her back against the headboard. "I guess we should get up. We're getting too used to sleeping in. Do you have any idea when Roger will open the office again?"

Lee tossed his pillow against the headboard and joined her. "I don't know. He's been spending most of his time at the hospital checking on Clint."

"Is he more relaxed now that Clint's had his operation?"

"Yes, but what's difficult for us to understand is why Clint had a tumor in the first place."

She took his hand and laced her fingers between his. "You have to remember that all of us are reincarnated. We planned our lives before we lived them."

"That's what I mean. If Clint planned this life, why did he put himself through this? I know Roger and Laura have to be together in order for something important to happen. But there had to be another way to get Laura to move here other than Clint having to go through hell."

"Who knows?" Hayley said. "Going through this pain might have been something Clint needed to experience."

Lee shrugged. "You don't seem to be as troubled as the rest of us about Clint's condition. I guess your gifts give you more of an understanding about life. They probably make things easier for you."

She met his gaze. "I don't think so. If you were seriously hurt or taken from me, I wouldn't be thinking there's a reason for everything. Even Grams wouldn't be able to comfort me. I'd close off and think life isn't worth living. No matter how much I believe and know there's a purpose, I wouldn't handle it as well as Roger does with Clint's condition."

Lee lifted her hand to his lips, kissing her fingertips.

"So, how's the romance between Roger and Laura progressing?" Hayley asked.

"He finally realized he's in love with her."

"And Laura?"

"She's been experiencing situations similar to yours," Lee

said.

"How's that?"

He climbed out of bed again, walked back to the window, and gazed down at the pond. "You're saving Abel's soul, and she's saving Clint's life."

Hayley pulled her legs up and wrapped her arms around her knees. "Okay, I'll go with that. But that's only one situation. What else is there?"

"She's awestruck, just like you."

"'Awestruck'?"

He turned. "You don't think I haven't noticed how you're walking around my home as if it's some sort of fantasy world? Well, you're not alone. Laura's wandering through Roger's mansion the same way. Between Clint's surgery and her new surroundings, she doesn't see Roger for who he really is. She doesn't realize he was born rich the same way you were born with your gifts. You don't see me walking around looking at you with wide eyes."

"Yes, I do."

"Well, it's not because I think your gift is a fantasy. Both Roger and I are waiting for you two to get over your infatuations and see our homes as just walls and a roof."

Hayley glanced up at the embossed tin ceiling. "I guess I am doing that." She got out of bed to join him and rubbed his back.

"It's not as bad for me as for Roger," Lee said. "You had a chance to get to know me before you found out I have wealth. So now you see me and not just my home. Laura has to separate Roger from his affluence, or she'll never know him. Underneath the wealth, he's just a man like I am."

Hayley embraced him. "You're not just a man. You're the man I love."

He placed his lips on hers. His kiss made her feel as if the

105

world rotated for only them.

When he pulled away, his mahogany eyes were filled with affection. "I love you, too."

The confession of his love sent warmth through her, the feeling of being home, with a contentment that reached her soul. But she knew he was right. If she'd known he was rich when they met, things could've been different. It might've made their knowing each other seem strained with insecurities, her feeling awkward in a world she'd seen only in fairytales. She knew how Laura felt. Hayley realized Lee had worried she'd never see past his wealth. *That's why he kept it from me until he brought me to the gardens.*

"At brunch, I'll try to get Laura to focus on Roger," Hayley said. "I know they're meant to be together anyway, but there's no harm in fanning the fire. Too bad I can't tell her they'll be getting married in less than a year."

"Tempting, isn't it?"

"Telling them might change the outcome. Now you know what I go through seeing the future and not being able to say anything."

After each quickly showered, Lee, wearing a white towel around his waist, went to his closet and pulled out a green designer polo shirt and blue jeans, while Hayley, dressed in a yellow cotton discount store robe, grabbed white shorts and a red halter top from the closet next to his.

"Any more headaches since your grandmother told you how to avoid them?"

"Haven't had one yet. Seems to be working."

He watched her take her clothes from their hangers, some of the few items she'd brought from home. "You know, that part of the closet looks pretty empty. Why don't you bring some more of your things over and fill up the space?"

"I could hang up every piece of clothing I own and not fill this space. Anyway, I'm visiting, not moving in."

"I'd like it if you decided to leave more things here."

"We're just having brunch. I have what I need."

"Maybe tonight you and Kathy can go by your house and get—"

"What's this leading up to?" Hayley interrupted.

"I thought you were psychic."

CHAPTER 16

After brunch, Hayley, Kathy, and Laura toured the second floor. When they stepped out of the music room in the north tower, they strolled down the hall toward the ballroom that overlooked the gardens in the backyard.

"Not only was his first floor designed for entertaining, but this floor as well," Hayley said, "except the guest bedroom suite now used as Jim's permanent residence. There's also the ballroom, dining, and music room, plus a few other rooms intended for visitors and social events." But how often and by how many? she wondered. "I've heard Roger plays the piano."

Laura smiled, nodding. "He serenades me."

"How romantic," Hayley teased. "Do you find Roger interesting?"

"Amazingly so. He's fascinated by my work. His library is a little smaller than Lee's, and has volumes of medical books."

"He gets that from his dad," Kathy said, walking at Laura's side. "His father was an avid anthropologist, and was obsessed with the ascent of the human race, body and mind. When Roger was a boy, his dad took him to Egypt on digs. It was an atmosphere Roger loved, you know, with the legends of life after death and the curses. Anyway, I'm sure some of those books belonged to his dad." Kathy brushed away a wayward blonde strand that had escaped the pink clip pulling her hair neatly to the back of her head.

Hayley had seen Kathy in every shade of pink. Today she wore light pink jeans with a ruffled white short-sleeved blouse and high heels. Her fingernails and toenails glowed pink as well.

"I don't know how you can wear those heels," Laura said. "Don't your feet hurt?"

"I've worn heels since I was two," Kathy said. "The only time I wear flats is when I'm on a date with Thomas, Lee's security guard, so I won't be taller than him, and when we go on a case. Then I wear sneakers."

Laura glanced at her own black pants, green blouse, and flat-heeled shoes. "I've spent my life in textbooks and hospitals. I've always worn sensible shoes."

"Even on dates?" Kathy asked.

"I've never dated much, just now and then. My job is my life. Most of my wardrobe is scrubs. If you've noticed, since I've been here I've worn a dress only once or twice. I've never been attuned to fashion."

"You're a brain surgeon, not a model," Hayley said as she opened the ballroom door.

They casually walked around the ballroom and hesitated at the window to admire the gardens.

"The view is beautiful," Laura said. "You can't see Roger's estate through all the trees, but it's directly across the lake."

"I remember that green dress you wore when we first met you," Kathy said. "You looked like a supermodel then."

"I didn't say I don't have taste. I just have a small wardrobe. In fact, I was able to pack everything I own that wasn't scrubs into two suitcases when I flew here from Oahu."

Kathy beamed. "I love to shop. Maybe sometime we can get together, and I can introduce you to the world of feminine footwear."

"That's a good idea," Hayley said. She looked down at her white shorts and red halter. "From the looks of Lee's wine cellar, he must entertain quite a bit. I definitely need new clothes. Maybe we can have a girls' day out and get manicures and have our hair done." She brushed her brown hair behind her ear. She liked her long hair, but Hayley needed to come up with some reason to coax Laura into a day of pampering.

It wouldn't take much to make Roger drool. Laura's stunning already, and with Kathy's help to enhance her wardrobe, Roger will be aroused to the point of madness.

"I've always wanted highlights. And anyway, if a man's going to serenade you, he'll think twice about playing an encore if you're wearing scrubs."

Laura blushed. "I don't think Roger looks at me that way. I'm a guest. He'd be just as attentive to anyone visiting his home. He's a gentleman."

"So you're not attracted to him?" Hayley asked.

Laura smiled shyly. "I never said that."

"You have to remember that Roger and Lee were raised in an upper-class atmosphere," Hayley explained. "Old school still exists among the elite. Manners are the measure of class. If Roger is anything like Lee, you'd better have lots of patience. I had to initiate our first kiss."

"How did you do that?" Laura asked.

"I thanked him with a kiss. It was short and appropriate, with just a little linger."

"What did he do?"

"It only took him a second before he was looking for a list of things to thank me for."

"That happened before the team met you," Kathy said to Laura. "We were on our way to Hawaii. She and Lee were inseparable from then on."

"By the time we came back to Sutterville, I couldn't take it anymore. I wanted him bad. After dining out one evening, I lured him to my room."

"You're kidding!" Laura said. "You had to lure him? He must have some kind of iron resolve."

"Not anymore, and I can blame that on you and Roger." Hayley led them through the ballroom's double doors.

"You lost me," Laura said.

"Remember when Roger was attacked by ants in the rainforest? Every time he said 'Ouch, ant,' you put gel on his bite."

"I remember."

"So do I," Kathy said. "That was funny."

"Lee and I snuck to the riverbank and came up with a kissing game. Lee would say 'Ouch, ant,' and I would kiss his imaginary bites."

"Glad you were having fun," Laura said.

"You were, too. I saw your face while you rubbed Roger's body with gel. Anyway, we had to wait to finish the game. Back here, one night after we returned to my home following a dinner date, I stood at the top of the staircase and picked up where we'd left off. Of course, I pretended my imaginary bites were in enticing places. He took the stairs two at a time."

"I don't think I could be so bold," Laura said.

"Just start with a thank-you kiss and see where that leads," Hayley suggested.

"Let's go shopping first," Kathy added. "You'll have Roger breathing hard."

Laura frowned. "I'm not good at flirting. I'm going to need all the help I can get."

"If you need anyone to talk to, I'm always available," Kathy offered.

"So am I," Hayley said.

After she finished giving them a tour of the ballroom, Hayley led them to the dining room where Roger, Lee, and Jim waited.

CHAPTER 17

Hayley glanced across the dining room to the right of the carved marble fireplace and saw Roger, Lee, and Jim with beers in their hands, knocking on walls and talking about secret passageways.

After seeing the girls, Lee looked over his shoulder. "Lewis, we'll be going over the documents we found. When you're finished clearing, I'd like you to join us."

"Yes, sir." Lewis sprinted around collecting their brunch dishes. With plates stacked to his chin, he hurried to the serving cart, set them down, and returned for the cups and glasses. Breaking into a trot, he wheeled the cart out of the room.

Jim blinked. "Did you see that? He was all over those dishes like flies on—"

"Jim." Lee nodded toward the women.

Hayley followed Laura to join the men, while Kathy walked to a chair where she'd left her research, picked everything up, and stood at the head of the table.

Once Lewis returned, the team congregated.

Kathy pulled out a list. "There's not a lot of information out there on the name Wheeler dating to the 1850s, with the exception of Major General Joseph Wheeler, who fought for the Confederate Army all over the south. After I researched the major general and his relatives, finding no connections, I broadened my search including other possibilities, and found three plantations associated with the name in Georgia, Tennessee, and Alabama."

Lee scanned the list. "This is good. Two of these are plantation owners. And, I guess, the other is a worker."

She nodded. "He was an overseer. I've researched the states closest to North and South Carolina, but this is all I've found."

Lee handed the list to Hayley. "Any clue where we should start looking?"

Hayley shook her head. "If there're only memories of the past left in the energy on the properties, I have to be physically there to detect it."

"Okay," Lee said. "We'll start with the plantation owners. Hayley and I will go to Tennessee and Georgia—Alabama later, if necessary. Meanwhile, keep searching, Kathy, and if you come up with anything else, let us know."

"I do have something else, but it's not about Wheeler." Kathy picked up the journal Jim and Lee had found earlier. Opening the cover, she carefully ran her fingernail along the top edge of the inner binding. The lining pulled away, revealing a hidden pocket. She slid a thin folded paper from its secret place and spread it on the dining table.

Lee stared. "The lost building plans of the foundation room!"

Carefully, Kathy turned the page over. "And a detailed drawing of the cave."

Lee looked at Roger and Jim. "We need to give this woman a raise."

"I second that," Jim said.

"Got my vote," Roger agreed.

Nodding thoughtfully, Lee sat back in his chair and turned to Hayley. "You know what this means. We'll be able to find Abel's remains."

"You might want to move slowly on this," Laura said, glancing from Hayley to Lee. "I know you plan on keeping this a secret, but think about it. If word somehow gets out about your discovery and you don't report finding human remains, you'll be breaking the law."

Lee peered down the table at Lewis. "I want no mention of Leech or Abel to my staff. And if the discovery of the remains gets out, I'm counting on you to keep the gossip to a minimum and not let any information leave the estate."

"I understand, sir."

"It's not just that," Laura added. "Once you notify state and local authorities, the medical examiner will start his investigation. The cave will be considered a crime scene until the state archaeologists determine the age of the remains."

"I can't imagine anyone going inside that cave while Abel's being influenced," Hayley said. "We won't be able to notify the police until I drive Leech away."

"Well, it shouldn't hurt to search the cave," Roger said.

Jim snorted. "I can't believe ya just said that. Hell, don't ya remember how Lewis was smashed against the wall? What do ya think will happen when we go inside Leech's den?"

"I'll bet nothing happens," Hayley said. "I checked out Leech after that bloody scare tactic yesterday. It had decreased to half its size. Right now, Leech's best defense is to keep away from us so we can't influence Abel's thoughts. Leech needs time to turn Abel's emotions from love back to hate so it can feed and grow."

Roger shrugged. "So, like I said, it shouldn't hurt to take a look. If we find the slave's remains, at least we'll know where they are when we decide to report them. And it'll give Laura a chance to see if there's enough DNA left to gather."

"If we find one bone, that's all I need," Laura said. "A tooth would be even better."

115

Jim shrugged. "What do we need DNA for? We're not makin' a family tree."

"You're forgetting he had a son," Roger said. "He might have other relatives somewhere."

"That should be 'bout as easy as findin' a raindrop in the damn ocean," Jim said.

"Who knows? Maybe we're meant to find them," Roger said. "Stranger things have happened."

"I'd love to find his heirs," Hayley said. "Can you imagine how Abel would feel to know he has descendants?"

Kathy gathered her research. "I have to get to the office. I'll start an interactive website, and maybe we'll get some feedback that will lead us in the right direction."

"Good idea." Lee studied the drawing of the cave. "Where do you think we should look, Hayley?"

She pulled the map of the cave to her and noted how the sketch showed fingers reaching south and west. Hayley closed her eyes, recalled her dream, and tried to sense the site of Abel's murder. Using her finger as a divining rod, she pointed, then opened her eyes. "We'll start here."

CHAPTER 18

In the foundation room, standing in front of the cave's entrance with her flashlight pointing the way, Hayley gazed into the narrow tunnel. Limestone, rich with iron oxide, gave the walls a reddish hue. The low ceiling looked to be no more than five-and-one-half feet high. Her muscles tensed while she nervously hoped she was right about the entity's retreat.

Clearing away her thoughts, she projected her senses.

Where are you?

In her mind's eye, she traveled deeper and deeper through the cave's maze. Nearly one-half mile away, toward the mountains west of Lee's mansion, she perceived the negative energy. Satisfied they were out of danger, she turned to the team. "All clear."

With his lamp held high, Lee stooped and led the way. Hayley followed, ducking and pressing her hand against the rock wall for balance. The stone floor sloped down for nearly the next fifteen feet. Then the tunnel leading into the cave widened and the ceiling rose, allowing them to stand upright.

As they continued to hike, the sound of loose rock being compressed beneath their feet echoed through the tunnel. Finally, they halted where the level dropped upon entering a small cave. Off to the right, tunnels led to other caverns that Hayley remembered envisioning while searching for Leech.

Lee jumped to the dirt and gravel below and steadied his footing before he reached out to help Hayley down. The other investigators, including Laura, followed.

In the middle of the chamber, Hayley turned in a circle amid traces of the past. Wooden chairs, rotted by time, rested on feeble legs. A rusted lantern sat on the dirt floor next to an empty wooden bucket with a ladle inside.

The stale air held memories so vivid Hayley wished the others could see them. All around her, men, women, and children—frightened but excited, nervous but hopeful, quiet but comforting one another—spoke in hushed voices.

"Can you see, hear, or feel any of this, Lee? It's like I'm invisibly standing in a memory."

While she spoke, she saw a dark-haired man with fair skin walk past her. Hayley was stunned. He looked like Lee's twin.

"No," Lee answered. "What are you seeing?"

"I think I'm looking at your great-great-great-grandfather."

"Seriously? His portrait hangs above the grand staircase. We look a lot alike. I envy you. Wish I could see him."

"I wish you could, too. We were right, though—this was part of the Underground Railroad." She pointed across the chamber. "And I see there used to be a tunnel in that wall."

He moved toward it and held up his lantern. "Looks like a cave-in." Reaching up, he wiggled out a stone, and a few more tumbled away. He motioned to Roger, Jim, and Lewis. "Give me a hand."

Laura stood aside with Hayley and watched.

Lewis pulled on the rock directly in front of Lee. It slid out easily, and he tossed it over his shoulder.

Jim jumped. "Watch where you're throwin' that, you damn goof."

"I can't help it if you're in my way, sir." Gripping a jagged stone with his fingers, Lewis tugged with both hands. It didn't budge. He placed his hands on his hips, took a deep breath, and tried again without success.

Jim threw up his hands. "You're as useful as dried spit, Lewis. Just move over and let me do it."

Lewis obliged.

"Ya gotta be smarter than the rock, Lewis," Jim said, stepping up to the wall.

"Then I believe you're wasting your time, sir." Lewis studied the blocked entrance, reached to Jim's left, and pulled out a protruding rock. The stone above the newly created gap slipped, and the wall lost its stability. Everyone leaped back. Half of the obstruction fell away.

Looking at Jim, Lewis tapped his head. "Need I say more?"

Jim scrunched his nose. "You're luckier than a squirrel in a nut house."

Lee held up his lantern and peered down a red-stone artery. "Jim, is this tunnel on our map?"

Jim took the map out of his pocket and checked the details of the cave. "Yup."

"How far back does it go?"

"Not far. I'd say a hundred and fifty feet or thereabouts."

Hayley stepped next to Lee and projected her senses through the tunnel to a small chamber, where it became a dead end. "Abel's in there, along with his remains. The entity must've lost its influence over him."

Roger looked at Hayley, then at the entrance. "Is it safe to go in? Will Abel attack us if we get close to his remains?"

"I think we'll be okay, but we should go slow," Hayley said. "If I can get Abel to speak with us, I'd like to try something."

"Like what?" Lee asked.

"I want to surround him with white light. Or at least his upper torso. I'm curious to see if the entity will react."

Jim stepped between Lee and Roger. "How 'bout askin' where the plantation is?"

Hayley shook her head. "If I mention the plantation, Abel will feed Leech with his negative thoughts, and I don't know how much feeding is needed before that thing takes control again. Hopefully, if the white light works, we'll force Leech to release Abel."

"Just make sure when ya chase that thing away ya steer it clear of us," Jim said. "I know what it's like to be possessed."

Roger gave him a stern look. "You do not!"

"Just ask Francine Schmitt," Jim said. "She'll tell ya. I was talkin' in unknown languages and vomiting green demon juice."

"Don't act like I don't know," Roger replied. "You faked your way out of your wedding commitment. I saw the cans of split-pea soup in your car."

Lee glanced at Hayley, shook his head, and turned back to the passageway. "Guess we better get this over with."

Hayley peered into the tunnel. "I'll go first."

Relying on her intuitive gift instead of her eyesight, she stepped over the rubble and guided them toward the site of Abel's murder. Behind her, the team's flashlights lit the fissures and cavities along the rock-ribbed passage. She walked slowly, not wanting to frighten Abel and cause him to flee. When she reached the dead end, she raised her hand, stopping the others in their tracks.

Hayley glanced at the team. "Wish you could see this. Don't move aggressively."

In the far corner, Abel stood over his remains.

"Don't be afraid, Abel," she said in a low, calming voice. "We're not here to harm you."

120

His deep-set eyes were filled with curiosity. His nostrils flared. "Why youse huntin' me?"

She knelt, folding her hands in her lap, trying to look less threatening. "We're not hunting you, Abel. We just want to talk."

"Talk 'bout what?"

"I was thinking about you and remembered you had a son. I was wondering when he was born. Do you recall?"

Below the tails of Abel's dirty white shirt, the entity's black mass clung motionless to his lower body, as if trying not to draw attention.

For a moment, Abel stared at Hayley, studying her face. Then his tensed massive biceps relaxed and softened. His dark arms dropped to his side. "Fift of Febary in fordy-seven. I'se 'member Emma put'n' li'l Noah in her lap, hol'n' 'im close, talk'n' to 'im, sing'n' 'im to sleep. Lawd, I do loves my boy."

"Did you live in a house in Ohio?"

"Yes'um. I builds it myself." His eyes narrowed. "Why's youse ask'n' me dese things?"

Hayley sensed Leech's influence building in Abel. His features hardened and his hands balled into fists. She closed her eyes and said a prayer for protection, mentally surrounding Abel's exposed body with white light. The entity screeched. Hayley noticed that its dark mass, where touched by the light, began to disappear. *Yes! This is so cool.*

But Leech reacted instantly, spurring Abel to flee. Abel's face contorted as if he were being tortured into submission. Then he leaped into the stone wall and vanished.

"Did you see that?" Hayley asked, turning toward the others. "Sorry, I know you couldn't see what I saw." She watched them, each with eyes fixed on the spot where Abel had disappeared. "Or did you?"

Lee glanced at her, then back at the wall. "Well, actually,

when you surrounded him with white light, we could see all of him but his legs."

"Damn cool," Roger said.

"Amazingly so," Lewis agreed.

Hayley glanced back at the wall, excited the others had seen him. "Wow! I'll have to remember that." She stood and brushed the dirt from her jeans. "The white light affected Leech." She took a deep breath, calming her excitement, smiling broadly. "Could you hear Leech shriek as its mass dissolved?"

"It dissolved?" Lee asked.

"Only slightly, where the light hit it," she said.

Jim shook his head. "Just saw Abel and his reaction, no audio. Guess Leech is pullin' the strings again."

"Not for much longer," Hayley said. "All I need is one more chance to surround Leech and Abel with white light, and I'm pretty sure Leech will choose self-preservation, release Abel, and flee." She walked to the corner of the cave and stood over Abel's remains. "I want to get Abel's permission to gather his DNA. We'll have to come back like Roger suggested."

Laura joined her and kneeled to examine what remained of Abel's corpse. "The sealed tunnel kept his bones in good condition. When we return, there shouldn't be any problem extracting DNA."

Hayley looked at Lee. "Now all we have to do is find Emma's remains."

A smile crossed his face. "Feel like taking a ride to Tennessee? Pack whatever you need. We'll take the SUV and leave in the morning."

"I'll be ready," Hayley said.

CHAPTER 19

Hayley looked out the window of Lee's Cayenne, remembering the last time she had driven across the Appalachian Mountains from North Carolina to Tennessee. It had been the day before her parents had died in a car wreck, the last day she'd spent with them when she was fourteen. It was around the same time of year — summer, in the morning, when warm and cool air collided over the mountaintops. Then as now, The Weather Channel showed thunderstorms had occurred during the night, drenching the mountain's highs and lows, crags, coves, and hollows. But by morning, much like today, the blue skies showed no signs of the storm.

With her elbow resting on the open window frame and Lee's car climbing a grade, Hayley noticed the mist settling in the mountains to the north. Like a smoky serpent, the vapor slithered down the mountainsides into the valleys. Above the hollows, majestic trees carpeting the mountain peaks punctured the mist.

She glanced at the clock on the dash. They were only a couple of hours into their five-and-a-half-hour drive. She grabbed the folded map from the dash and opened it.

Lee glanced at her out of the corner of his eye. "Where do you want to go first, the hotel or the plantation?"

"I need to go straight to the plantation," she said, studying the map. "Kathy said the house is in ruins, so there'll be no electricity. We'll have to get there while there's still plenty of daylight. I'll need time to walk around the grounds to see if I can sense Emma or any traces of Abel and Noah, and see if this is the right plantation."

~*~

Lee parked under the shade of an aged oak. They got out of the vehicle and looked at what remained of an old plantation home. Trees and twisting vines had invaded the ruins. Beyond the mansion, on the mountainside, workers harvested sloping fields of tobacco. Beside Lee's Cayenne, a silver BMW sat on the grassy drive.

"Looks like we're not alone," Lee said.

Hayley noticed County Realty on the car door. "I don't think we should say anything about why we're here. Gossip spreads in small towns. If this is where we find Emma's remains, I don't want it to be headline news."

"I agree," Lee said.

A middle-aged woman wearing gray dress pants and a white blouse approached through the overgrowth. Beside her walked a young woman with ebony hair and a fair complexion, who looked at Hayley and Lee, then glanced away and huffed.

While she watched the girl, who she guessed was nineteen or twenty, Hayley experienced a vision: an open casket, the body of an elderly woman inside.

"What's with the girl?" Lee asked.

"Her grandmother just passed away. I feel some kind of disconnection in the family because of a secret long held. Too bad we don't have more time. Could be interesting."

The woman in gray drew close, holding her hand out to Lee. "Hello. I'm Elizabeth Wade with County Realty. Can I be of some help?"

Lee shook her hand. "Just sightseeing. We're interested in old plantations, historical stuff. Do you know the history of this place?"

"It's the Henry Wheeler tobacco plantation, built in 1840. The place burned to the ground in 1859. It's been in ruins ever since."

"Is it haunted?" he asked.

"No. I'm sure I would've heard about it if it were. Now, if you're looking for somewhere haunted — "

Lee raised his hand. "No. I was just wondering, that's all."

Hayley studied the girl, who stood in the background with arms crossed, glaring at the realtor. Looking back at Elizabeth, Hayley asked, "Did the Wheelers have any other family in the area?"

"None surviving. The entire family died in the fire. Mr. Wheeler's brother, Zachary Wheeler, lived in Georgia and owned a sugar plantation. But he was murdered, I believe, before Henry and his family died, leaving no known heirs."

"I noticed the fields are planted," Hayley said.

"The land's been leased. Since there's no known family left, the plantation's administered by the Historical Society."

"Are any slave shacks still standing?" Hayley asked.

"There's just one left." She pointed. "Past the willow trees over there."

The girl cleared her throat loudly. Elizabeth glanced over her shoulder, then turned back to Lee and Hayley. A nervous smile crossed her face. "We're going to town. If you have any more questions, I'll be in my office." She offered them her business card. "Feel free to stop by."

Lee took her card. "Thanks. We will."

After the woman and girl left, Hayley turned to look at the old plantation home. Only the north brick wall and four crumbling pillars in the front remained standing.

She took a step. "Let's look around."

A Historical Society plaque stood on a pedestal close to the drive. It stated the name, year established, and a brief history of the estate. While ignoring the debris and No Trespassing signs, Hayley strolled through what should have been the front entrance. Standing where a staircase would have connected to the second floor, she closed her eyes, gathering energy from the past. After a moment, she opened her eyes, stepped over debris, and tried again.

She turned to Lee and shook her head. "Let's go beyond those trees where the slaves lived."

Lee followed quietly.

The slave shack had been constructed from rough split-log planks. A sign reading Do Not Enter blocked the open entrance. Through the open doorway, Hayley saw a wood floor lacking all traces of habitation. Searching for memories of Abel, Emma, and Noah, Hayley tried to detect their energy in the small room, but didn't sense their residual trail. Taking her time, she wandered the area, stopping, closing her eyes, then moving elsewhere, repeating her sensing effort again and again.

She shrugged. "I'm not getting anything. I don't think this is the place."

"That's a surprise. It makes sense this would be it. Ohio's so close. Tennessee would be a quick and easy place to sell their captives."

"I thought so, too," Hayley said. "But maybe that's why they didn't. If anyone went looking for Abel and his family, it would've been too simple to find them. It would've blown the cover off the con job Sam Digger was pulling."

"Well, it's not a total loss. At least we can mark this plantation off the list. Let's try his brother Zachary's plantation in Georgia."

"How long will it take to get there?"

"About three-and-a-half hours," Lee said. "It's too late to go now. We'll have to find a hotel and leave in the morning."

"Let's try to find a hotel that's not haunted," Hayley said, a sensual smile crossing her face. "I want you all to myself."

CHAPTER 20

In the morning, they drove south of the Appalachians from Tennessee into Georgia. Near their destination, peach orchards blanketed the landscape.

She studied the map to locate the Zachary Wheeler sugar plantation. "Kathy said we're supposed to look for an oak-lined lane. I think it's up ahead."

Lee turned his car near a green house trailer and drove down a well-kept dirt road covered by a canopy of giant oaks. In the distance, the plantation home seemed dwarfed. By the time they reached the end of the road, the mansion loomed in front of them. Lee turned onto the wide drive and slowed the car.

Green shutters covered every window of the white two-story Greek Revival mansion. Under a pillar portico, a locked front door barred the entrance.

Diagonally across from the porch, Lee parked beside a silver pickup truck with Tennessee license plates.

After he turned off the ignition, Hayley, in the silence, closed her eyes, sensing the surroundings. "This is the place. I can feel the past energy of Abel and his family. If we can't go inside, I can walk the grounds."

Lee got out and dashed around the car to open Hayley's door. While they stood in the drive planning their investigation,

Hayley did a double take as a slender girl with ebony hair and wearing jeans and red T-shirt walked toward them.

"It's the girl we saw at the other plantation," Lee whispered. "What's she doing here?"

"Let's not say anything about Wheeler until we know what's going on."

"Whatever you say."

The girl glared, then picked up her pace, storming toward them. Lee took a defensive stance in front of Hayley.

Her blue eyes narrowed as she neared. "You're following me! Did *he* send you to spy on me?"

Lee held up his hands, warding her off. "We're not following you. Who is *he*?"

"Daniel Smith, the damn lawyer."

"We don't know anyone by that name," Lee said.

"And I'm supposed to believe that?"

Hayley stepped out from behind Lee. "Did Mr. Smith happen to mention anything about a woman named Emma?"

"No. Who in the hell are you?"

Taking a deep breath, Hayley tried to figure out how to approach the girl without running her off. "Do you believe in coincidence?"

"No." The girl glanced at her pickup.

"Neither do I." Noting the girl wanted to leave, Hayley knew she needed to grab her attention. "I'm Hayley Johnson and this is Lee Franklin. I believe you'll need us to find what you're looking for. What's your name?"

"Brea Tyler. Don't act like you don't know. If you don't work for Mr. Smith, how would you know what I'm looking for, unless you're psychic?"

Lee matched her glare. "Yes, she is. And I'd listen to her if I were you."

Hayley put a hand on Lee's arm, then spoke softly. "We need to go somewhere to talk. Have you had lunch yet?"

Turning a shoulder toward the mansion, the girl planted herself firmly. "I'm not going anywhere until you tell me what this is all about."

"You're tracing your family tree," Hayley explained. "We're looking for someone's roots, too. Someone named Emma Smith. It's a long story, but we didn't just meet by coincidence. For some reason, we need each other's help. Okay?"

The girl let out a surrendering huff. "Okay, fine. But you don't have to keep lying. I know he sent you. He must think I'm going to cheat and bring back false proof. Why else would he send you?"

Hayley squeezed Lee's arm, cautioning him to stay quiet. "I noticed a diner just up the road. Would you like to follow or come with us?" Hayley suggested.

"I'll follow. But if I don't like what I hear, I'm outta here."

"Suit yourself."

They got into their cars and drove to the main road, turned right past the house trailer, and continued for one-half mile until they reached the country diner.

~*~

Lee pulled into a newly resurfaced parking lot and found an empty space between a red Ford Focus and a black Toyota Camry. As he and Hayley got out and locked the car, Brea pulled in, parking between two Harley motorcycles.

They gathered at the restaurant entrance. When they entered, a bell tinkled and heads turned in their direction. The restaurant had few customers. Some people sat at the counter and others sat close to the door.

Hayley chose a corner booth away from possible gossips. She scooted in, with Lee sliding in next to her. Brea, looking uncomfortable, sat across from them.

A woman in a pink uniform, her silver hair pulled into a bun and with a smile on her face, approached and set menus in front of them.

"'Afternoon. I'm Daisy. It's good to see new faces around these parts. Don't get many tourists nowadays since they closed up the old plantation."

"We just came from there," Lee said. "Any chance of getting a tour of the inside?"

"'Fraid not. The place has been closed since April. As I understand, the Historical Society took the place off the state's tourism register."

"Shame," Lee said.

Daisy glanced at the door when a young woman with two small children entered, and she waved. "My daughter and my grandkids. Let me tell you our specials for today and I'll fetch you some water." She turned toward a chalkboard hanging on the wall. "Might want to try our lunch special today — fried chicken, grits, mixed vegetables, and lots of hot biscuits. Our meatloaf is pretty tasty, too." She looked again at the woman and kids standing by the door. "I'll be right back with your water."

"Thank you, Daisy." Lee watched her rush over to greet her daughter and give the kids a hug. He turned to Hayley. "I wonder why they locked up the place."

"I'm wondering, too. But first things first." She glanced at Brea, then back at Lee. "We'll find out before we leave."

He nodded.

Daisy hurried back with the water and stepped away.

Before Brea picked up her menu and began focusing on the selections, Hayley started the conversation. "You go first. Tell us who this Daniel Smith is and why you thought we were following you."

"Why should I go first? You're the ones who brought me here."

"Because we need to straighten things out," Hayley said. "We're not who you think we are."

Brea took a deep breath and sat back, her arms folded in front of her. "Mr. Smith's some big-shot lawyer in Chicago. He called my dad just before my grandma died and said our family's related to his. My dad said the guy was trying to tell him that our great-great-great — oh hell, I don't know how many greats — grandfather raped his ancestral grandmother sometime in the 1850s and she had his child, making us blood relatives."

"So, what did your dad do?" Lee asked.

"He told that lawyer if he bothered him again, he'd file a complaint with the FBI."

"Did he stop calling?" he asked.

"Yes. Not long after that my grandmother passed away. I was helping with her belongings and came across a journal." She pulled a small book from her purse and opened it to the first page. "It was in her will that I should have this. I remember when she showed it to me years ago and said it had been passed down through the generations. See, it goes back to 1859. It looks like the first entry is the name Simon Tyler, but I can't read his middle name." Brea handed it to Lee.

He pulled his dark-framed glasses from his shirt pocket and studied the writing. "Not sure." He showed it to Hayley.

She placed her hand on the entry and closed her eyes. A vision of the past played in her mind. A man's hand wrote the name Wheeler after the first name Simon. Hayley opened her eyes and smiled at Lee, who nodded.

Brea took back the journal and tucked it into her purse.

"What happened then?" Hayley asked

"Mr. Smith came to Wisconsin and found my apartment. Said

he got my address from a friend of the family. It was a bad day. I'd lost my job that morning. I was mental. My rent was due and I had bills to pay. It really freaked me out when he showed up at my door. He made me an offer I couldn't pass up. Told me he'd help pay my bills if I could disprove or prove that we're related. I told him it was easy to prove and showed him the journal, but that wasn't good enough since some of the entries were illegible.

"He said the family connection had to do with the name Wheeler, and if I could find the family connection or disprove his claim, he'd give me five thousand dollars. On the computer, I searched for anything connected to the name Wheeler and the 1800s, and found the ruins in Tennessee. When I arrived in Tennessee, I rented a truck, found that realty lady so I could learn the ruin's history, and now I'm here."

"The lawyer sounds like a generous man," Hayley said.

Brea sat back and eyed Hayley. "I don't know about that. He said there might be an inheritance involved. I'm sure that's what he wants to get his hands on. Now, what's your story?"

"This might sound a little unusual, but I not only see ghosts, I can see the past, present, and the future."

"I knew it! What? Do you think I'm stupid? There's no such thing as ghosts, and I don't believe in psychics or mediums. My dad said they're a bunch of frauds."

"So why are you talking to us?" Lee asked. "I told you she was a psychic before we came here."

"Since you're working for Mr. Smith, you'll be reporting my progress. Like I said, I'm not stupid."

"I guess I'll have to prove I'm psychic before we tell you what we're looking for."

Brea crossed her arms. "This ought to be good!"

"Your grandmother's name is Martha May Tyler."

"Public record."

"She's a small woman—gray hair, thin. And she lost half a finger when she worked in a box factory."

"Public record."

"The last conversation she had with you was about the elm tree in her front yard. She said it was planted when your dad was born."

"I guess you could find that out, too."

"How would I know your last conversation? Okay. She showed you a ruby pendant, and told you that when she died she wanted you to have it."

"That was in the will. Mr. Smith's a lawyer. He could've found that out. Tell me something only she and I would know."

"She gave you new pennies, each from the year something special happened in your life. It was a way of sharing secret memories."

Brea turned pale and stared, unblinking, at Hayley. "I never told anyone. We talked about everything. When something happened she thought was special, she'd give me a shiny new penny. I'd write down my memory, and we'd put my note and the penny in an envelope."

"Your grandmother told you that everyone, no matter who or how insignificant they might be, makes a piece of history. Those pennies and your notes helped keep track of yours. It was her way of telling you how important you are."

She nodded. "At home, I have hundreds of envelopes full of my history. I never told anyone."

"Your grandmother's sitting next to you."

Tears welled in Brea's eyes. She gazed at the empty seat next to her.

Hayley pointed to the table. "She gave you a penny to keep this moment as a memory."

Stunned, Brea looked at the shiny penny on the table in front

134

of her. Tears ran down her cheeks. She picked it up, studied it, and checked the date.

"She says it's brand new — minted this morning. And she's sorry she doesn't have an envelope, but you can use the one in your purse."

"How did she know I have an envelope in my purse?"

"She's been with you since you found the journal. She helped you find it."

Brea, hands shaking, opened her purse and pulled out the envelope. After placing the penny inside, she turned and whispered, "Thank you, Grandma."

"She says she's going to leave so we can talk, but not to worry, she'll be around."

"Is she a ghost?"

"No. People who cross over can choose to visit whenever they like."

"Why can't I see her like you do?"

"Picture a divider with several layers separating two dimensions. In order for me to see her, she has to step through a few layers. If she stepped through a few more, you'd be able to see her, too, but only as a ghostly figure. She probably doesn't want to scare you."

"Is she gone?"

"Yes."

"So, are you ready to listen to our story now?" Lee asked.

"Yes."

Hayley told Brea about Abel, his family, and sensing Emma's presence at the plantation. "Emma's last name is Smith."

"Are you serious? She's the one who was raped, right?"

"Yes. Emma's the link between your family and Daniel Smith. Her son, Noah Smith, would be Daniel's ancestor, and the baby Emma conceived by Zachary Wheeler, the plantation owner, would be your ancestor. That makes Emma yours and Daniel's...." Hayley counted on her fingers. "Great-great-great-great-great-grandmother. I think that's close to right," she said, counting backward in twenty-year increments.

"But our last name's Tyler. The journal doesn't mention a Wheeler."

"The name's there. It's just not legible. Anyway, we want to investigate the property, but we'll need permission. If we help you find Mr. Wheeler's grave, maybe your lawyer can find a way to exhume his remains and extract a DNA sample. If you and Zachary Wheeler are related, it's very likely your family will inherit a share of the Georgia property."

"You're joking!"

"No. It would be perfect for us. I'm pretty sure Emma's remains are still on the plantation. We might need to do some digging. It'll be easier to get her DNA without going through the Historical Society if your family owned the property. I have a strong sense that we won't get anywhere if the Historical Society has anything to do with it."

Lee pulled a business card from his wallet and handed it to Brea. "Have Mr. Smith give us a call."

"Yeah, sure. When do you want to look for Mr. Wheeler?" Brea asked.

"As soon as we finish eating," Hayley said.

CHAPTER 21

After Daisy picked up their dirty dishes, she returned to refill their coffee cups, laid their check on the table, and began to dash away.

Hayley stopped her. "Excuse me."

Daisy wheeled around. "Can I get you something, honey?"

"No, we're fine, thank you." Hayley leaned forward, keeping her voice low, not wanting to make her question a topic for conversation. "We're interested in learning the history of that plantation you mentioned. Do you know anything about it or where we could get information?"

"It used to be a sugar plantation owned by a man named Zachary Wheeler," Daisy said, "and it's haunted."

"Haunted? Really! Do you think *he's* the ghost?" Hayley asked.

"More than likely," Daisy said. "Someone entered his home and murdered him. The law searched for the killer. The town was outraged and posted a large bounty. Someone got away with murder."

"Can you tell us anything about Wheeler?" Hayley asked. "What kind of a man was he?"

"I can practically recite the tour guide's entire oration. Zachary Wheeler held high status as lord of the plantation, the town, and all those around him. He was a saintly man. The church put him on the highest pedestal as a pillar of the community, a God-fearing man. Real shame he had to die the way he did."

Lee poured sugar into his coffee and casually stirred. "Why did they lock the place?"

"Mr. Wheeler's ghost is fighting to keep people out. It attacked and seriously injured two men earlier this year. Guess the Historical Society was afraid of a lawsuit, so they closed the doors. It's been quiet as a graveyard around here ever since."

"Is there someone we can talk to who might let us in?" Lee asked.

"There's Gil Meeker, the groundskeeper. I reckon if you make it worth his while, he'd turn his back, but you never heard that from me."

Lee nodded. "Where can we find Mr. Meeker?"

"He lives on the plantation. Just before you turn down the lane of oaks there's a house trailer. If he's not home, he's probably checking the grounds."

"We noticed the trailer on our way here. What does he look like?" Lee asked

"Skinny, about six feet tall, thinning blond hair, wears a brown baseball cap most of the time."

"Do you happen to know if Mr. Wheeler's buried on the property?" Hayley asked.

"No. He's buried in some fancy tomb behind the church he built for the townspeople."

"Where is that?" Lee asked.

"It's not far. I'll draw you a map."

~*~

Hayley looked over her shoulder through the car's rear window and saw Brea's silver Dodge Ram following close behind. Through the side window, she noticed a quaint 1800s white church with Palladian windows and a modest bell tower. Past the parking lot and behind the church, a cemetery covered the property. Beyond the headstones and statues, Hayley located an enormous crypt dominating the grounds.

"Looks like Mr. Wheeler had one hell of an ego." Lee laughed. "Did you see Brea's eyes when the waitress told us he's haunting the mansion?"

"She could freak out if she goes inside. If she does enter, we have to make sure we're with her. This haunting might be as dangerous as the one at your place."

"I agree."

Lee pulled in and parked next to the church. They met Brea at the iron gate leading to the cemetery and walked through the graveyard to the crypt.

By a twisted picket fence and a bent dogwood tree near the back of the cemetery stood a twelve-by-eight-foot concrete structure with a peaked roof. On either side of the oak-leaf-framed entrance, angels, each holding a cross, guarded the door. An engraved bronze plaque above the threshold resembled a scroll.

Hayley walked closer and read the name "Wheeler." She prayed for protection, covered herself with white light, then touched the wooden door to sense past energy.

Brea snorted. "So, what's she doing? She going to go into some kind of trance or something? This is so weird!"

"Quiet! She's tapping into the past," Lee said.

"This is way strange. I'm going to call Mr. Smith."

"You do that, but go stand by that tree over there so you don't disturb Hayley."

In Hayley's vision, a slave wrapped a newborn in a sheet while her master barked orders. He looked down on another woman, her breathing shallow, eyes closed, lying on the narrow

139

bed against the brick wall of a small room. A blood-drenched sheet barely covered her sweaty body.

"Clean this mess up, Liza. And after that, take that thing to the river and drown it." He looked sternly at the slave holding the baby.

Liza flinched away from him.

"Hear what I said, girl? I want that thing drowned. If you don't do as I say...." Clenching his fist, he moved toward her. "You'll not live to see tomorrow."

Liza nodded and drew the child close.

"After you do my bidding, come back and take care of Emma. If anything happens to her, I'll hold you responsible. Understand?"

"Yes, Massa. I'se be fast as lightnin'. Don't youse worry. She be just fine."

"Good girl, Liza. Now, I've got to go upstairs. I've got business to tend to. When I come back, you better be taking good care of her or I'll have your hide. Understand?"

Hayley's vision followed Wheeler out of the room and through a tunnel. At its end, he stepped up a ladder connected to the basement floor, propped open the trapdoor, and climbed out of the tunnel. Leaving the trapdoor open for Liza, he turned and went upstairs. She watched him go through the house and up to his library, where a man stood in front of the fireplace with his back to the door.

"I hope no one witnessed your arrival."

"Not a soul."

"State your business, Digger. I told you last week I no longer require your services."

"You inherited your brother's slaves—slaves he paid me boodle for with twelve hundred dollars of counterfeit money. Pony up, Wheeler. Cover your brother's debt and we're done."

"Balderdash. My brother was an honorable man."

"He deserved to die. No one hornswoggles me—not him, not you, no one." Digger pulled his gun. "Give me my due or I'll kill you the same as I killed your brother."

Wheeler balled his fists at his side, then relaxed them. "So it was you. My brother, his wife, and their boys."

"A splendid blaze." Digger grinned. "Don't think I don't know your secret, Wheeler. Abel's wife—is she so desirable you keep her hidden? What would the church think?"

Hayley sensed Wheeler's anger and heard his thoughts. *He'll not have you. You're mine. God favors me above all others. Because I am humble unto Him, you are His gift to me to do with as I please. I will not let Digger touch you.*

"Murder, now blackmail. Let's have done with this," Wheeler said. "I shall pay what's due." He walked to a desk near the window, controlling his fury. As he pictured Emma in his mind, her smell and taste filled his senses.

Hayley's vision jumped to Emma when Wheeler had first taken her as his sex slave, locked her in a storage room in a tunnel, and pleasured himself at will, committing lurid, perverted acts. His eyes had lit at Emma's defiance. "You are a temptress, my love. Fight me. It pleasures me more than you know."

His perversion engulfed Hayley's mind. Emma's screams brought tears to her eyes. She strained to control her vision as it moved forward, returning to Digger's demands.

She felt it as Wheeler's rage grew stronger. With his back to Digger, he opened the drawer, pulled out a gun, and turned. "You'll not have her," he hissed, and fired.

His shot found Digger's shoulder. Digger fired back. Wheeler dropped to floor, dead.

Abruptly Hayley's vision ended. Trembling, she pulled herself away from the crypt door. Lee rushed to her, wrapping his arms around her.

With her head against his chest, she spoke through tears. "He died protecting his captive, Emma."

"He's keeping her prisoner?"

"In death as in life."

"What do you want to do?"

She drew back. "We need to go to the plantation. There's a tunnel. I have to find out where it is and how far out from the house it goes."

"Are we going inside the mansion?"

"We don't need to yet. As long as we know where Emma is, I want to keep our presence a surprise. We have to get the team together. This isn't going to be easy. We'll need a plan. Zachary Wheeler's mean enough to kill, and thinks no one can get by him."

"He hasn't met us yet," Lee said.

Brea walked up behind them. "I spoke to Mr. Smith. He wants me to bring him all the details. He'll have to get a court order to open the crypt and gather DNA samples, which shouldn't take too long if there're no known relatives to give their permission." She handed Hayley a piece of paper. "This is my phone number, address, and information regarding the lawyer. I have to leave now, to check out of the hotel in Atlanta, drop off the rental truck, and fly home. So I'll call and let you know what's going on."

"Be sure to do that," Hayley said. "If everything works out and you want to go inside the mansion, you'll need us to deal with Wheeler."

"Yeah, okay. Maybe I'll see you later." She turned and left them standing by the crypt.

They watched her walk away.

Lee took Hayley's hand. "She's gone. Perfect! Let's get back to the plantation."

142

CHAPTER 22

Lee slowed the car when they reached the mobile home. In the front yard a truck sat, loaded with a lawn mower and garden tools. He pulled in next to it.

The screen door creaked open and a tall man wearing faded blue jeans, a T-shirt, and a cap with a John Deere logo stepped onto the porch.

Lee and Hayley climbed out of the car.

"Can I help you folks?"

"I think so. Are you Gil Meeker?" Lee asked.

"In the flesh."

"This is Hayley Johnson and I'm Lee Franklin. The waitress at the diner told us you're the groundskeeper at the Wheeler plantation."

"That's right."

"We could use your help," Lee said.

"Why don't we step into my office?"

They followed him through a gate in the picket fence surrounding a patio, and sat in folding chairs under an arbor laced with climbing white iceberg roses.

"So what's on your minds?" Gil asked.

"Hayley's a medium, and she'd like to walk the grounds. We were there earlier, but we didn't want to trespass."

"Ya must've just missed me. I was probably around back fixin' to open the shutters." He eyed Hayley. "So you see ghosts, do you? Want to go inside the mansion?"

Hayley shook her head.

"What are you looking for?" Gil asked. "Maybe I can help."

"It's a long story, one we don't want getting around," Hayley said.

"I can keep my mouth shut. I'm interested to hear what you have to say."

Hayley told Gil the entire story about what happened to Abel and his family, intentionally leaving out the information about Brea and her lawyer.

"I pictured him a nasty old man," Gil said. "I always wondered what made him so mean, and why he'd always try keeping me out of the basement." He scratched his nubby, unshaven jaw. "Well, okay then. No problem. You can wander anywhere you please."

"Our problem is Wheeler," Lee said. "We don't want him to know we're snooping around."

"So you want me to distract him?"

"Could you?" Hayley asked.

"I've been tormenting that demon for twenty-five years. I know everything that provokes him." Gil's shoulders shook as he chuckled. "Sure, I'll help you. I need a good laugh. How much time do you need?"

"About fifteen minutes."

"No problem."

~*~

While Lee drove slowly under the canopy of oaks toward the haunted mansion, Hayley thought about the vision of the tunnel and small room she'd perceived earlier at the cemetery.

"So what's your plan?" Lee asked, coming to the end of the

road.

Hayley glanced at Meeker's empty truck parked in front of the mansion, and knew he had gone inside. "I'll walk the grounds until I find signs of the tunnel. I'm hoping there's another way to get down there besides the basement entrance. It'll be impossible to get by Wheeler—he's too strong."

"Want my help?"

"No thanks," Hayley said. "I think I can handle it alone. I shouldn't be long."

"I'll wait by the car. If you need me, just wave."

Hayley pushed her hair behind her ears while staring at the mansion through the car window. Although Meeker had opened the shutters, the place looked deserted—drapes drawn, doors chained and locked. But no padlock, large or small, or curtains, thick or thin, could contain or conceal Wheeler's profane essence seeping though the mansion's outer walls from Hayley's sensitivity, intensifying her caution.

She focused on his whereabouts and envisioned Wheeler enraged, slamming doors when Gil told him that the plantation belonged to him now. "Whatever Meeker is doing seems to be working," she whispered to Lee. "Wheeler hasn't noticed us yet."

Lee parked the car a ways from the house by the south yard. Gil's truck sat in front of the pillared porch far up the drive. They climbed out, quietly shutting their doors.

Knowing Wheeler's attention could suddenly turn toward her, Hayley hurried to the corner of the house, glanced at Lee leaning by the car, then followed the perimeter of the house. She held her breath when sneaking past each window, praying Gil kept Wheeler distracted. Halfway to the backyard, she sensed a void underground—a tunnel.

The impressions led her to a well eighty feet from the house. A three-foot-high stone wall surrounded its shaft. A bolted-down cover shielded the well's interior. She sensed it was dry.

Hayley opened her senses to past energy. She stepped into a vision, viewing a scene replayed from the mid-1800s. In front of her, Wheeler stood facing his foreman, and glanced across the road at the recently purchased slaves being pulled from the wagon, his attention drawn to Emma.

"Free? How absurd. Everyone knows they're too ignorant to fend for themselves. Giving them freedom would be inhumane and cruel. It's my duty as God's servant to enlighten them, teach them obedience. I'll have the girl as my chambermaid. Let the boy work his craft. Give him to the smith. Put the child to work in the fields." Wheeler turned. "I'll use the dry well for storage, Clemens. I want a tunnel dug at its base, keeping it deep enough to tunnel under the basement of the house and allowing access to it through a trapdoor in the floor. Off the tunnel near the well's shaft there are to be three fortified storage rooms. Draw up the plans."

"It may take years to dig."

"So be it," Wheeler told him.

A second vision flashed before her.

In the darkness, Wheeler stood by the slave quarters behind the trees and peered out at the slaves playing music on their makeshift instruments and dancing. He watched twenty-two-year-old Emma, with her heart-shaped face, soft skin, and big brown eyes. Wheeler focused on the curves of her body swaying to the rhythm, her cotton blouse falling loosely across her full breasts, her dark sweaty skin glistening in the light cast by the fire pit. Trembling, he lusted for her.

"God has sent me a blessing. What of her husband's hindrance?" Wheeler glared at Abel. "The smith will make do without a second hand. I'll work Abel to the bone digging for years. He'll not have strength to touch her."

Hayley inhaled deeply and refrained from making judgments in order to relax and learn the truth.

Time flashed forward.

Wheeler paced in his upstairs study. He stopped, a smile crossing his face. "It'll work," he said to himself. "I'll take Emma, and if she resists me...." His heart pounded wildly at the thought. "I'll remind her once again that I'll sell her son and husband if she speaks of my love for her. Then, when Digger tempts Abel into fleeing with his family to the Underground Railroad, Emma will plead with her husband to go. Abel will run first and be told his wife and son will follow. Instead, Digger will take care of him. I'll lock Emma in a room off the tunnel and have her at my pleasure. No one will know she's there." He walked to the window and looked out. Seeing Emma hanging bedding, he felt his knees weaken. "I'll give her son to Digger for payment. Rumors will spread of their escape, my efforts to track them, and their deaths while resisting. My other slaves will be dissuaded from running."

When the visions of Wheeler faded, Hayley sensed Emma's ghost and remains trapped in a storeroom below. While hunting for the tunnel, shielding herself had seemed unimportant since Gil was distracting Wheeler. Now it was too late. Emma's agonized whimpers, cries, and screams consumed Hayley. The slave's physical and mental pain filled her and ripped her away from her reality, until her thoughts were no longer her own but Emma's. A seed of Hayley's awareness of herself flickered in the back of Emma's mind. Hayley/Emma stood trembling in the storage room below.

Wheeler yanked Emma's head back by her hair and ran his lit cigar down her neck. Pain consumed Hayley and she heard herself scream. She felt Emma's fear and determination as if they were her own, doing whatever she must to keep Abel and Noah safe. Wheeler licked Emma's ear, then, grabbing the back of her neck, his fingernails wedged in her freshly burned flesh, he forced her forward with his other hand and lifted the back of her skirt.

Revulsion turned Emma's stomach, as it did Hayley's. As Wheeler's pants dropped to the floor, a wisp of Hayley's own awareness floated across her mind. She felt someone carrying her. His arms seemed familiar. His muddled voice whispered.

Pain swept over her again. She screamed.

A voice called out. "I'm here, Hayley. I'm here! I love you! Hayley, I'm here. Hayley! Hayley!"

His pleas continued, taking her mind away from the pain. On the verge of finding her way back, Hayley felt agony engulfing her again and her own awareness ripping away once more.

As she stood in front of the fireplace in Wheeler's bedroom, enduring his torture, seeing a flash above her caused Hayley to look up. Light washed over her, caressing her. She felt herself pulling away from the past. Hayley's mind cleared. She resurfaced, returning to herself and the present.

Hayley opened her eyes, seeing Lee's face, his eyes closed and his body relaxed. While he sat cross-legged in the middle of the road under the canopy of oaks, she lay cradled in his lap, his arms around her.

"Lee?" she whispered.

His eyes sprang opened. "Hayley! Are you all right?"

She looked around. They were alone near his Cayenne. "How did I get here?"

Lee swallowed hard and took a deep breath. "I took you away from the well. For fifteen minutes, you wailed as if you were being tortured. Nothing I said brought you back. It scared the hell out of me." Putting his hand to her chin, he used his thumb to gently brush away the remnants of her tears. "I thought I'd lost you. I didn't know what to do, so I closed my eyes like you always do, said a prayer, and mentally surrounded you with white light. All I could do was trust I was doing it right."

"It was perfect. I'm sorry. I didn't think I needed protection. When I sensed Emma's presence, it was too late." Hayley reached up, covering his hand with hers, keeping the warmth of his touch against her cheek. "Her agony flooded me, and I totally became Emma. I didn't even know my own name until I heard your voice. But it was only for a minute and I was consumed again. Wheeler's a demon! Oh, Emma." Her tears followed a salty path down her cheek. "Then I looked up—you sent me protection."

He traced her jaw with his fingertip. His voice trembled. "I had to. My damsel was in distress." He softly kissed her temple. "Can you stand?"

She nodded.

He helped her up, led her to the car, helped her inside, and closed the door.

Gil Meeker drove up beside them.

"I have to thank him," Lee said.

"I'm fine. Go ahead."

Gil rolled down his window as Lee walked over. While they talked, Hayley rested her head against the leather seat, closing her eyes for a moment. The opening of the car door on the driver's side startled her.

Lee slid in and started the car. "I got his number in case we need him again." He reached over and brushed Hayley's hair behind her ear. "Are you all right?"

"Just a little tired, but I'm okay."

He put the car in gear. "Let's get the hell out of here!"

CHAPTER 23

The trip to the plantation the day before, plus the three-and-a-half hour drive home, took more out of Hayley than she wanted to admit.

Jim held the door for her and Laura while they entered the game room, Lee and Roger following. Inside, the early evening sunlight shone dimly through the second-floor windows of the south tower.

"Max, lights on," Lee said. The computer adjusted the lighting while Lee and the others crossed the room. He stepped behind the bar. "I had Lewis call and have pizzas delivered. There's pepperoni, ham and pineapple, and one with the works."

Glancing around, Hayley realized the game room hadn't been on her tour list when she'd shown Kathy and Laura the second floor. It hadn't entered her mind since she'd never been in this room. Not long ago, she recalled, before they began looking for Emma, Lee had taken her through the entire first floor, shown her Lewis's living quarters in the south wing, the culinary facilities in the north wing, and downstairs guest bedrooms initially designed for visitors in the late eighteenth and nineteenth centuries. *Pride and Prejudice* crossed her mind, and the scene emphasizing that the public commonly walked in the gardens, strolled the halls, and spent a leisurely day in homes such as Lee's.

Before sitting and getting comfortable at the bar, Hayley looked closer at the game room's decor. Hanging lamps illuminated a pool table in the center. Leather chairs surrounded game tables near the windows. The entertaining atmosphere made her remember the vast amount of wine in the cellar.

"Lee, do you entertain much?"

"Hell, he's a regular social butterfly," Jim said.

"Just once in a while. I'm involved with a number of charities. The end of October I'm having a costume ball to raise money for Children's Hospital."

Jim pointed across the room. "He's got his costume ready and waitin'. Ya might start thinkin' 'bout what you're gonna wear, darlin'."

Hayley, sitting next to Laura, swiveled her chair to see where Jim pointed. A suit of armor stood in the corner. She laughed. "My knight in shining armor. Perfect." Lee had called her his "damsel in distress" just yesterday. "This is still July. I'm sure I can come up with something by then."

Lee reached under the bar for bottles of soda and beer and set them on the counter. "I'll pour. Help yourselves to something to eat." He pulled a couple of plates from a stack by the napkins and lifted a slice from the box. "Pizza, Hayley?"

"Ham and pineapple, please."

"Laura, something to drink?" Lee asked.

"Sprite, thank you."

Lee poured her a glass and passed it to her. "Wine, Hayley?"

"No. I'll have a Sprite, too. A glass of wine would put me to sleep."

Jim raised a brow.

"We didn't sleep at all last night," Lee explained.

Jim held up his hand. "Too much information, Studly."

"That's not what I meant." Lee passed Hayley her drink.

"Yesterday, while we were at the plantation, I nearly lost her." He popped open a couple of beers and slid one to Roger and the other to Jim.

"What do you mean by 'lost her'?" Laura asked.

Hayley cringed at the thought, not wanting to talk about it. "Emma's emotions—her depression and pain—consumed me. I remember becoming her, experiencing her torture, and almost losing myself completely. If Lee hadn't helped me, I might be in a mental institution today."

Laura studied her. "How long was she out?"

"Almost fifteen minutes," Lee said. "It scared the hell out of me. Then last night, every time she closed her eyes, she woke up screaming."

"I don't like the sound of this. Any flashbacks other than last night?"

"No. As far as I know, I wasn't screaming while I napped on the way home from Georgia."

"You were restless," Lee said, "and that worried me."

Hayley raised her glass to her lips, then lowered it, speaking over its rim. "Well, you should sleep better tonight. I won't be here."

Lee's eyes widened. "What? You're going home? I don't think being alone is a good idea."

"I don't either," Laura said.

"I'm never alone. Grams will be with me."

Lee reached across the bar and stroked her cheek. "It's not the same."

"Do you think you might let me come over and stay with you?" Laura asked.

Roger nodded. "That's a good idea. I'll take Laura home to get whatever she needs, then bring her by."

Hayley took a sip, set her glass down, and looked at her pizza, wondering if she really felt like eating. She glanced at Laura. "I'd love to invite you over, but I haven't been home much at all the last few weeks. My guest room needs cleaning, and I'd have to go grocery shopping. I'm just too tired."

Lee came out from behind the bar and sat beside her. "Not a problem. I'll send Lewis over. He'll take care of everything."

"But—"

"If you think I'll be able to sleep knowing you're alone, you're crazy. Lewis will be happy to help. Where are your keys?"

"My keys?"

"If he goes now, everything will be ready when you get home."

"I'd go for it if I were you, darlin'," Jim said. "Ya look paler than ghost guts."

"Okay, fine." She handed Lee her keys.

"Now that's settled." Lee pulled out his cell phone. "Lewis, would you come to the game room? I need your help."

Hayley watched Lee meet Lewis at the door. Placing his hand on the butler's shoulder, Lee explained, then dropped the keys into his hand. Lewis nodded, smiling broadly. He turned, giving Hayley a thumbs up.

Looking satisfied, Lee walked back to the bar. "All set."

"So," Roger said, "you told us earlier that Wheeler made Abel dig a tunnel, held Emma prisoner, and had Digger convince Abel to run in order to murder him. Anything else we should know?"

"I don't get it," Jim said. "Male slaves as buff as Abel were worth lots of money. Why didn't Wheeler just sell him? And why would Wheeler keep Emma hidden? Plantation owners were known for havin' their way with slaves."

"Because the church forbade those sinful acts, and Wheeler had a reputation to uphold," Hayley said. "As for Abel, I've seen how he feels about Emma, and Wheeler knew as well. He was smart not to have sold him. If he had, I'm sure he knew, no matter where Abel ended up, he would've escaped and found his way back to the plantation. Wheeler probably surmised, too, that Abel would've gone through the tunnel, entered the house through the basement, and killed the scumbag for separating him from his family."

"You're right," Jim said. "And he would've found Emma locked up. Wheeler was a dead man, no matter what."

"Guess he killed two birds with one stone, so to speak," Roger said. "Giving Noah his son to Digger as payment so everyone would believe the family had fled."

"Mmm." Hayley held her finger up as she swallowed a bite of pizza. "Remember that photo of the bounty hunter and his men? Do you recall the slave boy with them? That was him, Noah—Abel and Emma's son."

"Do you think the lawyer's Abel's descendant?" Roger asked.

"Yes," Lee said. "And I'm curious to find out how he knew about his great-plus, plus, plus-grandmother being raped by Wheeler."

Roger nodded. "Me, too. I wonder if he knows where Noah's buried."

"Wouldn't that be great?" Lee said. "If he does, and we find Emma, we could bury her and Abel with their son."

Hayley reached into her pocket and pulled out a slip of paper. "We've got his number. Why don't we call him?"

Roger took the paper and stuck it into his shirt pocket. "I'll have Kathy contact him tomorrow."

"Then what?" Jim asked.

Hayley yawned. "I'm going to go down to the cave and free Abel from that entity. I want to give him something good to think about, so I'll show him the photo of Noah and tell him we're looking for his son's descendants."

"Is there some reason he has to stay in that cave?" Laura asked.

"I'm going to work on that, too," Hayley said. "When we go to free Emma, I want Abel to help us. I think it might be the only way to get Emma out of her prison and convince her she's free."

"We met a man who can give us a few ways to distract Wheeler," Lee said. "He's the groundskeeper, Gil Meeker." He chuckled. "One hell of a funny guy. He's been harassing Wheeler for twenty-five years, trying to find out what irritates the apparition the most."

Hayley yawned again.

"I think it's time to take you home," Lee said.

"I can wait. Why don't you guys play a game of pool and give Lewis a chance to work some miracles? I promise I'll let you know when I'm ready to leave." She held back telling him that she'd remembered her dreams on their drive home yesterday, and how she would rather stay awake than close her eyes again.

CHAPTER 24

Hayley's attempt to stay awake failed as her thoughts drifted, conjuring an autumn day. Leaves floated down from the canopy of oaks branching across the road leading to the plantation. In her dream, drawn to the well, she stood listening. Filled with apprehension, she tried to will herself away, to run to the safety of the old oaks. As if being pulled by a magnetic force, she tumbled into the darkness of the well, falling toward an angry voice and a woman's wail.

Abel's wife, her face swollen, hands raised in defense, trembled in a bloodstained blouse. Trying to protect Emma, Hayley stepped in front of her, shielding the woman from the bloodied fist of her master. But her plan failed. Instead, the slave's anguish consumed Hayley, Emma's identity usurping hers. Hayley screamed.

In the midst of losing herself, she heard a familiar voice calling her name. Appearing between the nightmarish dream and Hayley's consciousness, Grams intervened. "It's a dream, dear. The tortured emotions are not yours. Repeat after me, sweetheart: 'I will not own it, I will not own it, I will not own it.'"

Hayley repeated Grams's words, enabling her to free herself from the purgatory. Resurfacing from the dream state, she opened her eyes.

In her first moment of awareness, Hayley glimpsed Laura turning on the bedroom light and rushing to her side. "Are you all right? You were screaming."

While her eyes and mind adjusted to the abrupt awakening, Hayley sat up in bed, dragging her pillow behind her and against the brass headboard. "I had a nightmare."

"Same one as last night?"

Hayley nodded.

From her robe pocket, Laura extracted a medicine bottle. "Here, take one of these and you'll sleep better." She twisted the lid off and reached for the glass of water on Hayley's nightstand.

"STOP!" A disembodied voice, coming from nowhere, yet from everywhere, filled every molecule in the room.

Laura jumped. Sleeping pills sprayed, bounced, and rolled across the hardwood floor from the bottle in her hand. Amused, Hayley watched. Shaking, Laura crawled onto the bed next to Hayley, drawing her knees to her chin while her wild eyes raked the room.

Stifling a laugh, Hayley put her arm around her friend. "It's okay."

Laura stared at Hayley's Cheshire cat smile. "What's going on?"

"Watch."

While the temperature of the room significantly dropped, Laura rubbed her legs and arms to keep warm. Mist formed in the doorway. A transparent veil appeared a few feet above the floor, oscillating as it spread and rose, massing into a vague human shape.

"You've seen this before," Hayley whispered. "Do you remember? When we investigated that Japanese warship in the Pacific."

"An apparition's materializing," Laura said. While the doctor stared, a transparent figure of a woman solidified.

"Laura, this is my grandmother. Grams, this is Laura."

"She's a ghost?" Laura asked.

"No, a visiting spirit. She's in training to be my guide."

"She looks younger than me."

"I no longer have a decaying carcass, dear. One of the perks of crossing over." Grams moved closer. "Laura, you're trembling." She held out her hand. "Touch me. Once your mind tells you I'm real, you'll feel better."

Laura took Grams's hand. "You're as real as I am. How's that possible?"

"Have you ever heard of anyone moving an object with their mind?"

"Yes. Telekinesis."

"Thought is a powerful thing."

"So you *thought* yourself into reality?"

"Reality? Maybe your concept of reality." Grams extended her arm. While Laura observed, Grams's hand turned from youthful to old and wrinkled. Grams laughed at the stunned expression on the surgeon's face. "I used thought creation."

"You just concentrated?" Laura said.

"I can't go into detail. Some secrets are best kept. There's danger involved. What is created by thought can also be disassembled. That knowledge could destroy your world. I remember how many times I wished my husband would vanish."

"Grams!" Hayley said.

"Well, it's true. Even though I love him dearly, we all have our moments."

"Talking about disassembling something, do you think you can help me get rid of these dreams, Grams?" Hayley scooted to the edge of the bed.

"I was just about to do that," Laura said, following Hayley

158

and sitting next to her. "I have sleeping pills."

"Your sleeping pills won't help. When Hayley was at the plantation, she forgot to protect herself. She's infected, the same as Abel. The dreams are created to scare her, to give the seed of negativity something to feed on. If she took your pills, her nightmares would happen anyway, only you won't hear her screams. You'd see her sleeping peacefully, unaware she was being tortured."

Laura gasped.

"We need to get started, dear. This has to stop."

"What do you want me to do?" Hayley asked.

"You need to cleanse your chakras."

"Chakras?" Laura asked.

"On the top of your head, a vortex connects your being to the spiritual realm. Together there are seven vortices from the tip of your head to the end of your spine." Grams pointed to each area running down the center of Hayley's body. "They're called chakras. They receive energy and keep your body and mind balanced. The entity has planted itself in Hayley's chakra linking to the pineal gland in her brain. While it feeds on the fear it's creating in Hayley's nightmare, the negativity will grow and spread to her other chakras."

"Why would it need to create dreams?" Laura asked. She tightened the bottle's lid and slipped the pills back into the pocket of her robe.

"Negative entities consume," Grams said. "When Lee intervened at the plantation, the entity that consumed Wheeler embedded its seed inside Hayley. The seed's waiting until her guard's down, when she sleeps. If it takes control and matures, she'll lose reality. She'll become Emma in her mind, and relive the slave's tortured memories over and over. Then the negative entity inside her will feed endlessly."

159

"She could go insane?"

"Yes."

"So what are you going to do?"

"Hayley knows how to cleanse her chakras. It'll take about forty-five minutes. Then I'll help her with the next step to get rid of the entity completely."

"What about the rest of us? Are we in danger?" Laura asked.

"In order for Hayley to receive impressions, she has to open herself up to the energy around her. That's the problem. She leaves herself vulnerable. Usually, others with less sensitivity than Hayley naturally balance positive and negative energy without much difficulty. Of course, there are always exceptions, and that's why you have psychiatrists."

"Psychotherapy." Laura crossed her arms and narrowed her brow.

"Don't fret, dear. You and your friends have nothing to worry about."

As Hayley lay face up on the bed, Laura moved to the other side of the bed and watched.

"Let's get started, dear." Grams said a prayer, then placed her hands above the vortex on the top of Hayley's head.

CHAPTER 25

After Grams's intervention and Laura's return to her own room, Hayley slept better than she had in years. Climbing out of bed in the morning, she noticed her thoughts were clearer and her body free of stress. She sat at the edge of her bed and slipped on her fuzzy yellow slippers, then grabbed her yellow cotton bathrobe draped across the footboard. While she slid her arms into the sleeves, she thought about Abel. *Today's the day, Abel. You'll truly be a free man.*

She glanced toward the door, heard movement downstairs, and smelled bacon and coffee. Before joining Laura for breakfast, Hayley took her cell phone from her purse on the rocking chair and dialed Lee's number. "Hi. We need to call the team together. Strength in numbers might throw Leech's concentration off. Who's there with you now?"

"Lewis and Jim. I'll call Roger."

"What about John?" Hayley asked.

"He can't make it."

"That's okay," she replied. "We probably won't need him. Laura and I will be over after breakfast. See you in a bit."

~*~

Hayley started her car and glanced at the clock on the dash… close to ten. The car radio played "Home" by Daughtry. She waited for Laura to climb into the passenger seat and close the car door. Having her stay the night had felt comfortable, almost like having a sister visit.

Hayley flipped off the car radio. She loved the serene drive to Lee's estate, with the lake on one side of the road and the pine forest on the other.

Laura sighed as she looked out her window.

Out of the corner of an eye, Hayley glanced at her. "How are things going with you and Roger? Just good friends, or something more maybe?"

"We talk, we joke, we laugh so hard we cry, but that's all. I'm in love with him, but I don't think he feels the same way about me."

"Sounds familiar. I think Roger and Lee have a little trouble expressing themselves. Kathy was the one who told me how Lee felt. I never would've guessed."

"So you think Roger may have feelings for me?"

"He told Lee he's in love with you."

"You're joking!" Laura said. "Perhaps he knows something I don't. Maybe he thinks we shouldn't be together."

"Or maybe he doesn't want to rush things. You've only known each other a little over a month. He could be afraid of losing you if he moves too fast. I have an idea."

"I hope it's good."

"Why don't you move in with me?" Hayley suggested. "If he wants to see you, he'll have to make it obvious. No more casual dinners and chance meetings at home. You need to stop being a guest. When is Clint being released from the hospital?"

"It's a matter of days."

"Good. Tell Roger you were planning to live there only until Clint was on his feet again."

"That's true. I was planning to move once Clint no longer

needed medical attention." Laura rested her finger on her chin. "You know, this might be a brilliant idea. I guess I can tell him I'm staying with you to make sure your dreams don't return. How are you feeling this morning?"

"Great. Best sleep ever."

"Are you sure you want a boarder?"

"I think it would be perfect. You could stay as long as you want."

"It would solve the awkwardness I'm feeling at Roger's. It's sensible to move in with you. I know Lee would be glad you're not alone." Laura smiled, clearly remembering last night. "Well, I guess you're never really alone. Meeting your grandmother was beyond words."

Hayley pulled up to the gated entrance of Lee's estate. "Thomas, I'm here," she said into the speaker, then glanced at Laura. "Grams is just a whisper away. She's always here when I need her." The large gates swung open. Hayley drove through.

"Grams seems to be an insightful woman."

"Yes. She knows everything. In her dimension, knowledge is endless. I asked her what I should do to persuade Abel to leave the cave. Something that would convince him that he doesn't have to wait there any longer for Emma."

"And?"

"She said I should ask Ben to speak with him."

"Ben who?"

"I thought you knew Lee has a spirit in his home." They drove along the spruce-lined drive and parked in front of the mansion.

"I thought it was a ghost named Casper."

"Jim always calls him that, but it's Ben Franklin, and he's not a ghost, he's a spirit. When he died, he crossed over into the light. Ghost are spirits who have never crossed. Ben's just visiting."

"Holy — I'm going to meet *the* Ben Franklin?"

"In the flesh, so to speak."

"When?"

Hayley opened the car door. "Today. Ready?"

~*~

While Lewis approached the garden terrace, glasses rattling on his tray caught Hayley's attention. Unusual behavior for the perfect gentleman's gentleman, she thought, when she noticed the telltale sign. Then she realized the only time he'd lost his composure on the job was during a ghost investigation, or after seeing a spirit.

Lewis set the tray on the patio table and stood in his black tux with his hands behind his back, a grin crossing his face. She'd seen that look when Lee had asked him to join the team to descend to the foundation room. *Lewis isn't nervous. He's shaking from trying to contain his excitement.*

Hayley closed her eyes and mentally searched their surroundings for danger. Maybe the entity had broken free of Abel to find a new host in the mansion. When her senses swept through the house, she found the source that elated Lewis, and she smiled, too. *Great, it's Ben.*

"What's wrong, Lewis? Ya look like ya swallowed a damn canary," Jim said.

"Actually, everything is quite right. Mr. Hudson has arrived, and I've directed him to the terrace." He flashed Lee a mischievous smile. "Seems to be time, sir."

"Time for what, Lewis?" Lee asked. "Stop being so cryptic. What's on your mind?"

Lewis's white-gloved hands shot out from behind his back, and he became animated. "I was going down the hallway when I saw the library door open. I went in to see if you needed anything. Sir, Benjamin Franklin was, or is, in your library! It's really him, sir. He's a ghost. He was gracious enough to prove it to me."

164

"Not a ghost, Lewis, a spirit. He's the person who's been haunting my house since I was born. I wonder what's going on? He's never materialized before. Have any ideas what he wants, Hayley?"

"It's because I want to speak with him. Grams suggested Mr. Franklin should talk with Abel. She told him we need his help."

Roger walked out of the house and joined them at the table. "Why would Ben Franklin be haunting your house, Lee?"

"I know I've never mentioned this before, except to Hayley, but I was named after him. I'm his great-grandson many times removed. My first name's Benjamin. Lee's my middle name."

"Butter my butt and call me a biscuit," Jim said. "Ya mean to say you've kept a secret from us for all these years? Think we'd make fun of you? Well, most likely." He looked toward the library. "Why don't we go find out what Casper wants?"

"Don't call him Casper to his face. It's disrespectful," Lee told him.

"Ya know how many years I've been calling him that? If I don't call him Casper, he'll think I'm a half bubble off plumb."

"I'm sure if he's known you this long, the cat's already out of the bag," Roger said.

Jim smirked. "Ha. Funny."

They followed Lee to the library.

When Hayley entered, she saw Mr. Franklin standing at the window, staring out at the front yard. He wore a white lace silk shirt, brown velvet vest, dress pants, buckle shoes, and coat, his light brown hair pulled into a ponytail. Ben turned. Hayley thought he appeared younger than his portrait in Lee's dining room.

With a broad smile, he approached Lee. "Benjamin. 'Tis indeed the grandest of pleasures to speak visibly with my greatest of grandsons and his distinguished friends."

165

"It's an honor to finally meet you, sir. I always hoped you'd make an appearance." Lee motioned to the others gathering beside him. "This is Hayley Johnson."

When Mr. Franklin lifted her hand to his lips, his silk lace cuff flowed from his coat sleeve. The frosty touch of his fingers sent shivers up Hayley's arm. "My dear, you are indeed the most admired of all doers of good deeds. The angels on high praise your name. I am humbled to make your acquaintance."

"The pleasure is mine."

"This is Dr. Laura Song," Lee said.

Mr. Franklin bowed. "The stars in the night pale before your beauty."

He placed his hand on Roger's shoulder. Roger gasped and darted a nervous glance at Lee. Leaning to speak confidentially to Roger, Mr. Franklin gazed at Laura. "He who does not cast a net upon such a find is indeed mindless. Make haste, or you shall become a floundering fool."

Jim laughed. "I couldn't have said it better."

"You are impetuous to assume such notions, my good man Jim. Your mastery of the English language leaves the wisest of men breathless. And dare I say, your wisdom has left me in tears on many occasions."

"Gee thanks, Cas— Um, Mr. Franklin."

"I beseech thee," he said glancing around, "to call me Ben."

"We need your help, sir," Hayley said.

"You have only to ask it of me."

"Are you familiar with Abel's circumstances?" she asked.

"Most certainly." His brows furrowed. "I am concerned and grieved to see the wretched torture of his soul."

She nodded. "I am, too. I think he's tied to the cave for some reason."

"He is bound by trickery, but I am certain reason will break his bondage."

"Will you talk to him and help him leave the cave?"

"Indeed. His misery weighs upon him by his ignorance of free choice. The honor shall be mine to cure his deficiency of knowledge and free him of his prison. I shall enlighten him as you please."

"Should we go to the cave now?" Lee asked.

"Indeed. Let us not squander time. Lead the way, my son."

CHAPTER 26

The afternoon sun shone through the library windows, brightening the room. Lee brushed his fingers across the filigree on the rosewood paneling beside the fireplace, searching for the trigger to enter the secret passage. Laura grabbed her black leather bag containing a first aid kit and tools she needed to collect DNA samples from Abel's remains. Lewis handed the investigators flashlights to guide them through the darkness until reaching the basement.

With Lee's twist of the carved cluster of flowers, the wood panel door swung open. He looked over his shoulder. "Ready?"

Ben shook his head. "Nay. I am afraid my energy falters. I can no longer remain visible to your eyes."

Hayley motioned Lee on. "Go ahead. Take the others to the wine cellar. I'll walk with Ben." His presence awed her, and she knew he had a profound understanding of Abel's plight. She'd read that in Ben's last years he relentlessly spent months petitioning Congress to abolish slavery. By helping Lee find the key to the foundation room and the map of the cave, Ben had made it obvious to her that he cared about Abel's anguish.

Jim led the way through the narrow passage. Laura trailed, with Roger right behind her. Once Lewis and Lee followed and started down the stairs to the basement, Hayley watched Ben's transformation. His earthly appearance evanesced into spirit form, invisible to others, seen and heard only by her.

"Ready?" she asked.

Ben bowed. "Where thou goest, I shall follow." His footsteps were silent as he walked behind Hayley down the narrow stairway. When they reached the basement, Ben slowed his pace. "Are you aware of your impending peril?" he asked.

At the mention of peril, the hair on the back of Hayley's neck stood on end. "No. I can't foresee my own future. But I'm betting it's going to get rough."

"To say the least. My insight has allowed me to perceive your dilemma."

"Your choice of words makes me uneasy. Should I be nervous? Are we walking into a trap?"

"'Tis so, I dare say. But you must not speak of it. Your nemesis listens. You must act blindly and render your trust to my counsel. Likewise, you must beseech your friends to do your bidding without query. 'Twill not be easy. Lee is bound to protect you. 'Tis imperative he heed your word."

Hayley hesitated while Lee opened the wine cellar door and looked back in her direction. "Go ahead, Lee. I'll be right there." Once he followed the others inside, she turned to Ben. "Tell me what we need to do so no one gets hurt."

"Nay, I cannot divulge your dilemma without consequence. The entity surmises your plan. Your knowledge of its intent shall inevitably cause the entity to react differently. 'Tis the present intentions we most desire. Give mandate to your friends to follow your word, which I shall present to you at the most exact moment."

Her eyes met Ben's. "I trust you, and I'll do whatever you say."

"I am honored. I've pondered your plight and found free will to cause vast variances in outcomes. I've taken into consideration cause and effect to life's chain of circumstances. After much contemplation, I've found the moment to allow the best to be done. 'Tis a trick to know when a negative action is needed to perpetrate a necessary outcome."

Hayley nodded. "I'm familiar with life-links and how changing one thing can change the future. But destroying the entity and freeing Abel must be what's supposed to happen. Otherwise, why would Abel have attacked me in the garden in the first place?"

Ben gallantly extended his arm, the lace hanging loosely at his cuff as he motioned her forward. He continued as they strolled. "Positive and negative energy go hand in hand. You think wrongly to assume the demise of the entity. Neither positive nor negative can be undone."

She stopped in her tracks. "Grams said the same thing. But I saw parts of Leech being destroyed when I surrounded Abel with white light."

He shook his head. "Nay. 'Tis as water evaporates. You may believe the water exists no longer since your eyes perceive it not. Whereas, in truth, it has dissipated and exists beyond your awareness."

"What happens to it then? Will the negativity attack someone else?"

"Nay, it ceases to be an entity unto itself and returns to its state of balance in the universe."

"It seems a little scary to know it's still out there."

"Negativity 'tis in itself a catalyst. One shall petrify from contentment if not for unease. The spawns of negativity — want, need, boredom, et cetera — coax one to move forward."

"But the entity attacks people."

"'Tis key to curb negativity's hunger to know one's self.

One's free will with awareness will foil the assault."

"I think humanity's still working on that."

He raised a finger to his lips and nodded. "Alas, we must needs save humanity another day. Presently, let us make haste to free our good man Abel from his oppression. I must beg your pardon for, at the precise moment I give word, I must depart with Lee and your friends. If I remain, I will hinder the necessary outcome. Alas, you must face the entity alone. But fret not... resolve shall come swiftly."

"I understand."

As she and Ben entered the wine cellar, Lee met Hayley at the door, handing her a lantern. "Is Ben still with us?"

"He's right here."

"I guess we're ready to go. Any last-minute details?"

"Yes." She turned to the group. "I've been talking with Ben. He's foreseen what we're about to walk into. He wants everyone to promise on faith to do exactly as I say without question. That means you too, Lee."

Lee blinked with surprise. "Why do you think I'd have a problem with that?"

"Ben said you will. I have to face the entity alone — without you or Ben — in order to ensure the right outcome. Leaving me is going to be hard for you. Once we're in the cave, he'll let me know what you need to do. As soon as I give the word, react as fast as possible. I trust Ben completely, so if he says jump, I'll say jump — so jump! Okay?"

~*~

In the main cavern, a few feet from the tunnel leading to the dead-end chamber where they had last encountered Abel, they stopped.

Hayley stepped forward. "I'll go first." She closed her eyes and mentally surrounded herself and the others with a shield of white light. "Okay, stay alert."

Again she led them down the narrow tunnel until they reached the small chamber. At its entrance, before stepping inside, Hayley motioned the team to stop. Holding up her lantern, she spotted Abel poised for a confrontation in the corner of the cave near his remains, and clearly, she believed, possessed by the entity.

Hayley, ready for his signal, glanced at Ben. "Run," she shouted.

The team sprinted back through the tunnel. Ben stayed at Lee's side, running to safety, leaving Hayley alone.

Instantaneously, Hayley dashed inside the chamber, while Leech darted from its host, attacking the ceiling with blunt force. While her heart rate soared, rocks and soil cascaded, piling debris over the spot where she and the others had stood. Dust filled the room. With her hand over her mouth, Hayley frantically searched for Leech. Alarmed by a movement, she glanced up too late to avoid the large stone falling toward her.

A dagger of pain shot through her skull. Blood streamed into her eyes from her forehead. Unable to focus, she lost her protective shield. Blackness followed. She slumped to the ground, unconscious.

~*~

Hayley woke covered with debris, her arms pinned. Her head ached as she shook the dirt from her face. When her mind cleared, panic struck. She searched for Leech, relieved to see Lee standing beside her. "Lee." She wanted to feel safe in his arms, but rubble still immobilized her.

Slowly, the stones covering her rolled off, raked away by an invisible force. Her mind screamed, It's not Lee!

Terror seized her as Hayley realized Leech had shape-shifted into Lee's image. Freed from the smothering debris, she tried to turn over and crawl away, but Leech held her down by an unseen influence pressing against her shoulders.

"Let me go!" she shouted, looking up at the impostor.

The pretender, eyes fixed on hers, stepped across her body and straddled her. "Make love to me, Hayley," it moaned.

She trembled.

The illusion of Lee's face turned grotesque, its mouth broadening, sharp teeth dripping with mucus. While terrorizing Hayley, Leech inhaled her fear, licking its lips with a long, pointed tongue.

Hayley tried again to pull away, her battered muscles refusing to respond.

"Not yet, my love." Leech's facsimile of Lee returned to his handsome likeness and smiled evilly. Reaching down, it unzipped its pants, readying, Hayley realized, to rape her. Using its will, Leech unbuttoned Hayley's jeans. Through its teeth, it suckled the fear emanating from her.

As her pants unzipped and his invisible force began to slip her jeans off her hips, Hayley gathered her wits, closed her eyes, and shielded herself and Leech with white light. Leech threw its head back at the light's touch and released an agonized scream. The distorted fabrication of Lee's face disappeared, replaced by a jackal's. Leech's eyes flared red with anger, lips stretching across saber teeth while it shrieked.

Hayley concentrated her thoughts on the white light, knowing if she faltered Leech would bury her and go after her friends. Releasing her fear enabled Hayley to focus.

Engulfed in the light, Leech began to evaporate. The entity pulled away, taking the shape of a black mass, and hovered. Leech looked back at her from beyond the light's reach, and started to move toward her friends beyond the cave-in, then hesitated.

"If you plan on looking for another host, try another galaxy, because next time you won't escape," she vowed.

Leech's black mass took the shape of a human head, turned to Abel, then faced Hayley. "You are pathetic if you think you can defeat me. Your existence is brief, but I will survive throughout eternity. You cannot kill me. Keep vigilant, for I will return when you least expect it. And then we will see who will be outwitted." The entity's hostility filled every molecule in the dimly lit cavern, then it shot upward, vanishing through the ceiling.

Hayley flinched away from the falling rubble until the shower of dirt ceased. *Well, that went well. I just have to keep looking over my shoulder for the rest of my life, but I can deal with it.*

Silence engulfed the chamber, and the dust settled. With all her strength, she forced her aching body to sit up. Once she pulled on her jeans and fastened them, she stood, coughing, throat dry. In the dimness of the chamber, Hayley glanced behind her and saw the lantern still lit and on its side. She took a step, lifted the lantern, and peered around the cavern to find the entrance blocked, and Abel huddled on the dirt floor with his arms shielding his face.

"Oh, Abel, it's okay." She went to him, set the lamp down, and sat beside him.

CHAPTER 27

In the light of the lantern, Hayley surveyed her craggy oppressive prison. Abel's remains lay a few feet in front of her, exactly where he had been murdered over a century-and-a-half before. His ghost sat beside her on the dirt floor. Across the chamber, the cave-in blocked the entrance, leaving dusty air. So now she had to sit and wait. Ben had given his word that the situation would be resolved in a short time. She sighed. *But how long is short?*

Leaning forward, Hayley tried to avoid a jagged rock poking her lower back. She reached behind her, fingers searching for the stone's sharp edges. *Maybe I can —* Her hand swept across the back pocket of her jeans. *Oh, Noah. I almost forgot.* Gently tugging, she pulled out the photo Lee and Jim had found hidden in the secret passageway. Putting the picture under the lamp's light, she brushed off the dirt.

Abel looked at her with wondering eyes.

She held the photo out to him. "It's a picture of your son, I think. Does it look like Noah?"

"Yes'm, dat's my boy. Why's he wid Digger?"

"This was taken after you were murdered. Mr. Wheeler gave your son to Digger as payment for killing you. We've been trying to find out what happened to Noah after this picture was taken.

We might've found someone who knows."

"Es my boy dead?"

A lump caught in her throat. Tears pooled in her eyes, threatening to fall down her cheeks. She said softly, "I don't think you realize how long it's been since your murder. You've been in this cave for over one hundred fifty years."

He lowered his head.

Her tears struggled to find a path down her soiled face. She thought for a moment. *How am I going to ask him for his remains? The medical examiner has to be notified.*

She swallowed hard and took a deep breath. "We might have some good news. Nowadays, they can trace descendants by a thing called DNA. It's found inside your bones. We think we might've found your and Noah's relative. We'd like to find out."

He studied the picture. "My boy 'scaped from Digger?"

"Yes, and we believe he married and had children." She softened her voice. "Abel, we'll have to move your remains out of the cave. How do you feel about that?"

"Dey just bones, Missy Hayley. Dey ain't me no mo'. Youse wantin' to bury 'em?"

"In the cemetery."

"I'se seed a cemetery befo'. Dere be one 'n back of Wheeler's church."

"We won't bury you anywhere near Wheeler. We'll find somewhere nice. You can have a big headstone with your name on it if you want. I promise."

"Dat's mos' kindly. I'se tanks youse, Missy Hayley, I'se truly do." He looked up with sadness. "What 'bout my Emma?"

She hesitated, searching for the right words. If she told Abel that Wheeler was keeping Emma prisoner, he would want to rescue her now, and that was impossible. "There're a few things we have to do first before we find her. I brought a friend, Ben, who will help you leave the cave. You don't have to wait here for Emma anymore. He'll take you to the gardens, then show you how to leave the estate. You need to let him help you, Abel. We'll need your help soon, so you have to get free of this cave."

A grin crossed his face. "We's gonna find Emma?"

"Yes." She glanced up as Ben shimmered through the debris, then walked to them.

Abel stood, his eyes wide.

Hayley laughed lightly at the shocked look on Abel's face. "Abel, this is Ben Franklin. Ben, this is Abel Smith."

Ben bowed. "My good man Abel, I have heard you are in need of help. May I lend you my assistance?"

"Yes'sa, Massa Franklin. Tanks you mos' kindly."

"I am but a humble man as yourself. Please, call me Ben. Agreed?"

"Yessa."

"Let's take a walk, shall we?"

While Ben, in his next breath, began his teaching, he and Abel walked casually, disappearing into the wall of the cave.

Alone in the stillness, Hayley heard a muffled voice coming from beyond the cave-in. She stood and grabbed the lamp. Listening, she went to the cave's entrance, holding up the lantern.

"Move your bony butt, Lewis. You're really startin' to ruffle my feathers."

"I've always known you had a bird brain, sir. Thank you for your confirmation."

Hayley could not mistake those voices.

Pebbles trickled down from the blockage. Hayley glanced up. A rock the size of her head shifted at the top of the debris. She searched the chamber, looking for something to stand on. Surrounded by bits of stone, a large boulder rested in the corner. Walking to it, she used her foot to remove it from its bed, then rolled it toward the cave-in. With a final shove, she positioned the boulder, stepped up, and held the lamp high. She assumed that Jim or Lewis on the other side was wrenching the rock in front of her. Placing her dirty hand against its surface, Hayley pushed on the rock until it gave way.

The voices grew louder.

"Well, dip me in donkey dung and roll me in bread crumbs, Lewis," Jim said.

"I'd love to, sir."

"Lee, come here. Lewis broke through."

Hayley jumped down, standing back, straining to see, but dust filled the breech.

"You're skinnier than a tick's turd, Lewis. Think you can crawl through this?"

She heard Lewis gasp. "Sir, do I have to put up with these insults?"

"Hell, give him your worst, Lewis. You deserve to," Lee said. "But later. We have to get Hayley out of there."

Someone raised a lantern to the hole. She saw Lee's handsome face framed between the rocks.

"Are you okay?" he asked. She heard the concern in his voice. "You're hurt."

Hayley could only imagine how ghastly she looked with her face covered with blood and dirt. "It's not as bad as it looks. Nothing a glass of wine won't fix."

"Where's Leech?"

"Gone. And Ben's helping Abel."

Lee's frown turned into a reassuring smile. "We'll have you out in a minute."

Hayley sat back, listening to the rocks and dirt being removed. With the hole a little bigger, she saw Jim smile, his face caked with grime. "Have ya out in no time, darlin'." He turned. "So what's your worst, Lewis? Gonna throw a rock at me?"

"I've been putting up with your insults for years. I'm giving this serious thought."

"Might be painful." Jim tapped his head. "Your wheel might be turnin', but your hamster's dead." He reached up and pulled a rock from the obstruction.

"I suggest you sleep with your eyes open, sir."

She heard the grin in Lewis's voice.

Another boulder shimmied out of the debris. An avalanche of dirt, rocks, and gravel cascaded, opening up half the entrance. Lewis smiled triumphantly.

"Damn showoff," Jim said.

Behind them, Hayley saw a shadowy figure with a wheelbarrow making his way through the tunnel. *Roger.* "Roger, where's Laura?"

"She's in the main cavern. I'll get her."

"Ask her to bring her bag so she can gather Abel's DNA samples." She touched the gash on her head. "And her first aid kit."

Roger headed back through the tunnel.

A moment later, Laura worked herself through the gap and hurried to Hayley's side. "You look like hell."

"Hell—good description for what I've been through."

Laura gingerly examined the gash on Hayley's head. "Headache?"

"Just a bit."

She took a small flashlight from her bag, clicked it on, and held the light in front of Hayley's eyes. "Any dizziness? Follow this light. Don't move your head."

Hayley did as told. "No dizziness."

Laura glanced at Abel's remains. "Let's get this over with so we can get you out of here." She walked to Abel's bones and knelt. "Watch what I do in case I can't get access to Emma's remains." With Hayley at her side, Laura pulled gloves from her bag, then removed a small tool suitable for prying or loosening. She examined the skull and found a loose tooth. "Easy enough." Extracting it carefully with pliers, Laura placed it into a glass jar, screwed on the lid, removed her gloves, and returned everything to her bag. "Got it. Let's go."

~*~

Wearing a black tux and carrying a tray of drinks, Lewis stepped onto the veranda.

"Don't you look squeaky clean," Jim said.

With a dramatic gesture, Lewis set a drink in front of him. "I hope you enjoy this, sir."

Jim straightened in his chair. "What in the hell is that supposed to mean?" As Lewis walked away, Jim swapped his beer for the drink nearest his.

Roger reached for his glass. "What's this? Lewis, I asked for wine, not beer."

In midstride, Lewis stopped and turned, glaring at Jim.

With a Cheshire cat grin, Jim held up his wine glass. "Touché, Lewis."

Upon his return, Lewis placed a glass of wine in front of Roger and handed him a newspaper. "I thought you might like to see this, sir."

"Thank you, Lewis." Roger studied the front-page stories. "Well, well. Looks like we've made the papers. Seems Frank Thompson has sent his boys out looking for us. Since we haven't been going to the office, they put a tail on Kathy." He passed the paper to Lee. "Take a look."

Clearing his throat, Lee read out loud. "'Wonder what Paranormal Search and Analysis is up to these days? Kathy Lane, their historian/researcher, has been seen gathering information

180

pertaining to Lee Franklin's estate. Could Mr. Franklin have a ghost in his mansion? Among other topics Miss Lane researched were details of the Underground Railroad. Could it be that the past has come back to haunt our esteemed paranormal investigator and owner of the showcase Franklin mansion on Lake View Drive? We intend to find out.'" Lee ruffled the paper. "Damn it!"

"It's going to come out anyway as soon as you call the authorities," Laura said.

Lee tossed the paper onto the table. "Damn! We need to find the entrance to the cave. There's no way Digger brought Abel in through the front door. We'll have to block it off before I have a mass invasion on my hands. Hell, as it stands now, if anyone found their way into the cave they'd be able to get into my wine cellar and the basement."

"I can find it," Hayley offered.

"Great," Lee said. "We'll search tomorrow afternoon."

"Don't forget to notify the state and local authorities, including the medical examiner," Laura said.

"That's right. Lewis—" Lee said.

"I'll take care of it, sir." He turned and went into the house.

"Guess the manure's 'bout to hit the fan," Jim said. "It'll be a circus around here with all the lookie-loos. And you know Frank will be pesterin' us while gettin' his headline story."

Roger removed his ringing cell phone from his shirt pocket. "Hi, Kathy." He listened. "That's great. What time will he be in?" He glanced at Lee and smiled. "Thanks. See you in the morning."

"What's up?" Lee asked.

"The lawyer claiming to be Abel's descendant wants to see us. He's flying in from Chicago in the morning. Kathy told him to meet us in the office at ten."

"I'll need to be there," Laura said. "I have to get a sample of his DNA. I'll have both specimens sent to the lab at the same time."

"How long do you think it will take to get the results?" Roger asked.

"Hopefully in three or four days."

Lewis returned to the veranda with another bottle of merlot and began refilling glasses, starting with Lee's. "Sir, the police department is sending an investigator."

"Thank you, Lewis." Lee glanced around the table. "Jim's right. Let's make this easy. If anyone has questions, refer them to me. Otherwise, the only story we'll give is that we searched the cave, suspecting it had been used by the Underground Railroad, how Hayley got trapped in the cave-in when she followed a tunnel to see where it led, and that we had to dig her out. Don't elaborate. Keep it simple. We had a cave-in. Don't know how it happened." He peered at Jim. "Are we straight on that? No storytelling."

"Don't know why you're lookin' at me."

CHAPTER 28

Hayley lifted the morning newspaper from the stack in the center of the office conference table. A photo of human remains and the story of the police investigation at Lee's estate led the front page.

Across from her, Roger passed a copy to Laura. "Last night was a fiasco," he said to Kathy, who also took a newspaper. "The entrance in the foundation room leading to the cave is off limits now. There's a slew of investigators running around, from the police to the curators from the Museum of Man in Raleigh."

"I gave the curators the coded journal we found in the secret passage," Lee said, "and explained we were searching the cave believing it to be an artery of the Underground Railroad. They confirmed our suspicions, took photos, and tried to protect the integrity of the site while investigators and the press were present."

"When are they moving the remains?" Kathy asked.

"They're gone," Lee said. "Forensics took them early this morning to test for age. Meanwhile, Hayley and I will be searching for the cave's entrance."

Hayley glanced up from the paper. "Looks like we've kept Abel's presence a secret for now."

Roger picked up the remote control and glanced outside.

183

"We've been damn lucky so far. Hope Mr. Smith can keep quiet. We'll find out soon. He'll be here any minute."

When Roger pushed a button on the remote and closed the burgundy curtains, Hayley sensed his motive: to make a good first impression. With the curtains drawn, the room looked like an office rather than the car dealership it used to be. For that same reason, he had painted the walls a light gray and had decorated the office with plush burgundy carpeting, wall-to-ceiling burgundy draperies, and a black lacquer conference table. Visually, the room stated that Paranormal Search and Analysis was to be taken seriously as a professional business.

Hearing a car drive into the parking lot, Hayley waited patiently. Heavy footsteps approached the front door. Then Mr. Smith entered the office. Hayley stared in disbelief. He looked like Abel—almost identical; the same color and shade of skin, wide nose, deep-set eyes, and oval face with a strong jaw, the only difference being he wasn't as buff as his ancestor.

Roger stood.

Mr. Smith reached out his hand. "I'm Daniel Smith. Pleased to meet you."

Roger shook his hand. "Mr. Smith, I'm Roger Hudson. Glad you could join us. Let me introduce my team. Lee Franklin and Jim Newton are my business partners. Kathy Lane is our historical researcher. Dr. Laura Song is our medical researcher. And Hayley Johnson is our medium and psychic investigator."

"It's good to meet all of you."

"Would you like to take a seat, Mr. Smith?" Roger asked. "How about something to drink?"

"Please call me Daniel. Water would be good, thank you." He sat on Roger's right, placed his briefcase on the table, opened it, and pulled out a worn leather-bound book. "I guess I should start by showing you this. It's a journal I received last year in my grandfather's will. It had been passed down in our family from generation to generation. It tells the story of Noah, who is Emma and Abel Smith's son. The Smiths were slaves belonging to Zachary Wheeler, who owned a plantation in Georgia. The accounts were written by Noah."

"Wow," Roger said. "That will help immensely."

"How far back does it go?" Lee asked.

Daniel turned to the first page. "He wrote this while he was a soldier during the Civil War. One of the soldiers he fought alongside taught him to write. The journal starts at the time he and his family were seized by men on horseback in the spring of 1855."

Roger nodded. "We know about Digger stealing Abel, his wife, Emma, and their son from Ohio, then selling them to Mr. Wheeler in Georgia. We lost track of the boy when his dad was murdered and Wheeler gave Noah to Digger as payment."

Daniel's eyes widened. "How did you know Wheeler gave him to Digger?"

"Hayley can see the past," Lee said.

"Impressive." Daniel hesitated, as if collecting himself. Then he went on. "Noah didn't know about his father's death until he was much older."

Hayley shook her head. "No one knew except Digger and Wheeler. From the first moment Wheeler set eyes on Emma, he lusted for her. He never intended to keep Abel or Noah. Abel was put to work digging a tunnel on Wheeler's plantation leading from the base of the dry well to the basement of the house. After the tunnel was completed, Wheeler moved forward with his plans — having Abel killed, giving the murderer Noah as payment, and keeping Emma a prisoner in a storage room off the tunnel. No one knew. Wheeler told everyone that Abel and his family ran."

"How old was Noah when he was given as payment?" Jim

asked.

"He was nine when he and his family were taken from Ohio," Daniel said, "and ten when his father escaped by the Underground Railroad. With help from Digger's connections, Abel ran first, then Noah and his mother were supposed to join him later that day. Instead, Noah was taken from his mother and given to Digger."

Jim raised a brow. "Hell, damn Digger was paid in advance then, 'cause Abel wasn't killed 'til he reached the cave under Lee's estate."

"So all that time," Roger said, "Noah never knew that Digger killed his father?"

Daniel raised a finger. "Because Digger had helped his father, Noah believed he was an honest man. When Noah was fifteen, he found out how Digger and his men helped slaves run, then tracked them for bounty. That's when he ran away and joined the Union Army in 1862. It wasn't until years later that he learned Digger had killed his father."

Hayley looked toward the door when a man with a round face and a bent nose entered. Yesterday Frank Thompson had visited Lee's estate to get the rundown on the remains. According to Lee, Mr. Thompson unscrupulously hunted for stories, crossing the ethics line, stepping on toes, digging for dirt, and, a few years ago, ending up with his nose where it shouldn't have been and getting it broken.

Mr. Thompson strutted into the office, looking, Hayley thought, as if he owned it.

Lee leaned and whispered to Daniel, "I don't want to seem rude and not introduce you, but this is the man who owns the *Sutterville Times,* and I'd like to keep your name out of the newspapers."

Daniel nodded.

Frank, flashing a friendly smile, walked toward the conference table. "Ladies, gentlemen. I came by to ask Mr. Franklin how he liked the headlines."

"They're fairly accurate."

"Fairly? I hit the nail on the head."

"That's one man's opinion," Lee said.

Frank turned to Roger. "Good to see you're taking cases again. What's it been—nearly a month-and-a-half since you've been back? My readers are starving for ghost stories. Usually I can track down you and your team, but after I followed you to the airport last month, all of you vanished without a trace. I've never had such a hard time passing through the security gates. It all seemed rather strange."

"We were on vacation," Roger said. "Nothing strange about that."

Frank put his finger to his forehead. "Don't tell me. Hawaii. Right?"

Jim's eyes widened. "How in the hell did you know that?"

"I've got a nose like a dowser. It can find a story no matter how far down it's buried."

"Ya got a broken nose from stickin' it where it didn't belong," Jim told him.

"It's my business to know everything." With a shrewd expression, Frank studied Laura. "Why would a renowned neurosurgeon leave her lucrative practice and opulent estate in Hawaii to join up with a team of ghost investigators, unless something extremely interesting was going on?"

Jim banged his fist on the table. "Damn it, Frank. You know as well as we do that she's here because of Roger's nephew."

"I understand. With all your wealth, you wouldn't settle for just any surgeon. But the surgery's done with. The boy's fine. And she's still here. There's a story somewhere. I can feel it."

"If Dr. Song wants to have a little excitement to get away from her brain pickin', tumor pluckin', nerve-wrackin' job and help us out, it's her business," Jim said.

Roger picked up a newspaper. "We don't mind all the stories you run about us, but don't start making things up just so you can sell your paper. And don't ever come into this office and be rude."

"You're right. I am being rude." He turned to Daniel and extended his hand. "I'm very sorry. I haven't introduced myself. I'm Frank Thompson, owner of the *Sutterville Times*."

Daniel shook his hand. "Daniel Smith. Nice to meet you."

"Not Daniel Earl Smith, the lawyer from Chicago?"

Jim rose from his seat. "That cuts it! The only way you would've known that is by tampering with our mail. How'd you like your fat rear end behind bars?" Jim turned to Kathy. "Call the police, sugar. This scum bucket belongs in jail."

Frank raised his hands. "I never tampered with anything. I came into your office last week just to see when you'd be back. As I was leaving, I ran into Phil, your postman. I mean really ran into him. He dropped all your mail. Gentleman that I am, I helped him pick up a few envelopes and accidentally saw Mr. Smith's name on a return address." With innocent eyes, he looked at Kathy. "Just ask her."

Kathy nodded. "It's true."

Frank rubbed his chin and studied Daniel. "So you've hired a lawyer from out of town. Sounds like you have something to hide. Bet it has to do with the human bones found on your estate."

Jim shoved in his chair and walked toward Frank. "That's enough, Thompson. You're as rude as a damn fartin' pack mule, and you've got fewer brains than an Egyptian mummy."

"Mummies don't have brains," Mr. Thompson said. "They're sucked out through the nose before they're entombed."

Jim peered at Frank's nose. "Guess that explains why yours is bent. I think it's time for you to leave. Let me walk ya to the door." He put his hand on Frank's shoulder.

Mr. Thompson turned. "I know there's a story here, and I'm not giving up until I find it."

When Frank stepped outside, Jim locked the door and, with hands on his hips, watched through the glass while Frank climbed into his car and drove away. "Well, doesn't that just chafe your behind?" Jim said, walking back to the conference table.

"He's just blowing smoke," Roger said. "Who's he going to talk to?" He looked at Lee. "What about your staff?"

Lee shook his head. "There's not one I don't trust. They've all been told to stay quiet. But I'll tell Lewis to watch out for Frank and to pass the word." He straightened in his seat. "I'm sorry, Mr. Smith. Now, where were we? Oh yes, Noah stayed with Digger for five years."

Daniel nervously glanced toward the door, then spoke in a low tone. "That's right. He ran off and joined the Union Army at fifteen, which he wrote about extensively. After the war, when he was eighteen and free, Noah went back to the plantation to look for his mother. The place was deserted. Seems Mr. Wheeler had been murdered."

Hayley glanced across the table. "We know about Wheeler's death. The day Brea called to tell you that she found Wheeler's grave, I had a vision of Digger murdering Wheeler over a debt. Emma had just given birth in a room off the tunnel. Wheeler ran upstairs to meet with Digger. He was dementedly obsessed with Emma, and when Digger mentioned knowing where Wheeler kept her hidden, Wheeler shot Digger to protect his secret. Digger shot back, and Wheeler dropped to the floor, dead."

Hayley remembered the disturbing visions. They turned her stomach. "In his distorted mind, he thought he was protecting

189

her. He convinced himself he truly loved her. In reality, the only way he could pleasure himself was through torture and rape. Wheeler was a cruel, sick monster."

"Yes, Noah stated that in his journal."

"How did Noah find out 'bout all that stuff?" Jim asked. "He wasn't 'round to see it."

Daniel thumbed through the journal's pages, then stopped to read. "From a woman named Liza Chambers, Mr. Wheeler's housemaid. Someone at the church told Noah where to find her. She knew everything. She said Noah's mother was held prisoner in a tunnel under the house, how she was abused mentally and physically, then died giving birth to Mr. Wheeler's child. Noah went ballistic. For years after that, he wrote about how he wished he'd killed Mr. Wheeler himself."

Hayley leaned forward. "We know about Liza and that she was told to take the child to the river and drown it."

Daniel studied Hayley's face. "You're really amazing. You practically know more than I do. Well, Liza didn't harm the baby. She took it to the Tylers, a black family given their freedom in their deceased master's will, and who lived in the woods by the river."

"What was the child's name?" Lee asked.

"Simon Tyler. He was eight when Noah met him. Noah wrote that they became close brothers throughout their lifetimes. He talked Simon into keeping a record of his date of birth and also his family's dates, then passing that on to his descendants to keep track of their lineage."

"Brea told us about that," Hayley said. "There was a middle name written after the name Simon. We're sure it read 'Wheeler.'"

"Possibly. Liza told the Tylers that if Mr. Wheeler found out the baby was alive, he'd kill him. So Simon was given the last name Tyler to keep his existence a secret."

"That means Liza wasn't there when Digger murdered him," Jim said.

"Guess not," Daniel said. "She must've just made it out of the house before the shooting started."

"Did Noah stay in Georgia?" Lee asked.

"Yes," Daniel said. "He got married and had seven children. Of course, Simon got married and had kids, too. They both passed down their journals. Brea has Simon's, and I have Noah's."

"How much of her family history does Brea know?" Hayley asked. "Does she know she has black roots?"

"Yes," Daniel said. "She does now."

"Do you happen to know where Noah's buried?" Hayley asked.

"Yes. I took a trip to the town last mentioned in his journal, Macon. He's buried in a small plot tucked away near the edge of the cemetery. I pulled the overgrowth away and was lucky to find his and his wife's gravestones."

Hayley's emotions welled. This was what she'd hoped for. Now it would be possible to bury Abel and Emma's remains, if they found hers, with Noah's. *Hopefully, I'm right and Emma's in the tunnel.*

Roger turned to Kathy. "Are you getting all this?"

She nodded. "Got it."

"We have a photo of Noah," Hayley said. "Would you like to see it?"

Daniel's mouth gaped. "Are you serious? Yes, definitely!"

Hayley pulled the picture from her pocket. "That's Digger and his men on horseback. And that's Noah."

Roger passed Daniel a newspaper. "And this is a photo of Abel's remains."

Daniel took a moment to read the story. "How can you be sure about this?"

191

Jim pointed at Hayley. "Medium, remember? Abel's ghost and his remains were in the cave under Lee's mansion. She can see and speak to the dead. She converses with Abel a lot, and showed him that photo."

Daniel leaned back in his chair, shaking his head. "Damn! This is amazing!"

"You look just like Abel. You could be his brother," Hayley told him.

"I'd give anything to meet him."

"That could be arranged, but later, after we find Emma."

Daniel's brows drew together. He shook his head. "Not that I doubt you're truly gifted. You've proven your ability with facts no one could possibly know any other way. But introducing me to a ghost is beyond rational thought. I'll believe it when I see it."

"I understand," Hayley said. "But don't be too quick to judge."

"Yes, well, I'd rather think I'm levelheaded, not judgmental," Daniel replied, while studying the newspaper photo. "I'd like to get legal custody of his remains."

"We've thought about that," Laura said. "Before the authorities arrived, we took a loose tooth from the skull to collect DNA. I'd like to get a sample from you also."

"We'll cover all costs," said Roger.

"Yes. Perfect. I'm all for it."

"I'll need samples of mtDNA," Laura said. "The mother's maternal-line ancestry, known as 'mt' for mitochondria, is passed to all her children. Wheeler would have his mother's mtDNA, and that would show up in the Tyler family. When we find Emma, we'll test hers, then compare it with yours and Brea's to find out if you're related. To be accurate, we need DNA samples from all concerned to prove no one in either family had been adopted."

"Wouldn't Brea's DNA match her mom's?" Hayley asked.

"Yes. She'd carry the mtDNA from both sides of her family, along with a line of maternal ancestry," Laura replied. "It's complicated when you take into account the number of maternal signatures there are in a DNA strand. But the DNA specialists have come a long way. Recently, an entire town's DNA was traced back to its origins a thousand years ago."

Hayley watched Jim wrinkle his nose as if smelling a foul odor. "Ya heard Frank. Even if we're in Georgia, he'll probably be on us like flies on honey. Frank's gonna find out 'bout the testin' as soon as ya open Wheeler's tomb. Mr. Smith will be exposed. Maybe even Brea and her family."

"I don't see any way around that," Hayley said. "But no one has to know about Abel and Emma's spirits."

"We can hope, darlin'. Reality has a way of slappin' ya in the face. Only takes one bad apple to spoil the moonshine. That happens, I'd rather eat moose turds than hear Frank Thompson say, 'I told you so.'"

Hayley smiled. "By that time, Abel and Emma will have crossed over."

"Who's gonna know they left?" Jim said. "Hell, they're invisible."

"I don't foresee that as being a problem," Hayley told him. "But Frank's another story."

"How close are you to getting a permit to open Wheeler's tomb?" Roger asked.

Daniel pulled a folder from his case. "Actually, I've got it right here. After my visit with you, I'll be going to Georgia."

"Mind if we join you?" Lee asked.

"Not at all. That's a good idea. You'll be there to gather the DNA."

"Exactly what I had in mind," Laura said.

"While we're there, I'd like to have my historian, Kathy, look into Wheeler's estate." Roger turned to Kathy. "Up for a trip?"

"Ready when you are," she told him.

"We'll share our findings," Roger said to Daniel.

The lawyer opened his briefcase and put the journal away. He nodded. "Couldn't be better than that. I was planning to do some research myself, but your Kathy can save me a huge amount of time. I'm working on the Tylers' legal rights to the plantation."

"You'll get proof of their heritage within a week after opening Wheeler's grave." Laura reached into her doctor's bag, opened her DNA testing kits, and pulled out a swab. "All I need is a sample of your cheek cells."

Lee moved his seat back, stood, and glanced around the table. "After Dr. Song's through with Daniel, we can all go to my place for lunch."

"Great!" Hayley said. "I can introduce Daniel to Abel."

Daniel spoke a few indecipherable words while Laura wiped the swab against the inside of his cheek. Before he could speak clearly, the next swab was in his mouth.

"Done," Laura said. She sealed each specimen envelope and put them into her doctor's bag. "How's your blood pressure, Mr. Smith? You look a little nervous."

CHAPTER 29

When Lee drove up to his home, Hayley spotted Lewis standing outside. He looked much like a statue in his tailored black suit, his crisp white shirt, flawlessly knotted black tie, and impeccably fitting gray vest. With his chin in the air, he didn't move a muscle until Lee's car stopped. Hurriedly he opened Hayley's door, lending her a hand to help her out, then assisted Daniel with his door.

After Lee climbed out and walked around to join her and Daniel, Hayley sensed something unusual about Lewis's behavior. She watched him closely after he assisted the passengers out of Roger's car, hurried to the entrance, pulled the brass handle on the mahogany door, and stood aside to let everyone enter. That's when Hayley noticed his hands shaking: *A dead giveaway that he's containing his excitement.*

She hesitated before stepping inside. "Did you have a pleasant day today?" she asked him.

Lewis lost his composure. His eyes twinkled, and he took on the giddy demeanor Hayley had seen so often when he witnessed paranormal activity. "It has been a most exhilarating day, I must say." Glancing at Daniel, he resumed his stately stance.

With Lee, Daniel, and the others right behind her, Hayley stepped into the foyer, prepared to ask Lewis what was going on, but Jim hurried past her and stood in the butler's path.

"What in the hell's goin' on, Lewis?" Jim asked.

"It's a surprise, sir," Lewis said.

"So you're not gonna tell me?"

"Remind me to bring you a dictionary, sir, so you can look up the definition of 'surprise.' If you will excuse me, I'm in a bit of a hurry." He faced Lee. "Lunch will be served on the veranda, sir." Not waiting for a response, Lewis dashed off toward the kitchen.

"Damn weirdo," Jim mumbled.

"Follow me, Daniel," Lee said, heading toward the veranda. "Would you care for a drink before we eat?"

"Yes. Iced tea will be great, unless Hayley makes good on her introduction. Then I'd need a whiskey straight up." Daniel chuckled.

When they approached the end of the hall, Lewis held the door while Laura, Kathy, Roger, and Jim stepped out to the veranda. Hayley hesitated inside the door, along with Lee and Daniel.

"Drinks, Lewis," Lee said, "The usual for everyone, and bring Mr. Smith a double Macallan '39 straight up."

Daniel's brows rose.

When Hayley walked outside and across the veranda toward the others, the July sun felt good on her face. She looked out at the garden stretching to the lakeshore. Only a few days ago, she'd noticed heightened activity in the garden. Workers had trimmed the topiaries and boxwood hedges. In each flowerbed, they'd pulled weeds and planted new flowers where needed. Except today. Today the garden appeared serene.

She glanced around, looking for Abel and Ben, and saw them on the north side of the estate. They stood by the bridge spanning the pond.

Lee walked up to her, handing her a glass of sauvignon blanc. "Do you see Ben and Abel?"

"Yes, over there." She sipped her wine and pointed.

"Does Abel know Daniel's here to see him?"

"I told Lewis to tell Ben. I sense that Ben's been teaching Abel a few more tricks. From Lewis's reaction, it might be something that'll scare the wits out of Daniel. I'll have to talk with Ben and make sure their antics won't give Daniel a heart attack."

"How do you plan to introduce him to Daniel?"

"I'm going to surround Abel with white light. It worked in the cave."

Lee gazed across the garden, then looked over his shoulder at Daniel. "So, should we make introductions before or after lunch?"

"Before. That will give Daniel a little time to let his nerves settle. Then he can eat lunch if he's up to it." She took a sip of her wine. "I have to speak with Ben. I'll be right back." She passed her glass to Lee and descended the stairs to the garden, hurried along the pathways between evergreen hedges and toward the bridge.

Ben and Abel turned at her approach.

"Miss Johnson, how splendid of you to join us," Ben said.

"It's good to see you again as well." She faced Abel. "Has Ben explained that you'll be meeting your descendant?"

"Yes'em, Missy Hayley."

"So, Ben, I'm sure you've got something planned. Do you mind telling me what you intend to do?"

"Necessity has declared the day to be one of vision," Ben said. "Therefore, Abel shall materialize and will hence give a highly memorable debut."

"You've taught him how to materialize?" Hayley asked with surprise.

"Indubitably. He is most proficient. So kind is Lewis to willingly submit himself to our trials of surprise."

Hayley laughed. "He was more than happy to help." She glanced toward the veranda where the others had gathered. "Give me a moment to tell Lee your plan. As soon as I sit down, Abel, you make your appearance."

"Bless youse, Missy Hayley. Youse is most kindly—most kindly."

"Thank you, Abel." She turned and hurried back to the others.

Lee met her at the top of the stairs. "Well?"

She whispered in Lee's ear, "Abel's going to materialize."

"Seriously?" He returned her glass of wine. "We all get to see him?"

She nodded. "As soon as I take my seat." She looked over when Lewis appeared in the doorway. He carried a tray of drinks. "You better tell Lewis to wait before serving. I think Daniel will need that drink after the introductions."

Lee hurried to Lewis, stopping him as he stepped onto the veranda. Lewis turned a half-circle and walked back inside.

When Lee returned to Hayley's side, she asked. "Are we ready?"

"Not yet. Lewis wants to see this. I told him we'll wait until he joins us."

Lewis stepped outside and strolled over to Lee.

"Here we go." She walked to the veranda table, pulled out a chair, and sat. Three feet from Daniel the air wavered and a vaporous cloud appeared.

"What the...?" Jim laughed, then watched Daniel's face.

Daniel pushed his chair back, nearly falling backward. Rising out of his seat, he glanced nervously at Hayley. Hesitantly, staring at the mist hovering in front of him, he resettled into his chair. While it thickened, the vapor molded into legs, torso, arms, and head. The human shape became solid, forming muscles and facial features, until Abel stood before Daniel, appearing as real as the rest of them, who watched with amused grins.

"Daniel, I'd like you to meet your great-grandfather many times removed, Abel Smith." Hayley watched, hoping Abel had gathered enough energy to sustain his solidity. Thankfully, his dark form appeared as firm as Daniel's. He wore the clothes he had been murdered in. His eyes shone, and his smile was as big as the moon. "Abel, I'd like you to meet your great-plus-more-greats grandson, Daniel Smith."

Hayley saw Daniel's body tremble and his eyes well with tears. It took him a moment to compose himself. "Lord, help me."

"Youse sees me?" Abel asked him.

"Yes, amazingly well," Daniel said. With the back of his shaking hand, he wiped a tear from his cheek.

"My, my, my." Abel shook his head. "I'se blessed. Youse looks like my Noah."

"Yes. Yes, I do," Daniel said. "And like you."

Lee cleared his throat, walked to Hayley, and placed a hand her shoulder. She leaned back in her seat.

Lewis grinned, clapped his hands, then dashed inside, returning with a tray of drinks. He hurried over to Daniel. "Would you care for a drink, sir?"

"Yes. Please." He reached for the glass of Macallan, took a mouthful, and swallowed hard, never taking his eyes off Abel. Finishing his drink, he handed the glass back to Lewis. "I'll have another if you don't mind."

"Right away, sir." Lewis turned and hurried back into the house.

Hayley sniffled, holding back a tear. "Daniel, show him the journal and tell him about Noah."

199

"Yes. Yes, of course." He reached for his briefcase, placed it on the table, and looked at Abel. "Have I got a story to tell you."

CHAPTER 30

On the veranda, Hayley relaxed, sipping a glass of merlot. It had been a long day, and she didn't look forward to the hike to the cave's entrance.

She glanced at Lee, sitting at a table next to her, reading the local newspaper. "Today went pretty well, I thought," she said. "When Daniel came face-to-face with Abel, any remaining doubts for either of them were lifted. While Daniel told Abel what had happened to Noah, I could practically see the hole in Abel's heart fill. Now all we have to do is find Emma."

He set the paper aside. "I think we should plan on leaving about seven o'clock tomorrow morning. It'll take around three-and-a-half hours to get to the plantation."

"Where will we be staying?"

"In Atlanta where we stayed before. Mr. Smith and Kathy will have to meet with the Historical Society, and the courthouse is nearby. Kathy's making arrangements."

Lewis started clearing the lunch dishes. "Mr. Hudson, Mr. Smith, and Dr. Song have left, sir. Is there anything I can get you? More wine perhaps, Miss Johnson?"

She shook her head, took the last sip, and handed him the empty glass.

"Sir?"

"No thanks, Lewis. By the way, do you want to go with us tomorrow? You're part of our team."

"Thank you, sir, but I can't. I have to start planning the charity ball and mail out invitations. I'll be very busy for the rest of the week."

"Hayley and I will be taking a hike shortly. I need to know the location of the cave's entrance."

"Dinner will be served when you return."

"Thanks, Lewis." Lee reached out his hand to Hayley. "Come on, let's stretch our legs. We might have a lot of walking to do to find the entrance."

They strolled through the formal garden, passing the boxwood hedges framing a multitude of colorful flowers. *Irises, gladioli, delphiniums, geraniums.* Hayley realized she recognized a few dozen varieties of flora from all the research she had done for her own Victorian garden. As she admired the topiaries, she appreciated the masterful hands that had created the perfect circles, cones, spirals, and a few lions, tigers, and bears.

She and Lee followed the fragrance of lavender, sage, and fresh-cut lawn through the linear pathways. They turned halfway through the garden before its end at the riverbank. Their path led them to the arched bridge crossing the narrow channel feeding the pond with lake water. Midway across the bridge, they stopped next to the keystone. The steam feeding the pond rocked the flowering lily pads.

Hayley felt the garden's enchantment as the afternoon sunlight sparkled on the pond, which mirrored the azaleas, the copper beech, and cherry trees. She sighed. "Monet would've been jealous!"

Lee watched the swans swimming in the shadows of the weeping willow. "This is one of my favorite spots. The gardens have always been a special place. In the old days, before cars and planes, the riverboats took vacationers and locals on day trips to the estates along the banks. It was social etiquette for the rich to allow passersby to walk the grounds and relax in the grand hallway to get out of the heat. Back then, these gardens were filled with people."

"Since I lived in Sutterville in my past life as Richard, I wonder if I ever visited your home."

"That wouldn't surprise me," he said. "Up until I was a little boy, strangers were welcome to stroll in the garden. Eventually, due to the costs involved and the increase in vandalism, the home's grand hallway became off-limits. Then gradually, the social graces were replaced with 'no trespassing' signs."

She tried to picture Lee with his wavy brown hair, strong chin, broad shoulders, and toned abs as a little boy running through the garden, darting around passersby, probably playing hide and seek with Roger.

"It must've been an enormous amount of work to keep things up with so many visitors," she said. "The staff was probably glad to see the end to that tradition."

"Speaking of visitors.... I heard from Roger that Laura's moving in with you. Is it because you're having nightmares?"

She shook her head. "No. Grams helped me get rid of those the day Laura stayed overnight."

"I thought Laura enjoyed staying at Roger's."

"She's in love with him, but she doesn't think he feels the same way, and now she's uncomfortable being there," Hayley said.

She thought back to when she'd fallen in love with Lee. As always, foreseeing her own future had been impossible. Until she met Lee, she believed love at first sight was a myth. Instead of following her instincts, she fought them, not only because they seemed unrealistic, but because he was her boss. He, on the other hand, always presented himself as a friend, nothing more. In fact, she remembered, he went so far as to create a no-dating policy among the employees, including himself. How was she supposed to know he felt the same way about her?

With the gift to see the past, present, and future, she could envision life-links and foresee the chain of events in another person's life, how one thing leads to another and another. As if seeing a romance video play in her mind, she'd watched visions of natural occurrences unfold between Laura and Roger, and foresaw their coming marriage next year.

She gazed across the pond while remembering how she had told Lee about links, and that it was necessary for things to happen naturally without interference. If not, an event that was meant to be in that person's life could be altered or even eliminated. The moment Lee reconsidered the no-dating rule and asked her for a date would probably, she imagined, always be the biggest surprise of her life.

"When you invited Laura to move in, wasn't that manipulating her life-links?" Lee asked.

"I thought about that. I asked her what she would've done if I hadn't made the suggestion. She said she was about to ask me herself. Then I asked what she would've done if I had said no. She told me she would've found an apartment, but that she didn't want to leave North Carolina. So I didn't change her future. But I know what you mean. Because I can see things before they happen, it's hard to back away and not help things along."

Lee turned to her. "Roger's a little annoyed with you. He wanted her to stay."

"So he's mad at *me?* He ought to be glad she didn't go back to Hawaii. And if he doesn't start letting her know how he feels about her, she just might. The future I see isn't fixed. She has free will. If she changes her mind about staying, the life-link will be severed."

"I want you to promise me that you'll stay out of it," he said. "All relationships are different. Maybe theirs is supposed to have its ups and downs."

"So what do you want me to do—tell her I changed my mind?"

"No, just don't give her any advice. Let things happen on their own." He took a deep breath. "Roger's my best friend. I don't want to be put in the middle. As much time as you and I spend together, if Roger is mad at you, chances are the only time I'd see him is at work."

"You're asking me to break the universal genetic trait in every woman that has existed since creation—to stop her instinct to talk about men. I don't think it's possible for women not to discuss their flirting strategies while trying to rationalize a man's actions. It's like the same genetic strand males have that causes them to work on cars or watch the Super Bowl."

"I don't have that gene."

"Neither does Roger. Your first instinct is not to make the first move. Remember your no-dating policy, and your and Roger's pledges never to marry?"

He nodded. "Okay, okay. But we had good reason. After our parents' deaths, we decided never to marry and never to have kids. The possibility of losing family again was and always will be too devastating. It's been fourteen years since their deaths, and he's about to break his oath."

That vow had always haunted her. She cringed at the thought of losing Lee to that pledge someday. The same question gnawed at her as it had when he first confided in her. *How long will he love me before he walks away?* She shoved the painful thought to the back of her mind. *He loves me now. That's all that matters.* "So what should I do?"

"I just want you to think about what you say before you say it. Or at least make a pact with Laura to keep everything you talk about to yourselves."

"Done! A pact it will be." She hesitated. "But if I make that promise, will it mean I can't tell you about Laura's and my conversations?"

"I don't want you to do anything that will harm you. I'm not sure you can keep a secret from me without turning blue or exploding." He held up his hand to make an oath. "I, Lee Franklin, promise to keep secrets given to me in confidence by the woman I love."

She laced her arm around his and stroked his bicep. "That was sweet. Do you think you can promise to do something else?"

"What?"

"You're planning on wearing that suit of armor to the charity ball?"

He nodded.

"Do you think you could wear a prince costume instead? I'd like to go as a princess."

"So what's so bad about that? Why does it take a promise?"

"You'll have to wear tights."

His eyes widened and he stepped back. "Hell, no!"

"Is that a 'Hell, no, I'll think about it'?"

"No, it's a 'Hell, no hell, no! I'm not going to wear tights!'" Lee took her hand. "We need to search for the cave's entrance."

"We can talk about this later," she said.

"That's a hell, no, too."

She looked at him with pleading eyes.

"Stop it!" He gave her hand a little tug, ending the conversation.

~*~

On the far side of Lake View Drive, Hayley walked into the

forest with Lee. The canopy of trees appeared dense above her, but she knew from a vision that they would come to a clearing and their journey would end shortly. When they stopped up ahead, she recognized the surroundings.

Before her, in the midst of the forest, an outcrop of boulders led to a crag. In the mid-afternoon sun, shadows along the forest-covered mountains threatened to extend across the clearing. "This is it." Before she took another step, she realized something important. "We forgot to call Daniel," she told Lee. "I'm sensing trouble. Frank's youngest son is trailing Daniel, and he won't be able to leave without being followed."

"You're right. I forgot." Lee set down the backpack holding tools that Hayley had encouraged him to bring, reached for his phone, and made the call. "Daniel, this is Lee Franklin. Frank Thompson's trailing you. Have you noticed a young boy hanging around outside?" He paused to listen. "I think you should go to the lobby and extend your visit. If they get wind that you're leaving, they'll follow and then they'll find out what we're up to. It would be better if they think you're staying in town. Add about three more days. I'll pick up the tab. That ought to do it, and make sure the boy sees you so he'll go in and ask questions. Tonight when you drive over, he'll see you leave. When it's late enough and Frank's called in his boys, I'll have your car taken back to the hotel so in the morning, it'll look as if you're in your hotel room. That should confuse them." He listened and nodded. "Yeah, I think it'll work. Make sure you pack everything and leave it in your room. When Lewis takes your car back, I'll have Thomas follow him. Lewis can go to your room, get your things, and bring them here. Okay. See you then."

Lee hung up, then picked up the backpack. "Okay, lead the way."

Hayley led him to a narrow gap in the crag. In a crevice in the slab on the ground, shrubs and an oak sapling grew, hugging the sides of the cliff.

"Behind that growth, there's a gap in the rock. If we squeeze through that," Hayley said, "we'll find the cave entrance behind another tree."

He set down his backpack, unzipped it, and gathered a few tools. Turning sideways, Hayley followed Lee through the breach. Out of sight from passersby, the gap widened, allowing Lee to saw through the sapling blocking the entrance.

Hayley backed out of the breach, allowing Lee to clear the vegetation. While he dragged the tree away from the crag, Hayley slipped back to the cave. Putting her hand on the stone at the entrance, she envisioned slaves entering the cave at night, confirming its use by the Underground Railroad. She nodded to Lee when he returned. "Great place for an entrance. No one would notice someone entering."

"Let's see where it leads."

When he put the tools away, he took flashlights from the backpack, handed one to Hayley, then slipped the pack over his shoulders.

Hayley squinted into the cave. The babbling of a stream echoed in the darkness. Using her senses ability, she guided Lee through the tunnels, branching caverns, and finally to his wine cellar.

~*~

Once they finished dinner, Lee and Hayley walked with Daniel to the library, where they decided to have coffee and get comfortable by the fireplace.

"Last night, after the Thompson brothers went home," Lee said, "Thomas and Lewis dropped off my Cayenne at Roger's. In the morning, Roger will send a boat over to pick us up and take us to his place. When Frank's sons get here early tomorrow to watch the security gates and don't see us leave, they'll figure we're home instead of heading out of town."

"Sounds like a plan," Daniel said.

Lewis entered the room, went to the bar, and began fixing coffee. When the coffee had brewed, he loaded a tray with cups and served Hayley, Lee, and their guest. Daniel handed Lewis his hotel key.

"Thank you, sir. Thomas and I will leave at midnight. I believe Frank's boys should be in bed by then."

"Perfect," Lee said. "And make sure before you leave his room to hang a 'Do Not Disturb' sign on the door."

"Oh, and you should call the desk in the morning," Hayley told Daniel, "and tell them no calls, please. You don't have to explain. As far as I can see, this plan will work."

CHAPTER 31

After Hayley and Lee stepped away from the Atlanta Hotel's front desk, his cell phone rang. He pulled it from his shirt pocket. "Hi. What's up?" Lee listened. "Thanks, Lewis." He turned to Hayley. "Frank's been calling the hotel and can't get through to Daniel's room. He called my home to see if I knew how to reach him. Lewis said he would relay the message. I'll have Daniel give him a call from his cell phone. Frank will never know he's out of town."

"Maybe we should just invite Frank to the plantation next time we come, and introduce him to Wheeler. That would give him a story."

Lee chuckled. "You know, that might not be a bad idea."

They walked toward Laura, Roger, Kathy, Jim, and Daniel, all waiting by the Atlanta Hotel's restaurant entrance.

~*~

Lee wiped his mouth with his napkin and pushed his empty plate aside. "What's first on your list, Daniel?"

"I have an appointment at the church to open Wheeler's crypt in the cemetery there."

"Do the courts have their own DNA technician?" Laura asked.

"Yes. I'll be meeting him at the cemetery."

"Good," she said. "With the testing results of my DNA samples and theirs, there should be no doubt about the Tylers' heritage."

Daniel took a deep breath. "Yes, it'll help, but I'm afraid it might not be enough. In such cases pertaining to slavery, it's important to clarify their master's intentions. DNA proves the blood tie, but Wheeler's wishes would outweigh everything. The courts may find the evidence insufficient. Without the presence of a will, Wheeler's plantation may stay in the hands of the Historical Society."

"So all this is for nothin'?" Jim asked.

"I intend to fight," Daniel said. "I have the court's permission to go through all of Wheeler's belongings. That includes the mansion. If there's a will, I'll find it."

"So you're hoping Wheeler put Emma in his will?" Lee asked.

"Yes. But there's a lot to this. Interpretation of the will is a key factor. There's a chance Wheeler's actions might be what they called a sin-offering. He may have put Emma in his will to appease God and atone for his wickedness. If that's the case, we'll lose our argument."

"Tryin' to get property away from a historical society is like tryin' to string cranberry sauce on a Christmas tree," Jim said.

Daniel choked on his sip of coffee and laughed. "Great analogy. But no, it's the courts. Finances are tough nowadays, so the Historical Society is looking to rid themselves of unprofitable properties. Since they've closed Wheeler's plantation to the public and there's no more income, it costs them a bundle for upkeep."

Roger reached for the bill. "So, Kathy, you're going downtown to do some research?"

She nodded. "Yes."

"And Jim," Roger said, "you wanted to talk to the plantation groundskeeper, Gil Meeker. Mind if I join you?" He turned to

Lee. "Jim and I will drop Kathy at the hall of records, while all of you go to the graveyard. Once Jim and I get to Meeker's, we'll wait there for you."

"I'll take a cab to Meeker's place once I finish my research," Kathy said.

Roger took out his wallet. "Here, take the company credit card and call us when you're on your way back."

~*~

The thunder and lightning storm threatened to move down from the mountains. A breeze rustled leaves on the trees shading graves in the cemetery. Hayley stood beside Lee and Reverend Peters by the church's back entrance. She gazed across the well-maintained graveyard and past the old moss-covered headstones sitting crookedly between gnarled wood crosses, carved pillars, and other stones, tall or stubby, rounded or square. In the shadows of an oak, she saw the groundskeeper and another man open the door to Wheeler's crypt and move aside, allowing Mr. Smith, Laura, and the court's DNA specialist to step inside. Then they entered behind them, all wearing surgical masks and gloves.

Reverend Peters rubbed the back of his neck while he watched the crypt's door scrape across the stone. "I understand Mr. Smith is trying to find a family connection between Mr. Wheeler and his clients," he said.

"Yes. They're gathering DNA," Lee answered.

"It's hard to watch a sacred place of rest being disturbed, no matter what the reason. If you'll excuse me." The minister opened the church door and stepped inside.

"Reverend," Hayley called.

He turned.

"Do you have any records dating back to the 1800s?" she asked.

"Yes. We have an extensive archive."

"Anything we're allowed to see?" Lee asked.

"Yes. Public records like births and marriages."

"What about records of daily events?" Hayley asked. "It would be interesting to see what everyday life was like back then."

"It's been a long time since I've gone through our archives. But I do remember seeing something about Reverend Sims trying to help a cat out of a tree." His solemn face brightened. "Seems some things never change. You're welcome to study them. Let me know when you're ready."

"You're very kind," Hayley said.

"Will you excuse me, please?" The minister went inside.

Lee leaned toward her and whispered, "You've sensed something."

She nodded. "It's like a tug, a knowing that there's something here." She closed her eyes, trying to sense more information. "I can't see what it is. But I have a strong feeling it will help Daniel's case."

Over Lee's shoulder, she noticed the somber faces of Mr. Smith and Laura when they left the crypt and removed their surgical masks.

Daniel approached, grimacing. "Well, that was damn disturbing."

Laura, holding her doctor's bag containing Wheeler's DNA sample, stepped to Daniel's side. "Truly morbid," she said. "I took strands of his hair as well as some skin."

"It took two men to lift the concrete lid," Daniel said. "The smell almost knocked me out. Wheeler's hair and beard had grown after his death. His nails are grotesque — long and curled. And his skin…. I don't know how Laura could stand getting near it. The sight of it nearly made me vomit."

"Sorry you had to go through all that," Hayley said. "There

213

is a bright spot. The reverend said we can look through their archives. They go back to when Wheeler built the church before the Civil War."

"Hayley senses there's something you'll be interested in," Lee said.

Daniel raised a brow.

The pastor met them at the door and led them to a room behind closed doors in the back of the church. While they waited, he entered an adjoining room, returning with an armful of yellowed journals and ledgers, and set them on a table.

"There are more. Once you're finished with these, I'll bring you the rest."

Hayley gazed at the documents and smiled. "Thank you. We'll call you when we're done."

After he left the room, Lee spread out the documents, and Hayley held her hands above each one. Taking her time, she followed the thread of her senses through the sea of documents, then hesitated. Closing her eyes, she concentrated on a slight tug until she pinpointed its origin. Then, she picked up a heavy journal. "I think what we're looking for is in here."

Daniel pulled up a chair, put on his glasses, and slid the journal in front of him. He scanned the records, studying only the entries dated 1851 to 1864, while Laura, Hayley, and Lee stood waiting.

After five minutes or so of study, squinting at the one-hundred-and-fifty-year-old calligraphy, Daniel smiled widely. "I think I found it." He read the page carefully again and nodded. "It's a daily task calendar. This entry was made by a Reverend Dodds just hours before his own death. Says he witnessed a will written by Zachary Wheeler."

"Great. At least we know it exists!" Lee said. "But where?" He stared at Hayley's face and swore. "Don't tell me. It's in the mansion, and we'll have to get by Wheeler's ghost."

Hayley nodded. "And that isn't going to be easy."

CHAPTER 32

One by one, Hayley and the others entered Roger's hotel room, Jim carrying a brown bag. When everyone had sat comfortably, Hayley stood. "Here's the deal. Thought is energy. That means whatever we're thinking, Wheeler will know. When we call Gil Meeker, the groundskeeper, to let us into the mansion, we can't tell him we need to find the will. And once we're inside, we'll have to hide our thoughts."

"How will we do that?" Laura asked.

Hayley bit her bottom lip, then smiled. "Got it! First, the three of us women can go in as maids. It's something Wheeler would expect. We can keep our minds occupied by counting — counting our steps, number of dusting strokes, the number of pictures on the wall, anything to keep our minds busy. I'll go through all the rooms until I sense where the will is hidden." She paused. "I'll have to figure out a way to get the will past Wheeler."

"What about shielding everyone with white light?" Lee asked.

Hayley frowned. "Surrounding ourselves with positive energy would be like putting a spotlight on us. It would ruin our plan."

Lee stood, crossing his arms. "You're not going in there without me."

"Okay. Okay." She studied his handsome face. *How can he enter the mansion without Wheeler knowing what we're after?* "Do you think you can keep your mind on wanting to have sex with me and not think about the will?"

"I'm sure I wouldn't have a problem with that."

Kathy giggled, and Laura covered a smile with her hand.

"Good," Hayley said. "Because you'll have to enter the mansion as the handyman who has the hots for me. That should be believable to Wheeler. After I find out where the will is, I'll ask you to help me open the window in that room." She looked at the others. "We'll need a diversion. Who wants to keep Wheeler's mind occupied?"

Jim waved his hand. "Meeker and I can do that."

"What about me?" Daniel asked.

Hayley shook her head. "Daniel, I don't think it's a good idea. Wheeler might sense you're related to Abel." Because she remembered how meeting Abel's ghost had startled him, she worried how he'd react around Wheeler. Hayley studied his face, looking for traces of fear. "You could get seriously hurt."

With his jaw set firmly, he nodded. "I'll take my chances. What about you? If you're going room to room, sensing the presence of the will, won't he know?"

"I have to clear my mind to pick up past energy. Memories are left everywhere—on objects, papered walls, wood, granite, marble, even in the air. I just need to find the right room. When I do, I'll be vulnerable. I'll need the diversion."

Jim grinned. "With enough of us inside, Wheeler won't know where to strike first."

"Okay then. In the morning, we girls will go in as maids," Hayley said. "Daniel, you play yourself—a lawyer representing your client, who's claiming to be a relative of Zachary Wheeler's sister-in-law and trying to inherit the estate. Change your last name and use Jim as your assistant. Meeker will play himself, the groundskeeper, and show Jim and Daniel around while the workers clean. Roger, you'll have to stay outside. The only way we'll get the will out of the house is to throw it out the window. So you'll need to watch for an open window." She thought a moment. "I think I've covered everything."

"I've got somethin'." Jim opened the brown bag at his side. "'Cause Daniel looks so much like Abel, I took the liberty of bringin' a little somethin' just in case he meets Wheeler." He pulled out a bushy fake beard. "It's part of a costume I wore at the fundraisin' ball last year. Thought it might help."

"You're a genius," Hayley said. "I think you just saved his life."

"Just thinkin' ahead," Jim said. "And one more little detail. When ya had that vision of Wheeler's death, where in the basement did ya see him steppin' outta of that trap door?"

"Good question. I nearly forgot to tell you. It was about six feet from the west wall and about four feet in from the south, toward the front of the house."

"If I can, I'll check it out while I'm down there," Jim said.

"Guess we're all set then," Roger said, reaching into his pocket for his cell phone. "I'll call Meeker. He's going to love this."

CHAPTER 33

Hayley, counting softly, sat in the front seat of Lee's Porsche Cayenne, Laura and Kathy in the back. Following Meeker's truck, Lee turned down the drive toward the mansion. Ahead, rays of sunlight streamed onto the road through the twisted limbs and leaves of the old oaks arching across the road.

While Lee parked beside Meeker's truck in front of the columned porch, Hayley glanced up at the second-story balcony and saw the curtains in the front room close.

"Everyone act natural," Hayley said. She, the other two women, and Lee climbed out of the SUV. After Meeker, wearing his work clothes and acting nonchalant, stepped out of his truck, he pulled a utility tote filled with cleaning supplies from the truck bed and passed it to Hayley.

"We'll start in the living room," Hayley whispered.

She saw Roger, Jim, and Daniel approach slowly in Roger's Audi Q7 along the old oak-lined road, while Hayley and the others hurried up the porch stairs behind Meeker. After unlocking the front door, Meeker stood aside, letting the supposed maids in, leaving Lee outside by the door.

With his voice slightly raised to get Wheeler's attention, Meeker said, "Just let me know which rooms you want to air out and I'll open the windows."

When Hayley smelled a stench much like Leech's, it confirmed her belief that Wheeler had been consumed by a similar entity. Clearing her mind of that thought, she continued to count.

Hayley led Laura and Kathy to the parlor, set the utility tote next to the doorway, and glanced out the window to see Roger, Daniel, and Jim arrive. She handed each woman a dust cloth and they moved around the room.

Meeker spoke up. "Looks like we've got company. Go on with your cleaning, and I'll see what these folks want."

A small round table and four chairs sat in front of the living room fireplace. Scant furniture lined the room. Few pictures hung on the walls. Hayley cleared her mind as she walked the perimeter. A few feet from her, she heard Laura counting softly while dusting a high-backed chair. Kathy worked not far away. Near the window, Hayley stopped and studied a hinged writing desk against the wall. A slanted box holding paper, quill, and inkwell sat on the center of the desk with two sheets of yellowed paper on either side. Her hands swept the surface of the furniture as she dusted. Memories of Wheeler writing social letters flashed through her mind. She pulled her hand away.

Hayley felt Wheeler's ghost's penetrating glare from the hallway. She counted and strolled casually to the fireplace. Again, Hayley cleared her mind. She ran her fingers across the marble.

Out of the corner of her eye, she watched him approach. The air chilled. While she braced herself, keeping her breath shallow or holding her breath if needed to avoid gagging, she felt his cold misty body brush against her back. Her skin prickled. When he stroked his icy finger across her neck and moaned into her ear, bile rose in Hayley's throat. She swallowed hard and counted, hoping to keep her pounding heart from revealing her abilities to see and hear him. She glanced toward the door, seeing Meeker in the hall.

"Come in, Mr. Becker," Meeker said. "So you have some kind of legal documents saying you can look anywhere you want?"

Wearing Jim's fake beard, Daniel theatrically waved a sheet of paper at Meeker, pushed by him, and entered the parlor. "That's right, and I don't need you to look over my shoulder."

The space around Hayley warmed. She saw Wheeler's ghost hovering beside Daniel, who walked to the window and opened the desk drawer. With Wheeler's attention taken, Hayley motioned for Laura and Kathy to leave. Stepping into the hallway, she pointed across the hall. "That's his bedroom. We'll need to get in and out fast."

Once in the room, not bothering to pretend to dust, Hayley went straight for the fireplace mantel. She touched the shelf and brushed her hand down the mantel's side. Placing her hand on the marble face, she waited for an impression—nothing. Dashing across the room, she touched the bed's dark headboard and flinched. Putting her hand to her mouth, she held back the urge to vomit. Emma wasn't the only one Wheeler had abused. Visions of his wedding night flashed through Hayley's mind. *No one mentioned a wife.*

She whispered to Laura and Kathy. "Let's try upstairs."

When the women stepped into the hallway, Jim came through the front door. Hayley raised her index finger to her lips and led Laura and Kathy quietly up the staircase. She heard Jim clear his throat and ask, "How are things goin', Mr. Becker?"

"Slowly. I'll need more time. Looks like I'm going to be downstairs a while."

"I guess I can help by checkin' the basement," Jim said.

"Wait. Don't go down there!" Hayley heard Meeker shout.

"Oh yeah? And who's gonna stop me?"

"You'll be surprised," Meeker said.

"Don't think ya can scare me, Meeker. I don't believe in

ghosts."

Good acting, Jim. On the top landing of the narrow staircase, Hayley turned to Laura and Kathy. "The drawing room's in the front of the house. A bedroom's next to it, and over there's the library. Let's try the library."

Once inside, Hayley sensed Wheeler's hostility in the hallway below, his attention focused on Jim. She cleared her mind and ran her hand along the mahogany paneling and across the bookshelves. When she touched the fireplace, visions of Wheeler sliding open a secret compartment on the side of the mantel revealed the will's location. She counted while she searched the mantel, but couldn't find any trace of the hiding place.

Hayley gave Kathy, dusting and counting aloud next to her, a thumbs-up, motioned to Laura across the room, and stated loudly, "Guess we're finished in here. It's kinda stuffy. I think I'll ask the groundskeeper to open a window to let some air in."

Quickly they left the room and went downstairs. After Laura and Kathy stepped outside, Hayley hurried toward the kitchen, but hesitated, sensing Wheeler's ghost beyond the closed door. "Mr. Meeker, I'd like to air out one of the rooms upstairs."

"I'm real busy. Get the handyman outside. He'll help you."

"Thanks." She turned and saw Lee standing in the doorway. "Sir, would you mind helping, please? I need a window opened upstairs."

"Sure, no problem." Lee winked and strolled over to her.

She whispered in his ear, "Think about undressing me, Lee."

Returning casually up the stairs, trying not to draw attention, Hayley led Lee to the library. At the fireplace, she brushed her fingertips across the rough edges on the right side of the mantel. "There," she said cryptically, pointing to the area she'd envisioned. "I think it's stuck. I couldn't open it." Again, she hoped Wheeler would think she spoke of the window.

Lee crossed the room and opened the east window on the opposite side of the house from the dry well and the tunnel leading to the basement. Rushing back to the mantel, he reached into the toolbox, removed an awl, and ran its point across the painted seam. With little force, he carefully slid the compartment open, reached inside, and pulled out a long metal tube.

When Lee pried the lid open and tilted the container, a scroll of paper slid out. He shoved the tube under his arm, rolled back the paper's edge, and scanned the document. He nodded and smiled.

While he slipped the roll back into the container, a folded page fell to the floor. He picked it up, unfolded the sheet, and quietly read. "Unbelievable. It's a marriage license. Wheeler married Emma."

She raised her finger to her lips. "Not possible," Hayley whispered, not able to hold back. "Wheeler was already married. I saw it in a vision."

"Wheeler was married? Doesn't that ruin everything?"

A chill went up Hayley's neck. "Hurry, Lee. We don't have time to talk now."

Lee placed the papers inside the tube, ran to the window, tossed it down to Roger, and dashed back to the mantel.

"Hurry," Hayley whispered. She sensed Wheeler's ghost on the stairway. "Hurry!"

Lee tried to force the secret compartment to close. "It's stuck."

Trying hard to clear her mind, Hayley counted, nervously glancing at the doorway. She stilled a gasp. "He's—"

Before she could finish her sentence, Lee slid her snug between him and the mantel, covering the hidden compartment, and kissed her cheek.

Seeing Wheeler's glare when he came through the door, she swallowed hard. With his jaw firm and lips mashed together, the ghost stepped toward them.

Hayley tensed. She shut her eyes and steadied herself against the mantel, placing one hand on the shelf. The air grew cold. When her hand touched a small porcelain clock, visions of Wheeler as a child raced through her mind. She saw him as a four-year-old. An entity, spawn of the same negative energy as Abel's leech, showed him the joys of secrecy, while Wheeler presented himself as a little angel, hiding his real pleasures. She envisioned him smashing bugs and ripping the heads off caterpillars. Time jumped forward. At age seven, he loved killing rats and rabbits because they screamed. No longer able to stomach his grotesque actions, Hayley released the vision and counted.

The air turned frigid. The closer Wheeler approached, the more she smelled his horrid odor and felt the room's energy pulsating from his anger. "One hundred four, one hundred five, one hundred six," she blurted.

Lee's hot breath in her ear startled her. Her body stiffened. She felt his mouth move downward until his lips caressed her neck.

"Relax," he said, "everyone's in the basement. We're all alone."

At the word "basement," the air warmed. Hayley opened her eyes and glanced around. Wheeler had disappeared. With clenched fists she pounded Lee's chest, then smothered her face against him. "That scared the hell out of me. You couldn't see him. You had no idea how close he came to attacking us." She studied his face. "How did you know that would work?"

He looked toward the window. "I didn't have much choice. My only other option was to throw you out the window and jump, and I don't think Roger would've liked that."

They walked to the window. Roger waited below. With a nod from Lee, Roger turned with the cylinder in his hand and hurried toward his car.

Returning to the mantel, Lee worked on the compartment until it closed. He ran his thumb across the edge. "Perfect." Grabbing the toolbox, he reached for Hayley's hand. "Come on!"

Halfway down the stairs, he cautioned her to stop. Jim glanced through the kitchen doorway. Hayley raised a finger to her lips, then pointed outside.

Jim shouted back at the groundskeeper. "Ya pushed me down the basement stairs, Meeker. Don't think I'm gonna forget this."

Hayley and Lee dashed onto the porch. Laura and Kathy stood by Lee's car. Before stepping off the porch, Hayley glanced back and saw Jim and Meeker in the hallway.

"How could I have pushed you, you damn lunatic? I wasn't even near you."

"Mr. Becker, where in the hell are ya?" Jim shouted. "Are ya 'bout ready to leave?"

Daniel came out of Wheeler's bedroom. "Yes. I didn't find a thing."

They hurried out the door. Jim yelled over his shoulder. "Don't think this is the end of this, Meeker. We'll be back."

Through the Cayenne passenger window, Hayley saw Gil Meeker standing in the doorway. In the parlor window, Wheeler stared back at her, but soon vanished. The drapes slowly closed.

She saw Jim and Laura enter Roger's Audi Q7, heard Roger start it, and saw them leave the estate while Lee started his car.

On Roger's tail, Lee drove down the entry road with Hayley beside him, and in the backseat, Kathy and Daniel, who had pulled off the fake beard, examined the marriage certificate and will.

"This marriage license was signed by Reverend Dodds," Kathy said.

"It couldn't have been. Interracial marriages were illegal back then," Hayley said. "The reverend wouldn't have gone against his church. Plus, Wheeler was already married. I had a vision of his wedding night when I searched his bedroom."

"Did you know about that, Daniel?" Lee asked.

"Yes. I'm aware of his wife."

Lee glanced into the rearview mirror. "You're not holding out on us, are you, Daniel? I'd think that piece of information would kill your case if they had kids."

"I found evidence that the marriage was annulled," Kathy said.

"But the marriage was consummated," Hayley told them. "I saw it."

"I'm not sure that mattered," Daniel said. "There's more to the story than meets the eye. When we get back to the hotel, we'll compare facts."

CHAPTER 34

Returning home that afternoon, Lee, Hayley, Kathy, and Daniel drove up to the security gate and stopped with Roger, Laura, and Jim right behind them. Across the street, two of Frank's boys stretched their necks to see who waited to enter the Franklin estate.

At the entrance, Lee spoke as if talking to a friend. "Max, I'm home."

The gate opened.

"Your computer is connected to the gate?" Hayley asked.

Lee nodded and winked. "John's been expanding its abilities. You'd be surprised what Max can do."

"That almost sounds creepy."

Lee drove forward, following the curve of the drive. "Think less sci-fi—it's more like a German shepherd bringing your slippers."

"What else have you trained him to do?"

He looked straight ahead as the corners of his mouth turned up. "I'll show you later."

"Can I have a clue?"

"Nope."

At the end of the spruce-lined drive, Hayley glanced at the side mirror and saw Roger driving a car length behind. Along the front parkway, she noticed Lewis, wearing his black suit and tie, waving his white-gloved hand.

Lee chuckled. "It's always great to see Lewis's face. It wouldn't be home without him." He parked and popped the trunk.

"I know exactly how you feel," Hayley said.

Lewis hurried to open the passenger doors, assisting Hayley and the other two travel-weary passengers out of the vehicle. As Daniel climbed out, Hayley looked past him to see Roger, Jim, and Laura exiting Roger's car.

Rushing, Lewis went around to opened Lee's door and presented his butler's stoic face. "Great to see you home, sir. Dinner is being served in the dining room shortly. I'll see to your luggage."

He hurried ahead of them, opened the carved mahogany door, and stood aside, allowing everyone to enter.

With Hayley at his side, Lee led his guests to the grand staircase connecting to the second floor. "After you," he said, with the sweep of his hand.

Daniel went first, carrying his brown leather briefcase. Kathy walked next to him, clenching a spiral notebook. The others also followed Lee's gesture.

Hayley hooked Lee's arm and they climbed the stairs, following everyone to the landing.

"This way," Lee said.

In the dining room, seven of the thirty-two possible places at the table were set with gold-rimmed white china, linen napkins, fine silver, and stem glasses. While everyone sat, Hayley crossed the room to the windows facing the pond. Looking west over the copper beech and the cherry trees, she admired the sunset's pink blush announcing the coming of twilight. *Sunset — always so beautiful.*

She turned when Lee called her name. He pulled out her

chair. Stepping away from the window, Hayley took her seat next to Lee at the head of the table.

Lee began when his guests were comfortable. "Well, seems like we have another mystery — Wheeler's wife."

From a soup tureen on the sideboard at the far end of the room, Lewis ladled lobster bisque into bowls and topped small plates with pilot bread crackers. One by one, he served the guests.

"Thank you, Lewis," Roger said. "Wheeler's wife?" he asked, leaning slightly to the side as Lewis placed his bowl.

"Yes," Lee said. "While Hayley searched Wheeler's room, she had a vision of his wedding night."

"A young woman who looked to be eighteen or nineteen with long, strawberry blonde hair," Hayley added.

"I noticed you had sensed something in the bedroom," Laura said, lifting the soupspoon to her lips. "Mm, this soup is delicious."

"I concur," Daniel seconded.

"So do I," Kathy added.

"Lewis, give Velma our praises," Lee said.

"I'd be happy to, sir."

"Once we located the will," Lee continued, "we found another surprise — Wheeler and Emma's marriage license."

Lewis reached between Lee and Hayley and filled their glasses with iced tea.

"Lewis," Lee said, "you might want to hear this. It involves our case."

"You are correct, sir, I would." He set the pitcher of ice tea back on the side table and stood by the fireplace, his gloved hands folded in front of him. As each guest finished the soup, he collected the dishes, then excused himself from the room.

"We'll wait for Lewis to return before we go on," Lee said.

Lewis returned with their meals — prime rib with baked

229

asparagus. He served, replenished their drinks, then stepped away and stood by Lee at the head of the table.

"I noticed Reverend Dobbs had officiated at Wheeler and Emma's marriage," Kathy said. "It must've been highly secretive. At that time, everyone involved could've been hanged."

"Why would the reverend do such a thing?" Laura asked.

"Same reverend that died two hours after helpin' Wheeler with his will?" Jim asked. "Sounds damn fishy to me."

"We have more mysteries than we started with," Lee said. "It seems that Reverend Dobbs married Emma and Wheeler, which was against the law in itself, but he must've known Wheeler already had a wife. Did you get to study the will on the drive back, Daniel? Did Wheeler mention anything about Emma?"

"Yes. But first, allow me to clarify a few things. I have written first-hand accounts about his first wife." Daniel sipped his iced tea, set the glass down, and cleared his throat. "At the time Simon Tyler started keeping a journal, Liza Chambers asked him to write the truth about what happened between her and the newly wedded Mrs. Wheeler. Liza, Wheeler's black house servant, was twenty-two when Wheeler married, a month before he purchased the Smiths," Daniel said. "According to Liza, the night of Wheeler's wedding she heard screams coming from the bedroom. In the morning, when she entered the room to change the linen, she was shocked to see what she thought was an unusual amount of blood for a virginal consummation. But when she saw Mrs. Wheeler, the bride looked almost serene, with no signs of trauma.

"That morning, Mrs. Wheeler, Sarah, asked Liza to accompany her on a picnic at noon. Once Liza put a blanket, pillows, and a basket of food into a buggy, the two women drove to a hillside overlooking a gorge. Liza said Mrs. Wheeler walked to the edge of the cliff, enjoying the view. After lifting the basket and blankets from the buggy, Liza turned and saw Sarah jump to her death."

Hayley, Kathy, and Laura gasped in unison.

"Liza went for help. When the sheriff and his men found the body, they arrested Liza for murder. Wheeler stopped the hanging, saying he believed in her innocence. After that, Wheeler held her life in his hands, threatening to have her killed if she spoke a word about his personal affairs."

"What kinda personal affairs?" Jim asked.

"Liza said Wheeler knew Abel, Emma, and their son were kidnapped from Ohio. He purchased them only because he lusted for Emma. He never planned to keep her husband or son. Once the tunnel was dug, Wheeler had Liza take Emma to the storage room and lock her inside. From then on, she took care of Emma and witnessed the cruelty Wheeler inflicted upon her. There was nothing Liza could do. It was either Emma's life or her own. That's what she told Simon to write in the journal."

"How awful," Laura said.

"So why did Wheeler annul the marriage?" Kathy asked.

"He broke ties with her family, stating Sarah was insane—legal grounds for annulment," Daniel said.

"Damn Wheeler was Satan's spawn," Jim blurted, dabbing his mouth with his napkin.

"I can understand that," Kathy said. "He had to put the blame on Sarah to take the attention off Liza. Because many people still suspected her of killing Sarah and, back then, hangings were entertainment. He had to come up with a pretty believable explanation to save her."

"Did Liza mention anything about Wheeler and Emma's marriage?" Lee asked.

"No," Daniel said. "But her name's on the license as witness. And in the will, Emma's proclaimed to be Wheeler's wife."

"Liza witnessed the license?" Roger asked. "Was that legal?"

"Hell, the marriage wasn't even legal," Jim said. "I'd be interested in knowin' what dirt Wheeler had on the reverend to get him to commit a hangin' offense. Musta been somethin' eye-waterin'. Anythin' in the journal 'bout that?"

"Afraid not," Daniel said. "Guess we won't know what happened unless Hayley runs across something."

"I'll keep my antennas up," Hayley said.

"This is most interesting," Lewis said, clasping his gloved hands. He instantly altered his demeanor, waited for everyone to finish eating, and cleared the table.

"Would you like to join us for a drink, Daniel? A glass of Macallan, perhaps?" Lee asked.

Putting his hand to his mouth, Daniel yawned. "Excuse me. That sounds good, but I'm afraid it'll put me to sleep, and I can't risk it. I'm catching a flight out tonight so I can get back to my office. This case has more layers than an onion. I have to go over Wheeler's assets and determine their value."

"If Wheeler's will is binding, wouldn't that make you an heir?" Lee asked.

A smile crossed Daniel's face. "Yes. I'll plead my own case as well as the Tylers'."

"Then you'll be interested to hear the results of my research," Kathy said.

"Indeed I would," Daniel replied.

"Shall we take our conversation to the library?" Lee suggested.

Lewis placed a glass of semisweet Riesling in front of Hayley. "Miss Tyler left a message. She'd like you to return her call."

"Thank you, Lewis," Hayley said. "I wonder what she wants." Shivers of apprehension shot up her spine. *What's up now?*

CHAPTER 35

Hayley sank into the leather chair near the library's unlit fireplace. Even with the twelve-pane bow windows wide open, the early evening breeze didn't cool the room.

Lewis hurried to close the windows. "Max, AC," Lee said, taking the seat next to Hayley, while Kathy and Daniel settled on the couch. Jim plopped down in a high-back chair.

Once Roger and Laura entered the room, Hayley watched their body language. Her vision of their marriage still had ten more months before coming to pass, and she sensed nothing had changed its course. Roger's shyness to show Laura his feelings made Hayley want to shake him. When he took Laura's hand as they crossed the room, it didn't get past Hayley how long he waited before leading her to a seat. *It's about time he made a move.*

Lee followed Hayley's gaze. "Looks like Roger's got the right idea. Laura's not moving in with you until tomorrow. After that, it might take a couple of days before she knows where everything is and can manage on her own. How about staying the night tonight? Could be our last chance to be alone for a couple of days."

She glanced at his innocent-looking face. "You've got something planned, don't you? It's something to do with Max. I haven't forgotten."

Roger and Laura sat on the other couch.

"First things first." Lee glanced at Kathy. "What have you learned about Wheeler that we don't yet know?"

Kathy brushed a strand of her platinum hair from her face and opened her notebook. "You remember the real estate agent you two met in Tennessee when you first went looking for the Wheeler plantation? She said the burned-down plantation was owned by Henry Wheeler, and that he died after Zachary Wheeler, leaving no one to inherit the estate. But from Hayley's vision we know she was wrong. Wheeler was murdered after his brother and his family."

Between the pages of her notes rested a loose sheet of paper. Kathy lifted the document by its edges and presented it. "This is a copy of a witnessed letter I found in the Georgia Public Records archives addressed to the county clerk at the Tennessee Court House. It's from Zachary Wheeler's attorney. It states Zachary claimed the inheritance. That means there are two plantations among Zachary Wheeler's assets." She handed the copy to Daniel.

"I forgot about that," Hayley said. "Digger mentioned that in my vision."

"This is unexpected." Daniel examined it carefully, then rubbed his chin. "Another mystery. Why wasn't this listed with Zachary's assets?"

"May have been misplaced—information that accidently slipped between the cracks," Kathy said.

"If it comes down to it, Daniel, which plantation would ya choose?" Jim asked.

"The ruined Tennessee estate. The Tylers can have Wheeler's plantation. It requires too much upkeep."

"I would think you'd want your rightful share," Lee said.

"I'm not in it for the money. Tracing my roots has been my goal all along. Anyway, it doesn't matter. The land in Tennessee is worth a substantial amount. It's not as if I'm being foolish."

"Speaking of the Tylers, Daniel...." Hayley raised her glass as Lewis offered her more wine. "I returned Brea's call, and I think we've got trouble. Her father found out you've been talking with her, and he's raging mad. He's convinced you're a con artist. Brea says he might go to the authorities."

Laura leaned forward. "We need Mr. Tyler's DNA to prove he's Brea's father, and also to link him to Wheeler. And when he finds out Brea lied about the reason for taking his DNA sample that she sent to me, he'll most likely get a court order and have the specimen destroyed."

"I'm aware of that," Daniel said, "but I don't know how I'm going to convince the stubborn fool. How can I prove I'm honest? Any suggestions?"

"I've got one," Jim said. "How 'bout sendin' the Mr. and Mrs. on a free vacation to sunny Sutterville, North Carolina, compliments of a contest Brea can say she entered? Just call it a week's stay at a bed 'n' breakfast, and leave off the fact it's a haunted mansion. When they get here, we can ask Abel to help convince them that you're on the up and up."

"Lie to them?" Daniel asked.

Jim shrugged. "Just a little white lie. What's the harm?"

"I think there's a lawsuit there somewhere. If it doesn't work, I could lose my law license."

Jim grabbed another beer off Lewis's tray. "How are they gonna deny a ghost? Especially one who materializes before their doubtin' eyes."

Daniel studied Hayley's face. "What do you sense? Good plan or bad?"

"I can't influence your decision. It's up to you."

Daniel pulled out his cell phone and texted himself a memo. "Okay, I'll call Brea in the morning and we'll set this plan in motion. How soon do you think we can do this?"

"Now's a good time," Lee said. "Laura should be getting the DNA results in a couple of days. Speaking of evidence, I'll need a copy of the will and of that letter Kathy gave you about the brother dying first—a little down-to-earth reality to present to the Tylers."

"Certainly. Glad to share." Daniel handed Lee the paper, opened his briefcase, and pulled out the will.

"Lewis, would you please make copies of these?" Lee asked.

"Happy to, sir," he said, taking them from Lee.

"As long as we're sharin'...." Jim scratched his cheek. "When Wheeler shoved me down the basement stairs, I stumbled 'round, kickin' the flashlight like I was blind so I could get a glimpse of the basement. The floor's all brick. Good thing ya told us 'bout the vision ya had of Wheeler's death and the whereabouts of the tunnel's entrance. When I kicked that flashlight across the room, I 'bout made a hole-in-one. It stopped rollin' just inches away from the trap."

"You found the way into the tunnel?" Lee turned to Hayley. "Do you think we'll need to go through the basement to get Emma's DNA sample?"

She caught herself biting her lip. "I sure hope not. If anyone goes through the house, including me, and tries to go to the basement and down the tunnel, Wheeler will stop them. I thought maybe someone could lower me down the well to get to the tunnel, while a few of you keep him busy. I should be in and out in minutes. Laura showed me what to do when she took the sample from Abel."

"We'll move on this as soon as Brea's family leaves," Lee said.

"Mind if I join you?" Daniel asked.

"That would be great," Hayley said. "We'll need all the help we can get. In a few days we'll let you know when."

Lewis hurried into the library and returned Daniel's documents to him.

"Lewis will follow you to the car rental and take you to the airport," Lee said. "He's ready when you are."

Daniel filed the papers into his briefcase and stood. "I'm ready now. I'll keep you informed of my progress."

"We've got to be going, too," Roger said. He and Laura stood.

"I'll see you tomorrow, you two," Hayley told them. "Have a great night."

She noticed the glimmer in Roger's eyes and his soft stroke across the small of Laura's back, who responded by putting her arm around his waist. *Good girl. He's missing you already.*

~*~

After everyone left, Lee and Hayley walked hand in hand to the veranda. Under the moonlight, a candlelit table covered with desserts and wine awaited them.

Hayley put her arms around Lee's neck and kissed him. "A romantic evening under the stars."

"And dance lessons."

"What?"

"Well, that is, unless you already know how to waltz."

"Actually, I do. My grandfather taught me when I was five. I stood on his feet."

Lee led her to the table. "Velma baked us some goodies." He pulled a chocolate-covered strawberry from behind the blueberry cheesecake. Putting it to her lips, he whispered, "Open."

She took a bite and savored its sweet juices.

Lee kissed her wet lips. The tip of his tongue trailed across her cheek, its moistness warmed by his heated breath. "Would you like to dance?" he murmured into her ear.

Her heartbeat quickened; her knees weakened. "Yes," she managed to say.

Taking her hand, he led her past the azalea-filled urns and down the grand staircase to the soft grass. "Max, Strauss."

The computer complied by playing a surround-sound of music that emanated from camouflaged speakers hidden within boxwood hedges among the flowers.

"Max, lights on."

The topiaries throughout the garden twinkled with starry lights, and a pastel luminescence — blue, pink, purple, green, and yellow — bathed each flowerbed.

Hayley gasped.

Lee bent down and slipped off her sandals, then removed his own shoes and socks. Putting his hand on her waist, he whirled with Hayley to the rhythm of the waltz. Down the grassy aisles, between the boxwood hedges, a slight breeze blew in from the lake. The garden's perfume swirled in the air around them.

When the first of Strauss's pieces ended, Lee, with an elegant stride, guided her to the center of the garden. Bowing to her, he took her hand and kissed it. Once he pulled her close, another waltz began.

He dipped her and brought her up slowly. "I love you, Hayley Johnson."

She touched his cheek. "I love you, too, Lee Franklin."

They swayed to the tempo. After the music ended, they stopped and gazed into each other's eyes. He kissed her deeply. His lips caressed her neck, then followed the scoop of her blouse to the round of her breast. She trembled and moaned for more.

"Max, lights out," Lee said.

And the garden fell into a darkness filled with passion.

CHAPTER 36

Hayley and Laura stood looking up at the home's gingerbread details and cone-peaked turret. "Think you'll enjoy living here?" Hayley asked.

"What's not to like?" Laura said. "I love Victorian homes."

"Excuse me, ladies." Roger, luggage in hand, maneuvered past them up the pathway leading to the open stained-glass door. He turned. "Hayley, where should I put these?"

She pointed to the room above the wraparound porch. "Upstairs in the front bedroom."

Laura glanced around at the front yard. Tiny white sweet Williams covered the ground around the base of an old apple tree. Along the fence on both sides of the yard, hollyhocks, white daisies, Virginia bluebells, and foxgloves grew. "The view of the garden will be wonderful. I'm surprised you didn't take the front bedroom when you moved in."

"I think it's a déjà vu thing. I took the bedroom I had in my past life. I can't picture myself sleeping in any other."

"Hmm." Laura looked at the house, then back at Hayley. "Maybe you were reincarnated too soon after living here in your past-life, and didn't have time to lose your connection to this place."

"No doubt. I think timing has a lot to do with it. I've

heard stories about carrying over past-life experiences. Mostly phobias…fear of water, heights, and things like that."

They strolled toward the entry.

"What was it like, walking inside this house for the first time?" Laura asked. "Did anything look familiar?"

"It looked just the way I always imagined it. I've dreamt about this house since I was little. But reincarnation…I had no clue."

They stepped into the front hall.

"Any paramnesia when you met Lee?"

Hayley recalled her interview with Paranormal Search and Analysis when they first met. "Lee—he had a gravitational pull as powerful as the sun. I couldn't stop thinking about him. Talk about lust—" She recalled how she'd blushed every time she looked into his eyes. "If I had a penny for every time I thought about him."

"He's your love through eternity. You probably couldn't stop wanting him even if you had brain surgery to excise all desire for him."

While Hayley stared at the door, her memory flashed back to the night Lee brought her home after their dinner date. He'd stood where Laura stood now. Their investigative case had taken them halfway around the world. During those two weeks, she remembered how her mind, body, and soul had craved his arms, his touch, and his kiss. When they finally returned to Sutterville, she couldn't endure the temptation any longer.

She thought about having made love with Lee that night, her first time with any man. In the beginning, her insecurities had nudged at her, and bits and pieces of her troubled past flashed through her mind—how her peers had shunned her because of her strange behavior when her visions overwhelmed her, and how she'd talked to what others perceived to be imaginary people.

Psychiatrists her parents had forced her to see had diagnosed Hayley as being schizophrenic, and she'd bought into it. Feeling like an outcast, she had kept her hair long, pulling her bangs across her face, avoiding eye contact with men. But with Lee, she finally felt she could be herself. Once the heat of desire rose inside her with each moment of Lee's passion, her insecurities and painful memories melted away.

Her skin flushed at the thought of their lovemaking. While she visualized the sizzling details of their evening, she felt lightheaded. Everything around her disappeared — Laura, her home, and the floor she stood on. Sparks of light flashed in her peripheral vision. Without warning, her consciousness seemed to separate from her body and soar over parks, homes, and forests, then over the lake until instantly subsiding.

With the feel of solid ground beneath her feet, she glanced at her new surroundings. Across the room, sunlight peeked through the tower windows of Lee's sitting room. In jeans and white T-shirt, he sat at his desk going over papers. Stepping close, she felt his body heat.

Lee turned, gasped, and stared, wide-eyed.

"Hayley! Hayley, are you okay?" Roger's voice sounded distant.

In a blink, she again stood in the north side of town in her Victorian hallway, felt the floor beneath her feet, and saw Laura's face, brows furrowed with concern.

At Hayley's side, Roger reached out, steadying her as her body swayed.

"I'm okay," she said, her voice shaky. Hayley gathered herself, walked to the staircase, and sat on the lower step. Sensing Lee's call, she pulled the phone from the pocket of her white jeans and waited. When her phone rang, she put it on conference, letting

Laura and Roger listen. "Hi, Lee," she said.

"Is something wrong? Are you hurt?" Lee asked in a panic-stricken tone.

"I'm okay, I think. Something weird just happened. I thought about you one minute, and the next I stood beside you."

"I know. I saw you. Hell, I've never seen anything freakier. I thought you had died."

"My spirit was transported to you. It's called astral projection. Were you thinking about me?"

"Well, no. I was going through a list of entertainers for the ball."

"I could feel your body heat, Lee. I felt like I was physically there."

"Has this ever happened before?"

"I've read about it, but I've never experienced it until now."

"Exactly what were you thinking about me?"

Hayley's face reddened. "I'm sitting near Laura and Roger with the speaker phone on. I'd rather not say."

"Think you can do it again? Keep trying."

"Do you know what you're asking me to do, Lee? I have a very clear and detailed memory of what I can't tell you I remembered. If I keep thinking along those lines, you'll have to come get me."

He laughed. "Anything I can do to help?"

"Maybe I should try it again later."

"When?"

"I can't tell you. If you knew, you'd be thinking about me."

"Try visualizing me with clothes on."

"Lee, do you really think I always picture you naked?"

"I don't know how women think. When I think of you, I can't count the number of times I see you naked."

Roger cleared his throat. "If you don't mind, can we change the subject?"

"I think this is important, Roger," Lee said. "We need to work this out and see if Hayley can master this new talent."

"I agree," Roger replied. "But like Hayley always says, 'Things happen for a reason.' If this ability's meant to help her out when she's in danger, I don't think she'll be able to focus on intimacy."

"Hayley, do you foresee danger?" Lee asked.

"I'm not allowed to know anything about my own future, remember?"

"You'll have to try again to see if the thought of intimacy is the trigger," Lee said, his voice urgent. "And if it isn't, it could be a problem. I can't imagine what would happen if this occurs when you're facing Wheeler."

"If I confront Wheeler and project, he could seize my spirit and not allow me to return to my physical body. I have to master this astral projection before I go anywhere near him. I'll need Grams's help, or this could be disastrous. I'll get back to you, but I don't know when. Go back to your work. I don't know if it matters, but we should try to keep the conditions as they were before. Okay? I'll call you later."

She heard his concern when he said goodbye. While rising from the step, Hayley stifled the chilling "what if" thoughts, pocketed her cell phone, and focused on helping Laura settle into her new home.

~*~

Hayley placed her toothbrush inside the medicine cabinet and returned to her bedroom. Wearing a cool yellow cotton nightgown, she sat on the edge of the bed. "Grams, I need you," she whispered.

Without the theatrical oscillating vapor, Grams suddenly appeared in the rocking chair next to the fireplace. Her golden hair flowed over the shoulders of her flower print summer dress.

"You look nice today, Grams."

"Thank you, dear. You need my help?"

"Yes. Do you know what happened to me this afternoon?"

"Astral projection, dear. Your abilities are broadening."

"Yes. I know what it's called. But why? Am I in danger?"

"You know I can't tell you your future."

"Okay. Can you tell me if I need to strengthen that ability?"

"That would be wise."

Hayley bit her lower lip. *So I will be in danger.* "What should I do to make it happen again?"

"It has to do with focusing your thoughts on where you want to go or whom you want to see. It's not uncommon. Most people travel while they sleep and don't even know they're doing it. Your mind is more disciplined than that of others, so this is a natural progression for you. You just need to relax and let your mind travel, and your body will follow astrally."

"I read a little about it. But can I talk to Lee that way?"

"It depends on how much you practice. You won't be talking aloud. Your physical body will still be at its origin. Think the words with your mind. You'll be surprised how much energy thought can produce."

"Thanks, Grams."

The chair rocked on its own for a moment after Grams vanished. The bedroom felt still and peaceful.

Taking Grams's advice, Hayley lay on the bed, her head on a pillow and her body relaxed. With closed eyes, she began to focus on Lee.

CHAPTER 37

Hayley thought about her three attempts to project her astral body to other locations yesterday and four so far today, believing she was making progress. This time, while on the veranda with Lee, she'd focused her thoughts on Jim. Light flashed along her peripheral vision for only a second. Suddenly, she found herself in the ballroom.

Standing under the five-foot chandelier in the center of the room, she glanced around and noticed a blue plastic tarp spread on the floor about fifteen feet away. There she saw Jim, paintbrush in hand, stepping up the ladder. He dipped his brush into the paint can resting on the ladder's work platform. Jim touched up a small area on the wall to his right and laid down his brush. He descended the ladder and stood back, studying the celadon wall.

Before Hayley could clear her mind and return to her physical body on the veranda, Jim turned, saw her, and gasped. He stumbled back against the ladder. High on the platform, the paint can rocked precariously and fell onto its side. Celery-green paint cascaded over Jim's head and shoulders. Blasphemy blurted from his mouth.

Quickly, Hayley released her focused thoughts and returned to her physical self. She stood next to Lee, eyed the veranda doors, and bit her bottom lip.

"What?" Lee asked.

Without explaining, Hayley ducked behind him. Jim's execrations echoed throughout the hallways.

Lee glanced at the door, then over his shoulder. "What's going on? What happened?"

The doors flung open and Jim bolted onto the veranda. Paint dripped off his hair and down his face, dribbling from his nose, mustache, and chin. "Where is she?" he shouted, swiping his hand over his tinted face.

"You okay, Jim? You look a little green," Lee said.

He glared. "Where is that little—?"

"Did she scare you?"

"Do I look scared to you?"

Lee chuckled. "Not as scared as you looked yesterday."

"Damn right! Yesterday I thought she was a ghost. I didn't know if I should scream or go blind. Ya should've warned me. Hell, I could've had a heart attack."

Hayley put her hand to her mouth and giggled, remembering yesterday. Jim had been on a ladder then as well, placing lights on a topiary. When he saw her transparent image, she'd watched the blood leave his face and his eyes widen. The huge vat of cow manure had broken his fall. Once he'd climbed out, he ran, covered in muck, to the library to find Lee, while Lewis followed, shouting dignified curses.

"I see ya hidden behind his back, ya little troublemaker."

She glanced around Lee.

Lewis dashed out of the house with towels and hurried to Jim. "Sir, will you stop dripping on the veranda? Do you have any idea what a mess you made of the halls?"

"It's a no-brainer, Lewis. It cleans up with water."

Lewis looked at the puddles. "You are a menace to society, sir!"

"Not me, Lewis. Hayley's the damn menace!"

Lewis stepped back and shook his head. "Miss Johnson has been outside with Mr. Franklin all afternoon. You can't blame her because you're a doltish, bumbling klutz."

Holding her breath to stop giggling, Hayley tried to keep quiet, but the sight of Jim's green-stained face sent her into a fit of laughter.

Lee looked over his shoulder. "Stop it. You'll make matters worse."

With a look of disgust on his face, Lewis threw the towel over Jim's head and started to swab. Jim reached up, grabbed the towel, and threw it down. "Get the hell away from me, ya damn fool!"

Lewis put his hands on his hips. "Sir, do you know how long it took me to get the manure stench out of the halls yesterday? Now look. I'll be spending the rest of the day cleaning up your ghastly paint trail." Lewis draped the towel over his arm and straightened, raising his chin. "Since you have forgotten where to go to take a shower, I will gladly escort you to your room."

"Follow me to my room, ya little twerp, and *you'll* be turnin' green." Jim glared at Hayley. "I know you're supposed to be practicin' this projectin' stuff, but next time, use Lewis for your guinea pig. How am I supposed to get this place ready for the ball if ya keep tormentin' me?"

Feeling guilty, Hayley stepped out from behind Lee. "You're right, Jim. Sorry."

With a huff, Jim turned abruptly and went into the house, Lewis at his heels, their bickering continuing as they walked down the hallway.

Lee pulled his ringing cell phone from his shirt pocket and checked the caller ID. "It's Laura." He raised the phone to his ear. "Hi! What's up?"

While he spoke, Hayley walked to the table, poured two glasses of Chardonnay, returned to him, and handed him a drink.

"She called to let us know she received the DNA tests just in time for Daniel's court case tomorrow, and overnighted them to him," Lee said.

Lee shoved the phone back into his pocket and took a sip of wine. He followed her to the far side of the veranda overlooking the pond, and down a narrow flight of stairs to a flagstone path leading to the water's edge.

"What's our next step?" he asked.

"We need to get back to the plantation."

They strolled down the path toward a secluded resting area near a weeping willow.

"Do you think we should tell Abel?" he asked.

Hayley watched white swans glided across the pond, barely rippling the water's glassy surface while she sipped her wine and thought about Abel's reaction to the news. "No. It's better to keep him on a need-to-know basis. Once he knows where Emma is, he won't wait for us." She sat on a cushioned rattan chair a few feet from the pond.

"You're right," Lee said, easing himself onto the seat next to her. "We need to keep our plans a secret. He's waited over a hundred-and-fifty years to find Emma. He'll go right to her."

"No doubt."

"His ability to transport himself is similar to yours, isn't it?" Lee asked.

"Yes. Kind of eerie, isn't it? If we think our brains are where our thoughts originate, what about Abel? He lacks a material brain and yet he's intelligent. And he can transport quicker than I can."

"Talk about materializing. The Tylers will arrive Friday. Can't wait to see their faces when they see Abel appear from

248

nowhere."

"Me, too," Hayley said. "Maybe then Brea's dad will be a little more open-minded. We'll go to Georgia once they're gone. How about having a meeting tomorrow morning so we can plan our next step? Oh, and we may want to ask Frank to join our team, or he might ruin our plans."

"I vote yes. After the way he acted in the office and demanded to know what we're up to, I think he should get his wish and meet Wheeler. Maybe if he gets the crap scared out of him, he'll think twice about sticking his nose into our business, and won't be such a jerk next time. I'll leave a message for Roger about the meeting."

"A message? Can't you just call him?"

"I can, but when Laura called, I could hear him in the background. I'm not sure what they're up to, but I wouldn't go home too soon if I were you."

Hayley smiled. "Hmm."

"I'll know by the look on Roger's face when I see him at the meeting."

"Will Lewis be there?" she asked.

Lee grinned and nodded. "If he and Jim don't kill each other first."

Formulating a strategy in her mind, she held her fingers up. "Let's see. There are seven of us—three women and four men, if Lewis goes this time. Then there'll be Meeker, Daniel, and Frank. Ten—that should be enough of us."

"So what's the plan?" he asked.

Hayley glanced over her shoulder. "Abel and Ben are in the garden. We better not discuss this here. I'll tell you later."

CHAPTER 38

The team sat around the conference table waiting for Jim. While the curtains were pulled open, Hayley looked into the parking lot, watching the Thompson brothers sneaking peeks through the office window.

Jim drove in, parked, got out, and hurried into the office. "Sorry I'm late. I saw Frank watchin' the front gate at Lee's estate as I left there. When I noticed he was followin' me, I led him outta town. Last I seen of him, he was headin' toward the state line." He sat across from Lee.

"That's one of the reasons we're having this meeting — to find a way to get him off our backs," Lee said.

"I'll vote for that." Jim raised his chin and sniffed. "Coffee smells good. Guess I'll grab me some before we get started." He stood and crossed the room.

Hayley watched Roger and Laura's body language and leaned toward Lee. "I think you were wrong. Now that Roger's over his shyness, it looks like Laura's making him wait."

Lee shrugged. "You're right. If they had sex last night, Roger wouldn't be able to keep the grin off his face and his eyes off Laura."

After Jim returned to his seat, all conversations stopped.

"Okay, I guess we'll get started," Roger, standing at the head of the table, began. "We're here to figure out what's next in the Abel Smith case. Four elements need to be solved. First, get Abel and Emma back together. Second, trace the Tylers' ancestry to Mr. Wheeler. Third, get the Tylers their inheritance. And last, connect Daniel to Emma and her inheritance."

"I thought we already gathered Wheeler's DNA, and Laura's got Brea's family's samples," Jim said. "If that'll solve the question of inheritance, then all we gotta do is get Abel and Emma joined up. Right?"

"Yes, I know. I was just trying to summarize."

"Just get to what we need to do next," Jim said.

"Why? In a hurry? Got a date?" Roger asked.

"When do I have time for a social life? I've been busier than a one-armed paperhanger runnin' a slew of wirin' to China and back, helpin' John connect Max to the entire estate." He looked at Lewis, who quietly sat at the end of the table with Kathy and Laura.

Lewis's mouth opened. It looked to Hayley as if he were about to comment.

"What?" Jim asked.

"Well, sir, I was just going to say that I've always thought you were good for nothing, but lately you have been showing signs of intelligence. That baffles me."

Jim rubbed the back of his neck. "Damn, I can't tell if that's a compliment or an insult."

"I guess I was wrong about the intelligence," Lewis said. "I take it back."

"But seriously, Jim," Lee interrupted. "I know how hard you've been working getting things ready for the ball. Just say the word, and I'll hire as many workers as you need."

"I'm fine. There ain't nothin' I can't do. Every year, this ball is a pain in the butt. It's just the way things go." He glanced around the table. "Hell, if I knew this meetin' was gonna be 'bout me, I would've worn a tux."

Roger cleared his throat. "All right, well, Daniel went to court this morning and put everything on the table — the journals, the will, and all the DNA lab results. But the will states Wheeler wanted everything to go to Emma. So, the court has instructed Daniel to provide Emma's mtDNA to prove she's the Tylers' and Daniel's ancestor before the court considers the inheritance."

"I thought the Historical Society wouldn't let us do any investigating," Lee said.

"Daniel explained the situation to the judge and received unconditional access to the entire plantation," Roger said. "Now we don't have to sneak in anymore and maybe get Meeker fired. Once Hayley finds Emma, we'll have to find a way to make Wheeler leave the plantation so the authorities can get to Emma's remains."

"How soon does Daniel need the evidence?" Hayley asked.

"Eight days," Roger replied. "He's flying in Friday night."

She frowned. "Here's the dilemma. Last time we went to the Wheeler plantation, Lee and I came within inches of being attacked by Wheeler. The only thing that saved everyone from harm was putting our minds on something other than looking for the will. But this time, Emma is going to be on everyone's mind, and Wheeler will know what we're thinking. We'll need to buy the time while I'm lowered into the well to keep Wheeler from knowing and attacking me. I suggest we recruit Frank Thompson."

Jim stared into the parking lot at the Thompson sons, sitting on their skateboards, focused on the meeting inside as if watching a drive-in movie. "Great idea," he said. "It might be a little on the mean side, but it should work. Ya know how Frank Thompson wants an exclusive? How 'bout givin' him one? If we bring him here and tell him the inheritance story without spillin' Emma's name, we can get him to go into Wheeler's plantation and take pictures. If he doesn't know about Emma being down in the well, he's not going to be thinking about her, so he won't get attacked. Wheeler will be watchin' him and have his back to the well."

"Sounds good," Roger said.

Jim grinned. "We can have Meeker give Frank a tour of the place, and he can tell the unsuspecting pain-in-the-butt to take a few pictures of the basement. There's no doubt Wheeler's ghost will be throwin' Frank out of the house. Hell, Frank might even take off like a bee-stung jackass and never bother us again."

"Exactly what Hayley and I were thinking," Lee said.

Hayley closed her eyes. She envisioned Frank following them out of town. The team wouldn't be able to shake him this time. And it was inevitable he would show up at Wheeler's plantation during their investigation, putting a wrench into the works. The only way to make this investigation go as planned would be to invite Frank to join the team. "As it stands now, Frank will disrupt our case. If we let him participate, we'll be in control and won't have to worry about his interference."

"Everyone in favor, raise your hand," Roger said.

Hayley glanced around the room at Kathy, Laura, Jim, Lewis, Lee, and Roger. All, including her, voted to recruit.

"Okay. I'll contact him this afternoon," Roger said. "Any more discussion about Frank?"

Lee raised his hand. "Hayley will need about twenty minutes to get in and out of the well. Maybe we can call Meeker and see if he knows anything Frank can say or do to hold Wheeler's attention at least that long. We'll also need a secondary plan in case Hayley needs more time. It would be a good idea if a few of you wait outside until Frank leaves the house. Once he's outside, you guys can hurry in to continue keeping Wheeler's mind occupied."

Lewis clapped his hands together. "That's a brilliant idea. I volunteer to keep him distracted in the basement."

Jim looked up and shook his head. "Ya definitely have a screw loose, Lewis. Wheeler might break your scrawny neck."

"I'd be more than happy to risk my life, sir."

"You're a damn nutcase," Jim said. He turned to Hayley. "How many of us will ya need to lower ya down the well?"

"I'll need Laura nearby in case I have questions about gathering the DNA sample, plus Roger to lower me down, Daniel to be there to meet Emma, and Lee to stand by in case something goes wrong. That should be enough."

"I thought I was going down into the well, too," Laura said.

"I'd rather go alone," Hayley said. "I can contact you by astral projection if I need help."

A smile crossed Laura's face. "It doesn't take a brain surgeon to collect a DNA sample. You'll do fine without me."

"Wait a minute. If the authorities collect Emma's DNA, why does Laura need a sample?" Jim asked.

"Since Hayley needs to locate Emma's remains anyway," Laura said, "we can't let the opportunity to gather our own evidence slip away. If the tests come from two different places, the court's appointed lab, and the lab I'll be using as they did with Wheeler's DNA results, the evidence will be undoubtedly conclusive. When the findings are compared, the courts will have to rule in Daniel's favor."

"Okay. So Jim, Lewis, Frank, and Meeker will be in the mansion," Roger said. "And Lee, Hayley, Daniel, Laura, and I will be at the well."

"What about me?" Kathy asked.

"I'll need you to stay with Abel until we call," Lee told her.

"Does he know he's going to be with Emma?" she asked.

"Yes," Lee said, "but he doesn't know where she is. When we tell him, it should only take him a split second to translocate to the well. All he has to do is visualize where he wants to be, and he'll instantly be there. When that happens, Wheeler will sense Abel's presence. So we'll have to wait for the right moment before telling Abel where Emma is."

"Jim, give Meeker a call," Roger said. "Then contact Frank."

"Meeker's about as crazy as Lewis," Jim said, grinning. "Frank's in for one hell of a tour. Can't wait to see his face after he meets Wheeler. I'll get right on it."

"Won't take him long to realize he's been set up," Roger said, "but he'll get over it. The story of Abel, Emma, and Wheeler will feed his newspaper for weeks, not to mention the details of the Tylers' inheritance. Any other matters that need discussing?"

"Yes," Lee said. "The Tylers will be here Friday as well. I'm tempted to let them accompany us. It'll give them a chance to see the Wheeler mansion, to realize part of what they'll inherit when Daniel wins this court case."

Hayley closed her eyes and opened her mind to visions of the future. "Looks like they're in for an enlightening weekend."

"It's a plan then," Roger said. "Lee and I will take our SUVs and leave the company vans here. Don't want Wheeler to read our logo on the side and know what we're up to."

"Good idea," Lee agreed. "How about leaving after breakfast, around seven?"

"Okay. We'll tell Frank we'll swing by to pick him up, along with any cameras he may need. Then we'll run by the office to gather our tech equipment."

CHAPTER 39

When Frank Thompson entered the office, Roger took a seat next to Laura. The rest of the team sat quietly while Jim stood at the head of the table.

"Have a seat, Frank," Jim said. "We've got somethin' to run past ya. We decided to let ya in on an exclusive in trade for callin' off your boys. We've got a case ya might be interested in. The team wants ya to join the investigation."

Frank's eyes widened and his bent nose twitched. "Seriously? You want me to join your team?"

Jim twisted his mustache, and looked Frank square in the eye. "Ya said it yourself the last time ya came by. We owe ya a story. So we're offerin' ya one. But ya have to promise to call off your boys. They're annoyin' as a gnat up my butt."

"Yes. Sure. Right away." Frank looked out the window. His sons, staring into the office, had their noses pressed against a window. Frank motioned with his thumb for them to leave.

They turned, picked up their skateboards, and headed across the parking lot.

"I'm sure ya remember Mr. Daniel Smith," Jim said.

"Yes, yes, of course, the lawyer. Did he hire you?"

"That's what he was doin' here that day when ya so rudely — I mean, when ya came to our office. His clients are tryin' to prove that their ancestry is tied to a Georgia plantation owner named Zachary Wheeler. While the court's waitin' for more DNA evidence, it's granted us permission to investigate the estate. The place dates back to the mid-1800s. The history behind Wheeler and his descendants is one hell of a story."

"So, the place is haunted?"

"Oh yeah, almost forgot to tell ya 'bout that. Wheeler was murdered in the mid-1800s and his spirit stayed 'round. Well, are ya interested?"

"Damn right, I'm interested. What exactly do you want me to do? Will I need training?"

Jim looked back at Frank. "We thought ya could go in first and interview the groundskeeper, fella named Meeker, then take photos of the furnishin's. Daniel will be needin' pictures for his estate inventory. A newspaperman like yourself will get great shots. While you're lookin' 'round, Meeker will give ya a tour. We'll be investigatin' the hauntin' once you're outta there. Should be a piece of cake."

"Is that all? Just photos?"

"No. Ya might find out from Meeker if all the furniture belongs to the house. And while you're takin' photos, get some shots of the floor plan. The Tylers, they're some of the descendants, will appreciate that, since they won't be goin' in until we prove the place is safe. Oh, and they'll definitely want pictures of the basement. After all these years, that foundation must need some work. Think ya can do that?"

"Sure. Will I be able to publish the photos I take?"

"Yeah, and ya might want the back story on how Wheeler died. Meeker knows everythin' 'bout the place. I'm sure ya know how to dig up the dirt better than any of us."

"After that, will I be joining you while you're investigating?"

"Sure, if that's what ya want. We've got a few pieces of

equipment as easy to use as pickin' your nose. And ya won't be alone. We work in pairs."

"So when do you want to do this?"

"Tomorrow night," Jim said. "We'll meet here at seven to give ya some trainin'. Friday mornin' the Tylers are flyin' in. Then we'll be on our way to Georgia Saturday. Are ya in?"

"Hell yes. I'll be here. Thanks for the offer. I can't tell you how exciting this is."

"We've got a deal then, Frank. Just keep your boys outta our hair and don't be late tomorrow night."

CHAPTER 40

"They should be here any minute," Lee said Friday morning, looking out the tower window of his sitting room toward the security gate beyond the spruce-lined drive.

Hayley stepped next to him, her arm wrapping around his waist. "Should we meet them outside?"

"No, I think Lewis should show the Tylers to their rooms first. Let them settle in. We can meet them at lunch."

"And Abel? When should we make introductions?"

"It might be best if they meet before the meal, to give the Tylers a chance to calm their nerves before eating."

"It's not going to work," a disembodied voice said behind them.

Hayley and Lee turned in unison.

Grams materialized, wearing cream-colored dress pants and a powder-blue angora sweater, almost blending in with the color of the couch where she sat in front of the fireplace.

Hayley and Lee walked toward her. Lee rested an elbow on a high-backed chair.

"What's not going to work?" Hayley asked, easing herself into the chair Lee leaned against.

"Introducing Abel to Mr. Tyler. He won't buy it. He'll be convinced Abel's an actor and his appearance is a trick of the eye. Not to mention the argument he'll have with Brea, blaming her for bringing them here under false pretenses."

"Any suggestions?" Lee asked. "It's important the Tylers believe in ghosts. If they're going with us to Georgia, I don't want Mr. Tyler to cause a scene and ruin our plans."

"I'm aware of that. Let me join you for lunch. I know exactly what will convince Mr. Tyler, and put a smile on his wife and Brea's faces."

"Care to fill us in?" Lee asked.

She smiled devilishly and shook her head. "Let's say I've met someone lately who is more headstrong than Mr. Tyler, and she won't be denied."

"Who?" Hayley asked.

"You'll see, dear." Grams stood, her wavy blonde hair draping around her crew neckline. "I have to go. She learned to materialize only this morning. She'll need more practice to solidify and hold her shape before she makes an appearance. I'll meet you in the main hallway before you enter the dining room. Make sure Lewis sets a place for both of us. I don't want the Tylers to know I'm a spirit until they meet my guest."

"We'll leave it to you then," Lee said.

Before Hayley could stand, Grams vanished.

~*~

When she, Lee, and Grams walked into dining room, Hayley overheard Mr. Tyler's comment to Mrs. Tyler and Brea. "I bet this end of the dining table has its own zip code." When he glanced toward the door, his conversation stopped, he stood, and extended his hand to Lee as he approached.

Hayley and Grams accompanied Lee and stood at his side while he greeted Brea's father with a welcoming handshake. "Mr. Tyler, Mrs. Tyler, and Miss Tyler, I'm Mr. Franklin. So glad you've come." Lee turned. "This is Miss Johnson and Ms.

Heartman. They'll be joining us for lunch."

At the west end of the table, Lewis had placed six formal settings of white china rimmed with gold, silverware, and crystal glasses. The Tyler's had already been seated. Lee pulled out a chair for Grams and one for Hayley, then took his seat at the head of the table.

Mr. Tyler sat again while Brea and his wife smiled politely. "Brea entered our names in a contest," he said. "We've never won anything like this in our lives until now. We're excited to be here."

"The pleasure is all ours, Mr. Tyler," Lee said. "I hope all of you enjoy your visit."

"Is this the first time you and your family have stayed at a haunted house?" Grams asked.

Mr. Tyler chuckled. "I have to admit this is a beautiful home. How old would you say it is?"

"In three more years, it'll be two hundred years old," Lee said.

"My point being, Ms. Heartman," Mr. Tyler continued, "that over time a home's structure tends to falter somewhat, possibly confusing the inhabitants into thinking they hear moans, footsteps, or see unbalanced doors close, and fool a person into believing such happenings are supernatural. There are no such things as ghosts, Ms. Heartman. It's as simple as that."

"It is truly a debatable subject, Mr. Tyler," Grams said. "You should be well entertained by my friend, who will be joining us any minute."

Lewis came to the door and cleared his throat.

"You'll excuse me, Mr. Tyler, Mrs. Tyler, and Brea, if I may address you so informally," Grams said.

"Sure," Brea said. "I'd rather you did."

Grams pushed her chair back and stood. Once she left the

room, Mrs. Tyler glanced at the damask bordering the tablecloth and then at Lee. "I believe in ghosts. Just recently—"

Mr. Tyler glared at her and blurted, "Margret, this is not the time or place to show your ignorance."

Mrs. Tyler quietly leaned back in her chair.

"I believe in them, too," Brea said. "I don't care what my dad says."

"That's enough out of you, young lady," Mr. Tyler said.

"And that'll be enough out of you, Harold," said the woman entering the room. Hayley guessed her to be in her eighties. She wore a knee-length dark blue skirt, a blue long-sleeved sweater, and brown penny loafers.

Brea and her mom gasped, jumped out of their seats, and gathered behind Brea's chair, their arms around each other.

The woman crossed the room and stopped at Lee's side, while Grams walked around the table and stood across from the Tylers. The other woman glanced at Brea. "I told you I'd be around, honey." She reached into her pocket and pulled out a business-sized envelope. "I believe this is a five-penny event, my dear," she said, jiggling the envelope, then passing it to Brea.

Brea left her mom's side and rushed to her grandmother. "Is it really you? Can I touch you?"

Her grandmother held out her arms, and Brea embraced her. "Enough, honey. I have to control my emotions in order to hold this old hide together."

Brea stepped away, turned, and rejoined her mother.

Mr. Tyler's face had paled. He stared at the woman until his temper flared. "What kind of trick is this? How dare you impersonate my mother?" He pushed back his chair and stood. "I won't stand for this cheap Hollywood stunt."

"Sit down, Harold," his mom said in a stern tone.

His eyes widened and he sank into his seat.

She moved closer to him. "If you're so sure I'm not your mother, let me politely introduce myself." She reached out her hand.

He glanced at Brea. "Is this your idea of a joke?"

"Don't be so insulting, Dad. She's letting you prove your point."

Remaining seated, Harold Tyler huffed, turned to the woman, and begrudgingly offered his hand.

His eyes opened wider, while her hand in his lost its human touch and became ghostly transparent. He abruptly retracted his hand. "This can't be," he said in a low tone, his brows narrowing together, his darting glances finally focusing on her face. "Mother?"

"Yes, it's me. You don't know everything, Harold."

Mrs. Tyler giggled nervously, catching her mother-in-law's attention.

"It's good to see you again, Margret and Brea. Please sit. This won't take long. I can't hold this shape for much longer."

Brea and her mom slowly sat, their eyes fixed on the deceased Mrs. Tyler, who walked around the table to join Grams. "Before I go, I'd like to introduce you to the woman you've been speaking with the last few minutes. She's better known as Grams, Hayley's grandmother."

A high-pitched screech, followed by laughter, came from Brea's mom. Brea gasped, and her father raised a shaky hand to his mouth.

While Hayley watched, Grams's face began to age. Her blonde hair became shorter, its color changing to white. Her face turned plumper as her nose broadened. Fine lines formed around her mouth, while wrinkles appeared on her forehead and between her brows. Her blue eyes and pink lips paled, her neck and arms fattened, and dark spots formed on her skin.

As she aged, the fat in her face began to droop, causing her jowls to sag over her jawbone. As the aging process continued, her face thinned, her cheekbones protruded, and her eyes sockets appeared hollow. She looked gaunt and close to death. Hayley glanced away and saw Mr. Tyler passed out, slumping in his chair.

Lee jumped up and steadied Brea's father in his seat. "Lewis," he called over his shoulder.

"Oh, dear," Grams said. "I guess I went a bit too far."

Lewis dashed into the room. "I have just the thing, sir. Leave it to me."

Lee stepped aside, allowing Lewis to wave smelling salts under Mr. Tyler's nose.

Mr. Tyler jerked his head back. His eyes opened, although he still seemed unaware of his surroundings. "What, what…?"

"Just relax, Mr. Tyler. You'll be fine in a moment," Lewis said.

Harold Tyler glanced across the table at Grams. She hadn't returned to her youth. He looked at his mother. "Guess this wasn't a dream after all," he said.

"No, son. Sorry we had to be so abrupt with you. It's necessary that you understand the truth. You remember Daniel, don't you, Harold? Well, everything he's told you has been forthright. He's an honest man, son, and he's fighting hard to get us what's rightfully ours. I've been standing by listening to you call your daughter degrading names, when all she's been trying to do is to inform you of what's going on. She's told you about the slave, his wife, son, and their master, Mr. Wheeler. All she said was the truth. The slave's ghost lives beneath this house, and it's imperative that you meet him." Her energy wavered, and her solid form began to become transparent.

"I can't stay. My energy is limited. I'm afraid you won't be

264

seeing me again anytime soon." She glanced around. "I'll always be with you, Brea. Margret, if Harold gives you any more baloney about how he's the king of the family, remind him that you're the queen and don't take any more guff from him, or I'll be back." She glanced at her son. "Understand, Harold. Don't make me come back. And start loving your daughter a little more. She deserves it."

"Yes, Mother," he mumbled.

"Bye, Grandmother," Brea said. She held up the envelope. "This is more than a five-penny memory. It's priceless. I still can't believe you did this."

"I'll be off, too," Grams said, her face returning to its youthful appearance.

"Thanks, Grams," Hayley said.

"We really appreciate your help, Grams," Lee said. "Later tonight, after the Tylers have a chance to relax, we'll explain our plan to go to Georgia and we'll introduce them to Abel. 'Bye, Mrs. Tyler. Thanks for making an appearance."

"Glad to have helped. If you need me again, please let me know." She turned to Grams. "Ready, Julia?"

The two turned and headed toward the doorway, vanishing a little with each step until only the memory of them remained.

"Sorry, Mr. Tyler, for springing this on you," Lee said, "but it's important you know what you're about to witness."

"Witness? Know what?"

Lewis stood by the fireplace with his hands crossed in front of him. Hayley noticed his upper lip twitch and knew he held back a grin, secretly enjoying tonight's show-and-tell.

"We'll discuss our plans over dinner," Lee said. "Lewis, I believe we're ready to be served."

"Yes, sir. Right away." He hurried out the door.

"Let me refresh your memory about everything Brea has told

you," Lee said. "Do you recall the first conversation you had with Mr. Smith? It's true that your generational grandfather, Zachary Wheeler, raped Daniel's generational grandmother, Emma Smith. Emma and her husband's son, Noah, are Daniel's ancestors. The child Emma had with Wheeler, Simon Tyler, is yours.

"Noah joined the Union and fought in the Civil War. Once the war ended, he married and had a family. Simon also married and had a large family, who are buried in Jackson, Georgia. From Simon's line, only your family is left, and from Noah's, it's down to Daniel. There are journals from both of Emma's sons that you might be interested in seeing. That's why Daniel contacted your daughter and offered her a large fee for solid evidence to prove or disapprove the connection. Hayley and I ran into Brea in Tennessee, and then again in Georgia at Wheeler's plantation. That was about the time she started telling you what was going on, but you wouldn't believe her. She told you she'd met a medium. I'd like you to meet Hayley Johnson. She's able to see the past, present, future, and the dead."

Harold glared at her. "This burns my butt. I can't believe I was so gullible to fall for this free vacation hoax."

"Mr. Tyler," Hayley cut in, "it is extremely important that you keep an open mind. Daniel is putting his reputation on the line for your family, and the rest of us are putting ourselves in danger. This is not a joke."

"We'll just see about that," he said.

"Harold," a voice called out from across the table.

Mr. Tyler folded his arms. "Okay, fine, I'll listen to what you have to say. I have no choice. I'm surrounded by know-it-all women."

Hayley took a calming breath and glanced at Brea. *She's lucky to have an opinion at all, growing up around him.*

"As I was saying, Mr. Tyler," Lee continued, "Hayley has

an extraordinary gift. In a vision of the past, she witnessed the imprisonment and rape of Emma Smith by Zachary Wheeler. There's a tunnel running from the mansion's basement to the dry well. That's where Wheeler held Emma captive, and where she died. Tomorrow we'll be driving to his plantation in Georgia. Hayley will be lowered into the well in order to find Emma's remains and collect a DNA sample. So far, we have Wheeler's DNA and, along with Emma's sample, it'll prove your family's lineage and the entitlement of the inheritance as well. Lastly, it will connect your ancestry to Daniel's."

"So, you expect me and my family to go to Georgia with you?"

"Dad, if you don't cooperate, Grandmother will make your life unbearable," Brea reminded him. "I'm sure you wouldn't want that."

He took a deep, resigned breath. "You're right. I wouldn't want that." He uncrossed his arms. "Okay, I promise to keep my opinions to myself. That's all I can promise. If what Brea has told me about Mr. Smith's intentions to prove our rights to inherit Mr. Wheeler's plantation in Georgia doesn't pan out, I'll be calling him a fraud."

"That's all we ask," Lee said. "Now that your mother has proven her point, it'll be easier for you to accept that Wheeler's ghost resides in the mansion. It's our plan, as members of Paranormal Search and Analysis, to free Emma from her prison, unite her with her husband, whom you'll meet this evening, and trick Wheeler into leaving the mansion—unless you want to inherit a vicious ghost along with the estate."

"You wouldn't want that, Harold," Mrs. Tyler spoke up. "I've seen things like that on TV, and there's no way I'll step foot inside a place like that, inheritance or no inheritance."

"Cool your jets, Margret. I said I'd cooperate. If they want to rid the estate of a so-called ghost, I won't interfere."

Hayley leaned back in her seat as Lewis placed her meal in front of her. "When we finish our lunch," she said, "Mr. Tyler, Mrs. Tyler, and Brea, we'll retire to the library. By then Daniel will have arrived from the airport, and I'll introduce you to him and to Wheeler's nemesis, Emma's husband, Abel Smith. Do you think you can handle meeting another ghost, Mr. Tyler?"

"Yes, yes. Of course. What do you take me for, a simple-minded scaredy-cat?"

Hayley notice his hands shaking as he reached for his knife and fork, which reminded her. "We can't forget to pick up Frank before we leave town," she told Lee.

CHAPTER 41

Saturday morning, on the three-and-one-half hour trip to the Georgia plantation, Lee and Roger drove their own SUVs, Lee taking his Porsche Cayenne and Roger taking his Audi Q7. With their vehicles parked out of sight along the old oak lane, Lee and Hayley waited on one side of the road with Brea, Daniel, and Laura in the back seat. Jim, Brea's parents, Lewis, and Roger parked across the way.

Lee drove forward from behind the oaks until he and Hayley could see Frank and Meeker arrive at the end of the road and stop in front of the mansion's pillared porch.

"We'll wait about five minutes after they go inside so they'll have Wheeler's full attention," Hayley said.

"Do you really think this will work?" Lee asked. "Wheeler can read thoughts, and we're pretty close."

"I know," Hayley said. "I'm worried about that, too. I've told the others to try to occupy their minds, but I don't know how long it will take before Wheeler finds out we're at the well. After they get Wheeler's attention, we need to hurry." She read Lee's expression and saw that he worried she would be injured or, worse, killed. Hayley changed the subject.

"Brea," Hayley said, "you were really brave keeping your cool while your grandmother materialized in front of you and your parents. Your mom seemed to take it well, too, but your dad, not so much. I'm sorry he fainted."

"Yeah, well, Mom's a firm believer in ghosts, but I could still feel her shaking in my arms. Dad—nothing I said or did persuaded him that ghosts exist. I'm sure his mother was the only one who could convince him." Brea laughed. "Guess you showed him."

"I think he'll be a little easier on your mom from now on," Lee said.

"On me, too," Brea said. "It was hard hearing my dad call me a liar when I told him about Wheeler."

"He believes in ghosts now," Daniel said. "There's no doubt about that. But he still thinks I'm a crook and in it for the money."

"That will change after all this is over," Lee said. He glanced toward the back of the SUV. "We've got the rope attached to the hitch. I'll back as close to the well as I can. Hayley, let's get you harnessed while we're waiting."

They stepped out of the SUV, walked to the back, and opened the rear door. Lee helped her into a harness, tightening the leg and waist straps. Once she was cinched up, he fitted her with gloves and a helmet. They reentered the vehicle, and Lee drove down the oak-lined lane, followed by Roger's Audi Q7.

Before they reached the mansion and Meeker's truck out front, both Lee's and Roger's vehicles crossed the lawn to the well. Lee swung his Cayenne around and backed up, the rear of his SUV stopping about three feet from the well's wall. Roger parked, the front bumper of his Audi facing eight feet from the uncovered well.

Once out of the vehicles, everyone split into three groups, one team entering the mansion, the others helping Hayley, plus the spectators, the Tylers.

Harold eyed Daniel. "It's still hard to believe."

Daniel turned abruptly and walked toward the well.

"Dad!" Brea said sharply. "You promised to keep an open mind."

"She's right," Margret told him. "There's nothing unusual about any of this. I see it on TV all the time."

Harold crossed his arms and looked away.

While Jim and Lewis headed to the mansion, the others circled the shaft.

"Got the DNA test kit?" Laura asked Hayley.

Hayley patted her pocket and nodded.

Lee tapped her helmet. "Ready?"

She surrounded herself with white light and nodded.

Her heart pounded as she looked down the dark shaft. Stale air thick with the pungent odor of mildew filled the well in place of spring water. Hayley stared into the sixty-foot depth, Emma's agonizing screams tearing at her emotions. Flooded with determination to help, Hayley turned on her helmet light, its wide beam chasing away the darkness.

Hurrying, Lee secured the knot and foothold before hooking the lines to her harness. While Daniel held the rope tight, Lee helped Hayley over the wall, lowering her into position. While she steadied herself, Lee controlled the rope's tension.

Gripping the rope tight in her gloved hands, Hayley touched her foot against the shaft, stopping her sway and sending loose mortar and debris cascading. She relaxed, hanging loosely, while Lee lowered her.

Sweat from beneath her helmet ran down her temples. Perspiration soaked her short-sleeved blouse. Focused on Emma, Hayley ignored her pounding heart and slowly rappelled into the pitch blackness toward the slave's wailing.

Again, Emma's shrill cries sent shivers up Hayley's back. *You'll be free soon, Emma. I swear.*

271

Once her feet touched the damp craggy bottom, she pulled three times on the rope, signaling the others that she'd reached the bottom, then unhooked the rope and glanced around at the bricked well and tunnel leading away from the shaft. *Good job, Abel. It must have taken you forever to lay so much brick.*

She let go of the rope and stepped out of the foothold and harness. With a calming breath, she headed into the tunnel. Reaching out, she balanced herself against the walls, avoiding rubble lying in her path. On the right, two feet ahead of her, a rickety wooden door, tilting and appearing as if a stir of the musty air would upset it, barred a room.

Her footsteps echoed as she eased closer. Holding her breath, she glanced inside. Empty.

The screams turned to whimpers as she approached the next room. Hinges held the rotted door to a frame embedded in the brick. She turned the knob. *Locked.*

"Emma," Hayley whispered, her face against the door. "I've come to save you. Don't cry. I'll take you out of here, I promise."

She rattled the knob. Pieces of door fell to the floor. Slipping her fingers between the door's rotted planks, she ripped the splintered boards away, pulled the door open, then stepped inside.

The dark-skinned young ghost, eyes wide, cringed in the corner, her black wavy hair hanging to her shoulders. So young, so pretty, Hayley thought.

Emotions knotted in Hayley's throat. "I'm here to help, Emma," she said softly. "Don't be afraid." Glancing to her right, Hayley saw a bed collapsed on the floor, Emma's bones scattered, draped in remnants of rotted sheets. She flashed back to her visions of the young girl giving birth, then shook the memories from her mind. *I have to hurry.*

Hayley reached inside her pocket and pulled out the DNA

272

test kit. Bending down, she examined the skull. She brushed her fingers across the lower jaw. An incisor tumbled out. Quickly, using tweezers, she placed the tooth into the container and pocketed it.

She turned.

Emma's eyes grew larger. "Massa comin'!"

Hayley's heart beat wildly. She closed her eyes. Dropping her shield, she thought of Lee. Instantly, her astral body stood next to him by the wall encircling the well. "Get Abel. Wheeler... he's, he's coming!"

In a split second, she saw Lee toss his phone to Laura. "Call Kathy. Tell her to send Abel." He grabbed the rope, hurling himself over the wall and into the well.

Hayley returned to her physical body. The air smelled putrid. Wheeler's irate ghost appeared in the doorway.

Before she could shield herself from his rage again, he rushed forward, lifting her above his head, hurling her against the wall. When she plummeted to the floor, she felt a snap. Half-sitting, propped against the wall, she felt pain shoot up her right arm. *It's broken. How will I get out of here?*

"I will kill you," Wheeler snarled.

His putrid smell choked her. Bile rose in her throat. She looked up. His facial features were distorted with anger. Below wavy brown hair and black eyes, his nostrils flared and his jaw protruded. His mouth gaped, lips curled back, sharp teeth flashing.

While his semitransparent body gathered mass, his piercing black eyes flamed blood red. Before she could think, he struck her face, bouncing her head against the wall, her helmet absorbing the impact. Again he raised her above his head. She cringed, waiting for the pain.

Wheeler stilled.

Opening her eyes, she saw Lee standing in the doorway.

Lee's face hardened. "Let her go," he shouted.

Instead of releasing her, Wheeler flung her at her defender. She crashed into Lee, slamming him against the tunnel wall. Blood gushed from his scalp.

"Lee, Lee!" Hayley shouted. She rolled off her broken arm, the pain unbearably intensifying. She cried and held back a scream. Tears flowed down her cheeks as she reached out her other hand, caressing his face.

His eyes opened. He looked past her. Then his eyes closed again.

"Lee, Lee!" She glanced over her shoulder.

Emma stood between them and her master. "No, Massa, no!"

When Wheeler reached for his slave, a voice came from a few feet away.

"If youse touch my wife, I'se send youse to Hell."

Fully materialized, Abel stood in the tunnel. Rage filled his face. His dark skin glistened in the light from Hayley's helmet lamp. His huge biceps bulged.

Hayley knew he had waited for this moment.

CHAPTER 42

Outside her prison, in the tunnel to Hayley's right, Emma rushed to Abel, throwing her arms around him. To finally see them together brought Hayley to tears. Losing sight of Wheeler's ghost, she desperately searched through watery eyes for his shadow, an orb, or a vaporous cloud giving a clue to his whereabouts.

Sensing a movement, she listened. *Wheeler.* While she stared toward the well, straining to hear, her attacker came from behind. She turned to see his features distorting, alternating from the black mass of an entity similar to Leech to the form of Wheeler. He ripped her away from Lee's side, knocking the wind out of her, gripping Hayley like a rag.

She gasped for breath and cried out in pain.

With his hand clenched around her left upper arm, Wheeler dragged Hayley through the dark tunnel, her broken appendage hanging loosely, legs raking through the shards of broken brick and mortar, tennis shoes ready to slip off. The ground level rose with each step as the tunnel led them to the basement.

While piercing pain consumed her, she let out a blood-curdling scream, hoping to awaken Lee. Mustering all her strength, she twisted, struggling to break free. Desperate to escape, she glanced around, the lamp on her helmet bouncing its light against the walls.

She saw Wheeler raise his chin and suckle the air around him, as if feeding off her fear. Tree roots blocking their path withered at his touch. Mushrooms growing overhead shriveled, turning black as he passed. The moisture clinging to the tunnel walls turned to ice. The stench from Wheeler's apparition grew as his mass solidified. Hayley knew the ghost was readying himself for a fight, and perceived he wanted Abel to follow.

If the two battled, she had learned from Grams they would fight for eternity, matching strength with hate, although, with spirits no longer encased in human flesh, they'd be unable to harm one another. She'd told Hayley the negative entity was identical to Leech, and had consumed Wheeler while a child. In battle, it would feed from Abel's hatred and try to take him as another host.

After all her work in Sutterville separating Leech from Abel, Hayley was angered at the thought of his being consumed again by a similar entity. She knew Abel felt tempted to challenge his rival. While Abel hesitated to sort out his emotions, appearing torn between rescuing his wife and the desire to tear Emma's captor to pieces, Hayley hoped she'd have time to stop him from taking Wheeler's bait.

She cried out, "Abel, take Emma to Daniel."

He nodded, took his wife's hand, and they disappeared.

With a yank, Wheeler dragged Hayley farther along the ascending tunnel, her legs and arms numbed from the freezing cold.

Hayley gagged on her indrawn icy breath. Blood streaming down her forehead and into her eyes mingled with her tears and blurred her vision. Suddenly, her helmet lamp, the light that linked her to reality, went out. She perceived only a distant glow in the tunnel in front of the room that used to be Emma's prison.

Straining to focus, she saw Lee struggling to get up. He

276

grabbed the flashlight he had earlier dropped. The beam seemed to approach her, flooding her with hope.

Stumbling over debris and swearing, Lee continued toward her. "Let her go, Wheeler!"

Wheeler stopped abruptly and released her, propping her against a wooden ladder connecting to the basement, now overhead.

She looked up.

Above her, the ghost pushed the trapdoor open. The dim light now streaming into the tunnel broke any promise of her escape. Cringing, she waited for Wheeler's cold grip to drag her up the ladder and through the trapdoor, locking it to bar Lee's attempt to save her.

While her dread grew, the looming threat dissipated. After a moment, she noticed that Wheeler's stench had gone. Then Hayley realized she'd been only a lure to catch Abel, and Wheeler's plan had failed. He no longer needed her.

The only sounds left in the tunnel were Lee's footsteps and his labored breathing. As the beam of Lee's flashlight grew brighter and his footsteps drew closer, relief consumed her.

"Hayley! Hayley!"

"I'm here."

The heat of Lee's body warmed Hayley as he bent over her. His gentle touch explored her battered limbs. "Are you all right? Can you move?"

"My right arm's broken," she said through teeth clenched with pain. "But I can walk."

"Where's Wheeler?"

"He's gone. Your head — you're bleeding. You were out cold. I couldn't rouse you."

"I'm okay. Don't worry about me. Where're Abel and Emma?"

"They're with Daniel."

Echoes of footsteps and light filled the other end of the tunnel. "Lee," Roger called.

"We're over here," Lee shouted.

Roger rushed toward them. When he reached them, he set his lamp at his side and knelt. "You look like hell, Lee. How's Hayley?"

"Worse than I am."

Roger lifted her while Lee grabbed the lamp. They hurried back along the tunnel to the bottom of the well.

"I'll take her up," Roger told Lee. "You're in no condition." He hitched Hayley's harness to the rope and tethered himself, spooning her with one arm around her waist and the other holding the line. "Ready," he yelled.

"Will Wheeler be waiting for us when you reach the top?" Lee asked Hayley.

"No. Just like Abel was confined to the cave, Wheeler's stuck in the house or tunnel until he figures out how to leave. That will give us some time. I feel sorry for the men inside keeping him confused, because he's pissed."

She heard the SUV's engine start and knew Laura drove forward, slowly hoisting them. At the top, Daniel helped Hayley and Roger out of the shaft and lowered the line to Lee. Laura backed the SUV, allowing the rope to descend. Once Lee tugged the rope, she drove forward, pulling him up.

When Lee climbed out of the well, Frank Thompson left the second van. Bandaged around his head, he walked toward Lee and Hayley, his disbelief obvious to her. Stumbling, Frank reached out his hand and steadied himself on the hood of Roger's SUV. He stared at Wheeler's victims.

Brea and her family stood speechless between the vehicles.

The driver's door of Lee's SUV flew open. Laura hurriedly

climbed out, rushed to the rear of the vehicle, and gasped at the sight of Hayley and Lee. She opened the rear doors. "Sit," she ordered.

Lee wrapped his arm around Hayley, taking care not to touch her broken arm, and led her to the SUV. He eased her around, helped her sit, then stood back.

"You, too," Laura said to Lee.

Lee obeyed.

"We have to hurry," Hayley said. "As soon as Wheeler chases the men out of the house, we'll have to act fast. Once he starts concentrating on us and the well, he'll learn how to translocate."

"This won't take long." With a glance over her shoulder, Laura told Roger, "I'll need my supplies. They're in Lee's backseat." Carefully, she examined Hayley's right arm. It was swollen, slightly deformed below the elbow. "It's broken. You're lucky it didn't break the skin. You'll have to have X-rays."

Roger retrieved a white box with a red cross on its lid, brought it to Laura, and opened it.

Reaching into her medical kit, Laura pulled out a syringe and a small bottle. After giving Hayley an injection for her pain, she took a sling from its sealed plastic bag and ran the sling under the broken limb and around Hayley's neck to support the arm. She bent down to look at Hayley's legs.

Laura gently rolled up Hayley's blood-soaked pant leg. "You're lucky," she said. "Some punctures, but mostly abrasions that ruptured small veins and capillaries. All I need to do is clean and bandage them."

Hayley glanced toward the house, seeing Lewis, Jim, and Gil Meeker sprint out the front door, yelling.

"Hurry," she said.

Brea and her parents jumped out of the way as the men, out of breath, hurried past.

279

Appearing to be studying the situation, Jim stared and ran his hand through his mussed hair while he caught his breath. He sauntered over and lifted a brow. "You two look like ya had a fight with a wood chipper an' lost."

Hayley flinched in pain and forced a smile. "Thanks, Jim. Good to see you, too." She stood, testing the strength in her bandaged legs.

Lee started to rise.

"Wait," Laura said. "At least let me bandage your head."

"I'm fine. We need to get this show on the road."

"You might have a concussion. As soon as this is over, I'm taking both of you to the hospital to get checked out," Laura told him.

As the painkillers started taking effect, Hayley began to feel a little light-headed. She took the DNA kit from her pocket. "I forgot to give you this." She passed it to Laura.

"Thank goodness."

Hayley heard Harold mumble to Meeker, "This is unbelievable."

Gil glanced toward the house. "Wait until you meet Wheeler."

Hayley looked at Daniel, who stood next to Abel and his wife, oblivious to their presence. "Daniel, would you like to meet your ancestral grandmother?"

"You have to ask?" Daniel replied.

Unaware they were standing next to him, Daniel jumped when Abel materialized and Hayley placed white light around Emma, making her visible.

Brea's dad stumbled forward. "My God, it's true!"

His wife took his hand and pulled him to her side. "We told you so. Don't make a scene, Harold."

Tears glistened in Daniel's eyes.

Hayley glanced around, noticing everyone staring at the

phenomenon. She heard Frank bellow, "Who in the hell are they?"

Hayley glanced over her shoulder and saw Brea huddling with her mother. Mr. Tyler, face pale, gawked while standing as stiff as a mannequin.

Frank stared at the apparitions, then at Hayley. "What in the hell are you, a witch?"

"No, Frank, she's a medium," Lee said. "And if you print that in your newspaper, I'll sue you until I own your business."

"Okay, okay. But you owe me big time. You set me up. You knew I'd be attacked by that thing, didn't you? What else haven't you told me?"

"You'll get the entire story, Frank. I promise," Lee said. "Just leave Hayley out of it."

Instinctively, the newsman had found his camera and started taking as many shots as he could.

Emma and Abel's faces lit with smiles.

"Emma, this is Daniel, a descendant of Noah's," Hayley told her.

"I'se sees my boy in youse face, Daniel. It be fine meetin' youse."

"It's been an honor to meet you," Daniel said. "I've waited for this moment. I will never forget you."

"The son that you conceived with Wheeler didn't die. The Tylers, who lived by the river, raised him and named him Simon." Hayley extended her arm toward Brea. "These are also your relatives, descendants of Simon's, the Tylers."

"I do declare. May God bless all of youse," Emma said, gazing at them and Daniel. Then turning, she added, "And He be blessin' youse, too, Missy Hayley."

A lump formed in Hayley's throat and tears welled in her eyes. "We were all glad to help." She said to Abel, "We don't have much time. Wheeler will be here any minute. Do you see the bright light behind you? You must walk into it. It's the gateway to Heaven. Your and Emma's son is there, and also Simon, her other son, and family you've never met. But before you leave, you have to get Wheeler to follow. He will if Emma asks him to. He has to meet his Maker, Abel. It's the only way you'll find peace with all of this."

"And whats will happen to him den, Missy Hayley? Will he be sent to Hell wheres he belong?"

"Maybe, Abel. But if there's an ounce of good in him, maybe not. He will pay one way or another. I'm sure of it. I've been told so by a very reliable source."

Abel looked at Emma. She nodded.

"Remember when I freed you from the entity, Abel—the last moments when I covered Leech in white light?" Hayley said. "It tortured him. Wheeler will try to escape from the light, too, just like Leech. After he follows Emma and enters the light, hold onto him. Don't let him get away."

Abel smiled. "Yes'm."

Hayley and the others watched Abel and Emma walk into the light. Then Hayley looked up to see an ominous black mass hovering above the well. She sensed its intense hatred.

The mass swooped down until touching the ground, where it materialized as Wheeler, appearing as he had before his death in his mid-thirties. His dark hair brushed against the white collar of his cotton shirt. Dignity hung on him like the fake persona of an actor. He held his chin high, eyes glaring at Abel.

Frank lowered his camera, then slowly lifted it. Brea and her mother clung to each other, while Harold mumbled.

Emma called to Wheeler. "Come with me." She beckoned with a wave of her hand. "Please, come with me."

When Wheeler entered the light, Hayley saw, as she had

hoped, that his obsession for Emma outweighed his hatred for Abel. Before Wheeler could flee from the light, Abel wrapped his arms around him and held tight. Wheeler, thrashing to break free, shape-shifted, his nose and mouth elongating into the muzzle of a hyena, nostrils flaring. His curdling scream turned to a loud roar. Suddenly, the three vanished when the light disappeared.

Everyone around Hayley stood transfixed until a flash came from Frank's camera. "Hell, that was worth a dozen knots on my head." He turned to Lee. "You promised to tell me everything. I'm holding you to your word."

"Have patience, Frank. First things first. We need to make sure the DNA results stand up in court. In a couple of days, Laura will have the DNA lab tests back, and now that Wheeler's gone, the authorities can get to Emma's remains and officially gather their own DNA samples. Once the court makes its ruling on the inheritance, you'll have your story."

Hayley cleared her throat and raised her voice to get everyone's attention. She looked at Daniel. "Mind if we leave you, the Tylers, and Frank at Meeker's while Roger and Laura take us to the hospital? You can tell them the whole story while I'm getting a cast on my arm."

"Yes, of course."

"Me, too," Jim said. "I've got more stories to tell 'em than a camel's got spit."

They started the vehicles and drove down the oak-lined road. Roger drove with Laura next to him, while Lee, Hayley, and Lewis sat in the back.

"How long will it take for Hayley's arm to heal?" Lee asked.

"Usually six weeks, but with all her divine connections, who knows?" Laura said.

Lee grinned. "Just in time for the ball." He gazed at Hayley. "I'll wear tights if you want me to. I owe you that."

"I love you, Lee Franklin. I owe you. You saved my life." She smiled. "I'm picturing you in tights." She put her hand on his thigh. "We'll talk more about it when we get home."

CHAPTER 43

On the last Saturday of October, before the ball, Hayley took a deep breath and sucked in her tummy, while Laura tightened her corset's laces. Then Hayley slipped on the golden silk underskirt and Laura helped her into the seventeenth-century ball gown. Stepping around the gold-embellished cream-colored skirt that flared out from the waist, Laura tugged on the gold-embroidered bodice, trying to fasten the hooks up the back.

"You can breathe now," she said, standing aside.

Hayley exhaled. The corset fit like a vise, giving her breasts nowhere to go but up. "I can hardly breathe. And look." She pointed at the scooped neckline. "I've got bulging boobs. Is this really what women wore?"

"Yes," said Laura. "Back then, corsets were stiffened by whalebone called 'stays.'"

"Whalebone?" Hayley said. "I'm guessing a sadistic medieval tyrant invented it as a torture device for his wife." She walked toward the mirror, the gown's hem skimming the floor. Studying her reflection, she felt astonished by the gown's intricate details. "Beautiful!" She straightened the shoulder, then ran her hand down the gold-and cream-striped puffed sleeve to the buttoned lace cuff. "So elegant."

"And you can thank King Louis XIV for the neckline," Laura

said. "He insisted all women wear their necklines low to pay honor to him and to God."

"Seriously?"

Laura nodded.

"If I hiccup, I'll be arrested." Hayley turned away from the mirror. "Tell me how men back then could wear tights. One look at a woman and it would be totally obvious what they were thinking."

Laura laughed. "No. They were covered with codpieces." She explained. "But it doesn't matter. Roger told me that your dress and Lee's tights were worn during two different centuries — yours in the seventeenth and his in the sixteenth. He's wearing shorts that cover his dignity."

"I thought Lee and I were going as a couple — prince and princess from the same era. He knew that's what I wanted."

"Didn't you choose the costumes?"

"My arm was broken, remember? I couldn't go shopping and try anything on. Not to mention, you can't just walk into any store to find something like this. So I was more than happy for Lee's help — that damn sneak!"

"You think he planned this?" Laura asked.

"I know he did. He sent over a costume designer and I was measured. Now I know why that bald-headed little man took so much interest in the size of my breasts. I thought he was a pervert."

"And the plan was?"

"Because I'm making him wear tights, he's making me wear boobs. But he took advantage. He covered his assets. Look at mine." Hayley sighed heavily and glanced at Laura, who broke out in laughter. "So what are you wearing?"

"I gave up looking. I've been so busy at the hospital I let Roger decide. He sent over a costume designer...." Laura's eyes widened. "Oh, damn!"

"A bald little man?"

Laura went to her garment bag and unzipped it. An illustration of the costume lay inside. She lifted the picture. "Cleopatra. How bad can that be?"

She pulled out a golden-colored bra and a collar ringed with gold, blue, burgundy, and turquoise beads. The picture showed the rings of beads draping over the bra. Laura slipped into it, then put on a hip-hugging, multi-striped skirt, its waistband falling far below her bare belly button. The costume's final piece, the blue-beaded loincloth, modestly covered the top of the skirt's split front seam.

Laura brushed her hand across the fabric. "It feels like thousands of large scales."

"Is it comfortable?"

"Yes. It's lined in silk. It's pretty snug. I don't think I'll have a problem with the skirt slipping down any lower. If it does, I'll be in the same jail cell with you."

A knock came from the open front door downstairs.

Hayley yelled down from the middle upstairs bedroom. "We're up here, Mrs. Ida."

Arms piled high with a cosmetic case and hatboxes, a woman in her late forties with cherry red hair entered the room. Setting everything on the bed, she reached for one of the boxes, opened it, and pulled out a pretentious curly brown wig. "You can probably figure out whose this is," she said, looking over the rims of rhinestone-embellished glasses on the tip of her nose.

Hayley carefully lowered herself into the chair in front of the dresser. In less than thirty minutes, her hair and makeup were finished. Then Laura took the seat. Mrs. Ida brought out a black wig and a beaded headdress. She pulled Laura's hair up into a net, then slipped on the wig and headdress, finishing with a bejeweled gold cobra crown. Minutes later, dramatic makeup completed her guise.

"Done," Mrs. Ida said. "There's a limo waiting outside."

~*~

Hayley and Laura arrived hours before the guests. Lewis met their limo when it pulled up and led them to the library. Once he opened the carved wooden door, Hayley saw Lee, her prince, and Roger, a Roman soldier, standing by the elongated windows.

Lee hurried across the room to join her. "You're beautiful! You look like a queen." He offered his arm, then led her across the room.

Roger's face reddened as he stood speechless, staring at Laura. "I think you stopped my heart," he finally said. They followed Hayley and Lee to the windows overlooking the front yard.

"Drinks?" Lewis asked.

"Wine. Thank you," Lee said.

After Lewis closed the door, Hayley stood back, examining Lee's costume. His golden tunic was as embellished as hers, sleeves ornate, alternating between billows of striped silk, and embroidered form-fitting velvet leading to cuffs trimmed with lace. He wore gold-and cream-striped onion-shaped shorts. White tights covered his muscular legs, and he wore white slippers.

"Nice bubble pants," Hayley said. "I pictured you wearing only a tunic and tights."

"I had an advantage. I knew what you'd be wearing. If I only wore tights, everyone would know what I was thinking about, despite a codpiece." His eyes fixed on her breasts.

"My boobs." She gestured toward her neckline. "This is embarrassing. Don't you see enough of these?"

He reached for her hand and brushed his lips across her fingers. "Never, my love."

"You're incorrigible. And I'm mad at you. We'll have to talk about this later."

She glanced at Laura. Beside her, Roger's Roman steel silvery cuirass covered a military tunic. Below his waist, covering his tunic, he wore studded leather lappets, leaving his lower legs bare. He wore leather sandals laced up his calves. A red cape, pinned on his left shoulder, crossed his chest and draped over his right shoulder.

"Great costume," Hayley told Roger.

"Thanks. I had to leave the helmet at home. Its plume bent when I climbed into the Mercedes."

"You look fine without it," Hayley assured him.

Once Lewis returned with their drinks, they accepted their wine glasses, climbed to the second floor, and followed the hallway to the rear of the mansion.

Lee stepped aside as he opened the ballroom's double doors. Inside, the walls were newly painted shades of pale green trimmed with gold. On the ceiling panels, frescos depicted the gardens of Florence. Five chandeliers, the largest in the center, hung in the rectangular room, which spanned nearly the width of the mansion. Tables covered with white linen bordered the dance floor and filled one-third of the ballroom.

Hayley glanced toward the stage, seeing members of the orchestra bringing in their instruments. She walked with Lee, Roger, and Laura across the ballroom to the twelve-pane windows and looked onto the gardens. An orange-and-golden sunset painted the sky. In the twilight, Max lit the garden with twinkling lights strung around the topiaries and illuminating all flowerbeds with pastel fluorescence. A goshawk circled the garden as if admiring its beauty, Hayley imagined, then flew toward the lake.

Lee turned to Hayley. "The second hour after the guests arrive,

I'll be making an announcement. Because this is a costume ball, I'll be doing a little theatrics. Medieval trumpeters will announce our arrival." Lee pointed behind them to two thrones against the far wall near the stage. "I'll lead you to your throne. Before you take your seat, I'll address our guests and introduce you. Then I'll thank them for coming and tell them how much money our event raised for Children's Hospital. After the applause, I'll turn and we'll sit."

"Do you mind if I try out the throne? This dress is a little full. I'm curious to know what will happen when I sit."

"Not at all, my queen." Lee held out his arm and escorted her across the ballroom. "I didn't place the thrones on a platform because I intend to have a few drinks tonight. I've had visions of missing the step up and falling on my face."

Hayley handed Lee her drink and settled onto the throne. "I'm more than glad about that." She looked down at her low neckline. "If I were to trip and my you-know-whats popped out of you-know-where, I'd have to kill you in front of everyone."

Lee looked at her with his big brown eyes and flashed an innocent smile. "You worry too much. I assure you, if you even appear to be ready to have an accident, I'll be all over you."

Hayley's gaze went up his white legs and fixed on the crotch of his billowing shorts.

He caught her stare. "You're going to drive me insane tonight. This is going to be a long evening." He sipped his wine.

She rose and, with arms wide open, turned a circle, taking in the grandeur of the ballroom. "It won't be a long night for me. I've never been to a ball. It's going to be unforgettable."

"You have no idea."

"What?" Hayley asked.

"Nothing," Lee said, quickly taking a sip of wine and handing Hayley her glass. He turned to look at Roger and Laura, standing by the window. "Don't they make a good looking couple?"

"You changed the subject."

"Did I?" He called to Roger and Laura. "We'll see you two later. We're going downstairs to welcome guests."

CHAPTER 44

While valets outside the main entrance opened car doors for guests, Lee and Hayley met a stream of costumed people entering the mansion. Lewis, wearing his butler attire, directed the ballroom guests unfamiliar with the home. Kathy, dressed as Marilyn Monroe in Marilyn's infamous white halter-top dress, standing with her date, Thomas, Lee's security guard, impersonating Joe Dimaggio in his Yankees uniform, also greeted guests.

Thomas turned to Lee. "Thank you, sir, for giving me the night off."

"You're more than welcome. You've been working long, hard hours with Lewis prepping for this party, and deserve to have some fun."

The partygoers walked beneath a double-tiered empire chandelier hanging from the vaulted ceiling in the center of the foyer, and followed a grand staircase leading to the second floor.

Hayley and Lee followed the last of their guests upstairs, through the opened doors, and down a sconce-lit hallway to the ballroom at the rear. In the main hallway running the length of the ballroom, guests chatted.

Glancing around, Hayley marveled at the array of costumes. George Washington walked with Marie Antoinette. A fairy escorted a hobbit. Among the couple of hundred guests, no two had dressed alike.

Upon entering the ballroom, Lee took two glasses of red wine from a waiter's tray and handed one to Hayley. Music played, while waiters served drinks and hors d'oeuvres. With her hand in his, he led her toward the mayor and his wife to mingle.

"It's a splendid turnout," Mayor Webster said.

"Yes, I'm very pleased," Lee replied.

The mayor's wife touched Hayley's arm. "I just met a man who looked like Ben Franklin. He wouldn't give me his real name, but such a gentleman. He took my hand and kissed it. His cold hands gave me the shivers."

Standing on her tiptoes, Hayley scanned the room. Beside the thrones, Grams, dressed as a gypsy queen, and Ben, dressed as himself, looked her way. They waved.

"Lee, Grams and Ben are here." She waved back.

"Glad they made it." He turned back to his guests.

"Please, see to your other guests," the mayor said.

"Thank you, Mayor and Mrs. Webster. Please excuse us," Lee said, stepping away.

He led Hayley to the windows overlooking the gardens. On the veranda below, candlelit globes flickered on a multitude of tables covered in white linen. Some guests strolled through the garden, while others stood on the bridge over the pond.

When she and Lee turned toward the entrance, Kathy, escorted by Thomas, entered, waved, and joined Ben and Grams.

Jim, wearing wide, knee-length canvas trousers, a white linen shirt, a blue single-breasted collarless jacket, and a striped waistcoat, approached them. He wiped away a bead of sweat rolling from beneath the red kerchief on his head. The beard he had lent Daniel as a disguise at Wheeler's framed his chin, and a black patch covered his right eye. In a green sash around his waist, he carried a pirate's flintlock pistol. He wore shoes with buckles.

"Ya make a grown man's eyes water, Hayley," Jim said, smiling, flashing a couple of blacked-out teeth.

"Thank you…I think."

He scanned Lee. "Ya look like a damn fool. Ya need to let some air out of those britches."

"Thanks a lot."

Hayley giggled. "I bet if you poked a needle in his pants, he'd fly around the room."

"Okay. Have your fun. Have you seen Roger and Laura?" Lee asked.

"Yeah. Roger's a stammerin' idiot. Can't take his eyes off Laura." He pointed. "They're over there." He looked around the room. "Same crowd as last year." Another bead of sweat fell from his forehead. He grabbed the lapel of his waistcoat. "Damned hot. I'm goin' to my room to take a couple of layers off." He made a move toward the door. "Be back shortly."

When the band began to play a waltz, Lee turned to Hayley. "Care to dance?"

She held out her hand, and he led her to the dance floor. While they glided and whirled, she glanced often at her plunging neckline to make sure her assets remained hidden. "I can dance all night," she said.

"I can think of better things to do," Lee said, winking.

Looking over Lee's shoulder, she noticed Jim returning.

When the music stopped, Lee gave Hayley his arm. "It's time," he told her.

Men and women, all the same height, all dressed in red-and-gold tunics with red tights, each wearing a similar light brown pageboy wig, filed in through the double doors. They eased guests off the narrow red carpet leading to the throne and formed a line along its edges. Standing at attention with their long trumpets at their sides, they waited.

On cue, they raised the horns to their lips. The trumpets blared and Hayley thought they were heralding the announcement.

Lee took Hayley's hand and, as the minstrels lowered their instruments, he led her to the thrones. The room fell silent, all eyes watching them. They stopped and faced the guests. Lee dropped Hayley's hand and stepped forward.

"I'd like to welcome each of you to my home for the annual Children's Hospital Charity Ball." He reached back and took Hayley's hand again, bringing her to his side. "I want to introduce my hostess and the love of my life, Hayley Johnson."

Her heart pounded. *Lee just told everyone he loves me.* Cameras flashed. To her left, Frank, dressed as a court jester, took photos for the *Sutterville Times.*

"I can't tell you how much of an honor it is to have you here tonight and to share in this special occasion." Lee turned, facing Hayley.

"What are you doing?" she whispered. "Do you want me to speak? You didn't say anything about—"

He knelt before her.

He isn't! She glanced around nervously. Waiters swept through the crowd with trays of champagne. One of the minstrels stepped forward carrying a red pillow. On top rested a small black velvet box. Hayley's eyes widened. *He is!* She trembled.

Frank's camera flashed repeatedly.

Lee took her hand and looked into her eyes. "A moment in time is too short to give you my love, and eternity is not long enough. My existence would crumble and evaporate on the winds without you. In front of God and all my friends, I ask for your hand."

The minstrel held out the pillow, offering the small velvet

box to Lee. He took it, opened it, and showed her a diamond ring.

She held her breath. *It's the size of Alaska.*

He stared into her eyes. "Hayley, will you marry me?"

She remembered to breathe and held out her hand. "Yes, Lee. I will."

He placed the ring on her finger, stood, and embraced her. When her lips met his, Hayley felt like the rest of the world had vanished until applause filled the room.

The guests raised their glasses. Roger made a toast. "Here's to the best friends in the world. Nothing I can say could express how much happiness I wish for them."

Laura raised her glass. "Congratulations!"

"I second that!" Jim shouted.

Beside Jim, Grams brushed a tear from her eye. At her right, Ben pulled a handkerchief from his vest pocket and offered it to her. Next to him, Kathy jumped up and down, clapping her hands.

Lee gave a gesture and the band began to play. He led Hayley to the dance floor. While dancing, she tried without luck to picture her future. She slowed their pace and looked up at him. "Grams once told me that everything that exists vibrates. My rate of vibration is unique. It causes my aura to glow more than others'. That's why I attract the dead."

"And why are you telling me this?"

"Are you sure you want to marry me? Ninety percent of the time when I'm around you, I have my beacon turned off. That's not the real me. Life may get kind of scary if you make me your wife."

"I already know that." He stopped dancing and his eyes met hers. "I love you, Hayley Johnson, from the tip of your marvelous mind to the bottom of your small feet. I want all of you."

"I love you, Lee Franklin. Better hold on. Your life is about to get a little wilder."

~*~

By midnight, the guests had left. Lee and Hayley walked Laura, Roger, Kathy, and Thomas to the door. "Good night, guys. Thanks for coming."

Kathy's red Toyota GT was parked at the front curb behind Roger's black Mercedes-Benz SLK. She waved before she and Thomas climbed into her vehicle.

After both cars left, Lee turned to Hayley. "Were you surprised?"

"Totally. You were very poetic."

"Everything I said is true." Lee tilted her chin and softly kissed her.

She looked into his loving eyes. "I know. I feel the same way about you."

His glance followed the curve of her neckline. He ran his finger across her bulging breasts. "Mind if I help you get out of that dress?"

She smiled.

They walked toward the elevator. As they rode up to the third floor, he unfastened the top hook of her dress.

"You know what will happen if you do that?" Hayley said.

He smiled. "I've been waiting for it all night."

The End

ABOUT THE AUTHOR

Shirley lives in Northeast Ohio. She turned to writing after taking an early retirement to care for her mother who had been stricken with Alzheimer's. While writing first started as a pleasant form of stress relief for Shirley, it soon became her creative passion. She thanks God for her family and her close friends, who have given her support and inspiration.

www.ingramcontent.com/pod-product-compliance
Lightning Source LLC
Chambersburg PA
CBHW020256200626
46816CB00001BA/321